SIXTEEN HORSES

GREG BUCHANAN

MANTLE

W

First published 2021 by Mantle
an imprint of Pan Macmillan
The Smithson, 6 Briset Street, London EC1M 5NR
EU representative: Macmillan Publishers Ireland Limited,
Mallard Lodge, Lansdowne Village, Dublin 4
Associated companies throughout the world
www.panmacmillan.com

ISBN 978-1-5290-2717-4

1 3 5 7 9 8 6 4 2

A CIP catalogue record for this book is available from the British Library.

Typeset in Sabon by Palimpsest Book Production Ltd, Falkirk, Stirlingshire
Printed and bound by CPI Group (UK) Ltd, Croydon, CR0 4YY

MIX
Paper from
responsible sources
FSC® C116313

Visit **www.panmacmillan.com** to read more about all our books
and to buy them. You will also find features, author interviews and
news of any author events, and you can sign up for e-newsletters
so that you're always first to hear about our new releases.

SIXTEEN
HORSES

Greg Buchanan was born in 1989 and lives in the Scottish Borders. He studied English at the University of Cambridge and completed a PhD at King's College London in identification and ethics. He is a graduate of UEA's Creative Writing MA. *Sixteen Horses* is his first novel.

For Charlotte

SIXTEEN HORSES

The woods are lovely, dark and deep,
But I have promises to keep,
And miles to go before I sleep,
And miles to go before I sleep.

'Stopping by Woods on a Snowy Evening'
Robert Frost (1922)

1.

Tufts of cloud burned black before the sunrise, the horizon littered with the flotsam of old and rusted silhouettes. They were alone.

'Chemtrails,' the farmer had said to Alec, early on their walk. Other than this, he had been silent.

And now their torches revealed the edge of a bank, right before the crest of a shallow stream that cut through the farmer's reclaimed marshland. Along its muddy edge and all around, the reeds sang with flies and crickets and buntings.

'Where are they?' Alec asked, shivering. It was 6.55 a.m. He'd left his jacket in his patrol car.

'There weren't any sheep over here,' the farmer said, ignoring the question. He leapt over the bank, his boots slipping slightly on the incline. 'They normally love coming over here.'

Alec stared at the mud, and the farmer grinned, his cheeks ruddy beneath his dirty white beard. With that thick wax coat and that gut and that voice, he could have been a lunatic Santa Claus. 'You won't fall,' he said. 'Not afraid of a little dirt, are you, Sergeant Nichols?'

'No.' Yes. 'I just hope you aren't wasting my time. And these flies . . .' Alec swatted one away from his rolled-up sleeve, a great bulbous thing that had nestled on the hairs of his forearm. He was food for this whole place.

'Try covering up next time,' the farmer said.

Alec grimaced. He stepped back, tensing before rushing over the ditch. He came down with a thud, right into the thick and gelatinous mud. He splattered his black trouser legs and the farmer's jeans.

The other man tutted, smiling. 'What have we come to, eh?'

Alec brushed at the muck around his ankles, but this only spread it further. His palms grew filthy.

The farmer walked on.

He gestured past a large, half-empty water tank around two hundred feet away, its translucent plastic grown stained with time, the smear of a smile where fluid had lapped within. 'We found them near there.' His face fell.

Alec checked his watch. 7.06 a.m.

The sun would soon rise.

They kept on, the silence drowned out by the buzzing of the flies and the distant hellos of scraggly sheep out there in the semi-darkness.

'Jean's moving out,' the farmer said. 'Did you know?'

'Who?'

'Jean . . . The lady who lives down the lane,' the farmer said, frowning. 'She's moving out, selling up her farm.'

'Oh yes, Jean . . .' His voice drifted. 'I saw the sign.' Alec had driven past it on the way here, a farm twice the size of this one, its animals and land and people in far better condition. He had not known the name. He knew few out here. One more reminder that he did not belong, he supposed.

'They're selling up to live with family, so she says.'

'I think I saw them in town a few times,' Alec said. They were almost at the water tank, at the smile. 'Were they the ones who made those wagon wheels? They'd mix sausage meat into a kind of – well, kind of cinnamon swirl, I suppose. It's delicious. Did you ever try one?'

He swatted another fly away from his face.

'No,' the farmer said. 'I'm a vegetarian.'

'Really? My wife tried doing that a few years back, and—'

'No,' the farmer said, and the conversation died.

The world was still dark, even if only for a little while. The sun was almost free. The day had almost begun.

ॐ

Fifty feet away, the field gave way to freshly tilled brown soil, forming mounds everywhere on the uneven earth. Chalky rocks littered the plot in every direction. Each step in this place was as muddy and wet as the last.

Further still, a thin metal fence marked the edge of the land, clots of wool decorating the wire like fairy lights where the sheep had once tried to break through.

But there were no animals in sight now. There was nothing but detritus.

'I don't see what—'

'There,' the farmer interrupted. 'In the ground.'

Alec looked down. For a moment, he saw nothing but dirt.

'I don't—'

Alec stopped talking, a breeze moving past them both. Something shook along the soil.

He removed his torch and stepped forward, pointing its light at the source. Just three feet away, almost the same colour as the mud itself, there lay a great mound of black hair, coiled in thick and silken spirals.

He moved closer and knelt down. He wiped his hands on his trouser legs, reached into his pockets, and pulled out a pair of latex gloves. He tried to pull them on in one smooth motion, but his fingers – clammy, damp from the walk – clung to the latex before he could get them fully in. He had to inch each one into place before he could touch those cold dark circles. He stared at them all the while.

He lifted some of the hair up, surprised by the weight of it, its coarseness. He held it higher and ran his fingers along the strands, gripping at intervals. Towards the base of the spiral, where the rest of the hair still lay upon the ground, he felt flesh and bone.

Alec put it back carefully. The sun continued to rise. There was something else.

It was black, almost like plastic in its sheen, a thin half-moon of dulled white at its rim. It looked past him.

There was an eye, a large sad eye in the earth.

Alec stepped back.

'My daughter found them,' the farmer said. 'Shouldn't even have been out . . .'

Alec shone his torch across the area. There were others – some close together, some alone. He walked until he was sure he had found the whole set. He paced back and forth, a hundred feet all around.

He counted sixteen submerged heads, all apart, all with only the barest strand of skin on display, all with a single eye left exposed to the sun. One of the heads had been dug up a little more than the others, revealing the neck, at least. It was unclear how much of the corpse remained beneath the surface.

There were footprints everywhere: his, the farmer's, the daughter's, no doubt. He hadn't been told any of this . . . He hadn't known . . .

'Who could do this?' the farmer croaked, blinking. 'Who could make themselves—'

Alec looked up suddenly, acid rising in his throat. The sky was growing brighter, its red spreading like fire, the clouds shifting blue. Still the flies and crickets screamed across the reeds, though nothing crawled along those dead eyes. Nothing seemed to touch them.

There was a stone house half a mile away along the horizon.

'Who lives over there?' Alec asked.

'No one.'

Alec stared at it a moment longer. It was a lonely-looking place.

'Have you ever seen anything like this?' he asked. 'It's—'

Grotesque.

Beautiful.

'No. Have you?'

Alec shook his head, stepping back, staring once more at the hair. It was all tails, he could see that now.

'That's murder,' the farmer said, his voice soft. 'Just look at them. Look.'

It was in fact criminal damage, a mere property crime.

If you decide something isn't human, you can do almost anything.

Alec looked at the house again, dark and cold in the distance.

'Do you know anyone who might have a grudge against you? Anyone who might try and cause you harm?'

The farmer tried to smile. 'Apart from my wife? No, no . . . I get along with folk. Always have.' He paused. 'What do I do?'

'We need to get a vet in.' Alec stood up. 'We need to get post-mortems performed, if we can. I wouldn't touch them until we know more—'

'Can't afford any of that,' the farmer said.

'You wouldn't have to—'

'And besides,' the farmer interrupted. 'Someone buried them, didn't they? Horses don't just get that way themselves.'

'What about the mud? If this used to be wetland, maybe they . . . I don't know, maybe they—'

'No,' the farmer said, firmly, without elaboration.

Alec paused, looking back down at the eyes. But for the lack of motion, they might have been alive.

He got his phone out to take some photographs of the scene. They would have to do until help came. 'Try and keep your other animals away,' Alec said. 'If you can keep your other animals inside or—'

'What about the owner?' asked the farmer.

'Of what?'

'Them – these—' The farmer gesticulated, wincing.

'What?' Alec glanced down at the heads and up again at this man. 'Were you stabling them?' He paused. 'We'd need to contact the—'

'NO,' the farmer spat. 'No – no – no—'

'Hey, it's OK,' Alec said, stepping closer as the farmer turned away. 'I'm sure it's covered by your insurance.'

'You don't understand. I don't keep horses – I've *never* kept horses. That's what I tried to tell the girl on the phone—'

A fly landed on the rim of an eye.

'I've never seen these horses before in my life.'

2.

A dead man sits in a room. His hands are tied behind his back; it's why he hasn't fallen. The air is full of dust and gas. There is something moving inside his stomach. His right eye is no longer there.

His hunger outlives him. His teeming gut, his microbiome aflame with bacteria and symbiotic juices, they carry on. All that life within him continues consuming and breathing until it can breathe no more. He digests himself.

It smells like rancid pork mixed with sugar. It smells like a nightmare of food. It smells like the worst thing in the world.

A dead man sits in a room, but he isn't alone.

Two detectives watch as a sample is taken from the body. It isn't from the victim, it isn't even human.

Three white cat hairs, found in blood.

Cooper clutches her mask to her face, the stench unbelievable, but still she carries on. She won't run to the window and vomit. She won't give any of these smug pricks a reason to doubt her.

It is the first time Cooper has ever seen a dead body, but you wouldn't think it.

She focuses on the cat hairs, and only the cat hairs.

She ignores everything else. It is no time to get emotional.

These cat hairs are going to solve the case. They're going to ID a man no one could ID. They're going to—

🐍

'Why are we here?' her therapist asked.

There was no clock in the small, fluorescent-lit white room. Cooper had a black smart watch on her left wrist, though. It needed charging once a day. It was bulky. It had a red trim. It was hard to use and it was far more trouble than it was worth.

The watch was not something Cooper could easily check the time on without being accused of fidgeting. The therapist used anything against her. She was relentless.

'Why are we here, Cooper? I want to go back to why we're here.'

Cooper narrowed her eyes.

'You want me to express what I'm feeling?' Cooper straightened up a little. 'I'm expressing what I'm feeling.'

'I want to go back to something you mentioned before. That "it was no time to get emotional".'

'I was at the scene of a murder,' Cooper said, anger entering her voice. 'It was the first time I'd ever been called out to one. What was I supposed to do? Cry?'

The therapist just stared back at her. She was not like Cooper's previous therapist: that woman had been warm, filling out big green jumpers with smiles and echoes of whatever Cooper was feeling. There was sympathy, empathy, everything. This woman . . .

Her eyes were cold.

'I was twenty-five. I took the hairs from the crime scene, I looked over the rest, and I made it five feet from the building before I poured my guts out into the grass.' Cooper angled forward a bit. 'I did a good job.'

'Do you think you were prepared for it?'

'Of course I was prepared. They wouldn't have let me be there if I wasn't prepared.'

'You're not a police officer. You're not CSI. You're—'

'I was prepared,' Cooper interrupted. 'I'm quite a professional, actually.'

'You're a vet.'

Cooper looked away. There was silence for a time, so she raised her wrist and stared at her watch.

2.18 p.m.

2.19 p.m.

'Those cat hairs we found on the victim's leg – they were from a friend of the man's brother-in-law. We found a small quantity in the sister's house, we traced his associates, we found the friend. The evidence helped us to convict him of the murder.' Cooper paused.

The therapist said nothing, and Cooper's muscles tensed.

'I still don't think you understand exactly what I—'

'Why did you focus on the smell? I'm curious about that.'

'You ever smelt a dead body?'

The therapist shook her head.

'Not much room to think about anything else.' Cooper picked up her water bottle from her feet and drank a bit. 'Part of us lives on after our death, all right, but it's nothing like a soul or anything. It's just our gut.'

'You said we eat ourselves.'

'We do. The bacteria inside us, they start breaking everything down.'

'So it's not *us* then, exactly.'

'We're sixty per cent water. There's room in us for a lot of things.'

Cooper straightened herself and looked at her watch again. 2.23 p.m. The therapist was studying her notes.

'Why did you become a vet?' the woman asked.

Cooper looked at her.

'Why did you make that choice?'

'I wanted to help animals.'

'Is that true?'

'Yes.'

'Is that all the truth?'

There was a pause.

'If you wanted to help animals,' the therapist said, 'you'd be helping animals. What you do, it's different than that, if I understand correctly.'

Cooper nodded.

'So, why do you do it?'

'Because I didn't want to be polite for a living.'

'To who do you not want to be polite?'

'To whom.'

'Cooper . . .' The therapist sighed.

'To everyone.'

'Tell me what you mean.'

'What I mean is, most people don't think about the fact they're going to die one day.'

'Do you actually know what most people think?'

'Yes,' Cooper said. 'So do you. It's your job.' She snorted. 'You honestly think most people truly understand the nature of dying? You see it in their faces when you bring it up. "Oh, I'm not worried about death, it's fine, as long as I don't feel much pain then I won't know I'm dead so what's the problem?"'

'What *is* the problem?'

'The fact you won't know,' Cooper said. 'The fact any of us won't know, that "knowing" won't even be a thing any more, that all of this we're experiencing right now – every moment of my life – it will be as if it had never even happened. The end will just be absence.'

'Others will live on,' the therapist said.

'Does it matter?'

There was silence for a time. Cooper did not look at her watch.

'I went to vet school because I didn't know what else I wanted to be.'

'And now?'

'Now I'm thirty-one and I haven't practised on a live animal in years.'

'How does that make you feel?'

'It doesn't make me feel anything.'

'Do you have regrets?'

'No. I . . .'

The therapist wrote something down. 'Go on.'

'I love what I do.'

The therapist put her pad down on the table. 'The way you're sitting – the way you just said that – it clearly bothered you to say you love your job. That's interesting to me.'

'I'm glad you're having fun.'

'Cooper . . .'

The light had faded a little outside.

'I can't work with you if you don't work with me,' the therapist said.

'I don't want to work with you. I'm only here because I have to be here.'

'As you've said.'

'As I've said.'

'I thought you were worried about wasting your life, Cooper. It seems like you're choosing to do so.'

'It does seem like that, doesn't it?'

The therapist tensed up, hesitating before she spoke again. 'Tell me about—'

'Did you know that a veterinary surgeon is four times more likely to kill themselves than the average person?' Cooper paused. 'It's not a recent statistic either – we've been dying for years.'

'Why do you think that is?'

'We know how to end suffering.'

There was a long gap, then, where neither woman said a thing. Where both looked at the other, not entirely angry, not entirely civil. Where Cooper's breath was faster than she'd like.

Finally, the therapist spoke.

'Why are we here, Cooper?' She paused. 'I asked you twenty minutes ago – why are we here?'

'I answered you.'

'No . . . No, you didn't. The real reason. Not stories you tell yourself. Not any of this . . .'

Cooper stared.

'I need you to say it.'

'Because the people I work with decided I wasn't coping. Because they thought this would be a good fit for me. Because they don't know me at all.'

The therapist sighed. 'I'll ask you again, and I want you to be honest this time.'

Cooper said nothing.

'Why are we really here, Cooper?'

There was movement in the hallway. She looked at her watch. 2.38 p.m. Not much time to go.

She looked up, her eyes tired, her body still tense.

'The horses,' Cooper said. 'We're here because of the horses . . .'

The van moved through the night.
'It's happened again.'
They met no one on that road.
'And it's going to keep happening, isn't it?'
The driver did not answer.
'Tell me.'
Ahead, there were fireworks in the sky.
'Would you rather be careless or cruel?'

PART ONE:
ILMARSH

Day One

CHAPTER ONE

'Legs, eleven,' the voice called. 'Does anyone have legs, eleven?'

No answer came.

Seagulls perched on top of paint-flaked facades and black iron lamp-posts. Neon logos screamed ST GEORGE'S CHARCOAL GRILL, TROPICAL CAFE, CAESAR'S PALACE. Empty amusement arcades blared *waka waka waka* chiptune and flashing lights. It was all for no one, no one at all.

The sky was grey. Waves lapped against the shore.

In twenty-four days, two torsos would be discovered upon the sand.

§⊙

A couple of hours after the horse heads were found, a man leant against the side of his caravan with a cigarette in his right hand, a stained cotton vest stuck to his thin, freckly body.

The morning bingo had woken Michael up – it did so every couple of days at this time. The repetition, the questions, the sheer suicide-inducing tedium of the announcer's voice, all of it was more effective than any alarm. It drilled into his skull. The day was cold and the air smelt of ash.

He dropped his cigarette down onto the cement and flattened it with his foot, exhaling deeply and then coughing.

'Queen Bee. Under the tree. Lucky three.'

He went inside the caravan for a few minutes and emerged dressed for his work: the same vest, but with a checked shirt over it, a faded, thick blue-black. He locked the door and walked onward, putting as much distance between himself and the bingo as possible.

He'd left Annie at Joe's Tyres, had given the eponymous Joe some money each day to make sure she was OK.

It wouldn't bother Joe, of course, but a favour was a favour.

His friend had a whole patch of land right outside his garage, you see, beneath the looming towers all around; it was just perfect, far better than tethering Annie to the caravan like he'd used to do. And truth be told, the customers kind of liked it. Joe too. Trotting around as they waited for their cars to be repaired. Coming to the fence for treats.

There was something about a horse.

People loved her, and they loved Michael for the access he granted. Business wasn't that busy this time of year, but they still got the odd kid wanting to travel along the beachfront in their little carriage. Teenagers used the horse, too – some of them would pre-book a ride at night, an Annie-drawn date in the dark. It was the highlight of their young lives, everything else surely a disappointment.

In the summer, well, his business did gangbusters. They were a team.

He'd take Annie out every morning before work, even when there would *be* no work. He'd sit with his horse by the sea as she grazed on grass nearby. He'd let her sun herself while he read his paper, sometimes even a book. He'd go out there for the same reason the empty arcades opened their doors, the same reason a bingo hall played to a crowd of six.

He reached Joe's Tyres and let himself round the back gate.

'Annie,' he croaked, too quiet at first. His throat was a bit raw from the night before. 'Annie!' he said, cheerful, slightly louder.

He rubbed his tired eyes. There was no answer.

He walked out into the field, taking a wide berth. It wasn't a large plot, but there were trees everywhere and backs of buildings she could have gone around, grey bleached hotels that had shut down years ago, strips of coloured cladding to revitalize them for a new purpose. Some of them had started to take in the dispossessed and the vulnerable, all shunted here from other towns. Housing was cheap.

This field was in their shadow, just a few minutes' walk from the sea. Perhaps it had been a garden, once. The fences were cast iron, black, ornate. He kept going.

He walked the length of the field. A car passed with a distant hum, followed by another.

'Annie?'

Nothing. He couldn't see her anywhere.

🕉

All your old favourites. ICE CREAM, TEN FLAVOURS.

PAPA TEA.

SHOE & KEY REPAIR. WHILE YOU WAIT.

AMERICAN CHIP SALON (they had forgotten the extra O, and the name had stuck).

MILITARY SURPLUS, with an angry man reading an angry newspaper, glaring up at all those who dared walk past.

All around lay litter from the night before. Cigarette butts. Receipts. Gum. Thin wooden skewers, stained with chip oil. Sparklers, set aflame then discarded.

Motor scooters ambled along through the square, coalescing together, moving apart, the haggard, swollen faces of the riders pointing towards the ground. These men had once stood on oil rigs as the black seas had raged below, or had once brought back thousands of tons of fish a year. They had smiled at the boys and girls on the beach, all the businesses booming, their arms thick, their hearts strong and glad.

They kept their faces down, now. They barely spoke to each other. Half of them could not remember who they were, not really.

Seagulls swooped from roof to roof. Middle-aged couples sat on benches, mostly silent. The air smelt of dust, salt, skin, tobacco.

Beyond the anonymous, crackling buildings that encircled Market Square, a song played from tinny speakers. When music is that far off, when it thuds from the innards of some shitty pub, you can't make out the words any more.

'*Czy Alexey wciąż leży w łóżku?*' a woman asked, shopping bags at her feet, her phone pressed against her cheek. '*Powiedz mu, żeby wstał z łóżka. Musi iść do szkoły.*'

Her conversation was quiet, but others noticed. Most didn't look. One old woman did. It bothered her.

'*OK, ja ciebie też kocham. Zrobię później klopsiki, dobrze?*'

The Polish woman put the phone back in her pocket and briefly caught the gaze of the old stranger. She took her shopping bags and went over to TEA SARAH COFFEE (ROLLS).

'Milk, two sugars,' the Polish woman said, her English barely accented. She smiled as she took her tea, nodding in thanks. She picked up her shopping bags and left.

When she was gone, the old woman murmured to her partner, pained. They talked about votes.

The day continued. People came and went.

At 12.02 p.m., a police car came through the square, stopping at the corner of the car park. This was not that unusual. It would be unusual if you saw one in the night. They left the town to itself in the night.

One of the policemen got out – it was the handsome older one; George, the old woman thought his name was – and he went over to the market tents. He disappeared for a bit. The metal letters above the arch – ILMARSH MARKET – they were grimy, they only shone when the sun was properly out.

Minutes later, George emerged and got back into his car. He drove off.

Over the next hour, people started talking.

The old woman knew something was different – people were gesturing to each other. She saw two motor scooters stopped, their owners deep in conversation.

Something had happened.

She said as much to her friend. 'Something has happened, Derrick.'

Her friend just nodded. It was unclear what he was thinking about.

She turned her head, twisting her body in awkward, dramatic motions that had come to her with age. She looked a little scared, a little delighted. 'Something has happened,' she repeated.

෨෯

Rain had been forecast for the day before, but it had never come.

It came now.

They hammered nails into tents around the horse heads, dividing them into three roughly distinct sites. They left their police cars closer this time.

Sixteen horses, Alec had said. *And the tails – they're all cut off . . . They're in a pile . . .*

The way the tails clung together, slightly wet within the growing rain. The way the eyes, even now, even after wind, still watched from the ground. And the spacing . . . the almost-but-not-quite circles they formed . . . it did not feel like a crime scene.

It felt like a wish.

No uniformed officers had been available that morning. Alec

shouldn't have been. He was a detective sergeant. He was CID. He was meant for more than this.

He had been having trouble sleeping.

Alec got on the phone as the head vet drove off.

The man had given him a name and a number, a referral for a specialist just a few hours away. Someone with forensic experience, apparently.

'Might be worth it,' Alec said to his superior. They'd only need her for a little while.

Earlier that day Alec had been laughed at for suggesting they plaster-cast the footprints found at the scene ('You want some luminol with that, Poirot? How about we get COBRA on the phone and—'). Now, now the situation was different.

All these people, phoning into the station. Not just the owners of horses.

Something had happened. Something was happening. The day was cold and the wind blew and the rain was pouring.

'OK,' the inspector said, staring at a photo of the crime scene. Harry held the dark images in his hands, saw the captured tails up close, the clotted blood. He saw the white bone. 'OK . . . I'll make a call.'

CHAPTER TWO

The journey took a few hours, enough for the specialist to feel queasy without travel sickness pills. Trains weren't normally too bad, and driving herself, that was fine, but the carriages heaved at slight angles along the rails. Her body, her mind – they lost their balance. The world sank into nausea.

Her bags, full of her tools and instruments, rested on the racks nearby. She had a plastic cup of red wine in front of her, abandoned for a while now. It had stained her lips just a little. She had tried watching a movie in the muddle of all these people, but surrendered quickly, staring out instead at the smear of the passing world. The carriage spat itself out at various stations, until there were only thirty minutes left, until Ilmarsh.

She'd read about it online.

It had been a pleasure town, once. All lettered rock and candy floss by the sea.

A place to escape. A place to drink clean air, to recede from the grind of daily work.

She closed her eyes in a light doze, the table finally hers, folding her coat so she could wedge it into a pillow against the glass.

She drifted. Down the carriage, a door opened and closed. People shuffled in with their bags. A stranger laughed at something on their phone. Another stranger talked softly. The minutes passed. She woke.

They had come to their final destination. Sixty miles had passed in a dream.

When she gathered her bags and stepped onto the platform, there was no one else around. From the look of the announcement board, trains only arrived every couple of hours. There were posters for films that had come out over a year ago. Old advertisements with faded colours. You could see the soul of an area in how hard it was sold to. How it was rated. How much there was to spare.

There were no barriers or guards, no one at all. Just a platform, a shuttered waiting room, and a small island of red and blue flowers out on the street.

Her cab arrived a few minutes later. The driver was polite enough, quiet, didn't want to talk, which was fine.

They reached their destination, much closer to the sea now, though still no water was visible.

She'd been given the address by the police.

There were trees in a field outside. Oaks. Dark, unwashed hotels loomed against everything, their original white stucco muddied with the grey of a hundred years, a small splash of colour on each. The car-hire building itself was low and red in this strange road, JOE'S TYRES emblazoned on the front.

She went inside. The place smelt of ash and cigarette smoke. Car air fresheners stood in a rack next to the counter. A teenage boy sat behind it all, shuffling through a pile of keys.

'You Joe?' she asked.

He looked up, vaguely confused. 'What?'

'Are you Joe?'

'Why would I be Joe?'

She frowned. 'The sign outside.'

'What sign?'

'The sign, outside the—' She sighed, scowling before trying to turn it into a smile. 'You know what? Doesn't matter. I'm here to pick up a car.'

'What sort of car are you looking for?'

'A rental. It's been booked for me – it's—'

'By who?' He stopped sorting.

'The local police.'

'What happened at the farm,' the teenager said.

She didn't nod, didn't shake her head. She just waited.

'Name?'

'Cooper Allen.'

He handed her the keys. 'Four days,' he said.

＆

It was already dark by the time she reached her hotel. Fairy lights dangled from the street lamps along the seafront, COATES INN painted in old letters upon the building's side.

It was raining, but Cooper didn't bother pulling up her hood for the short walk. She smoothed her dark hair as she went through the front door, a little fleck of moisture remaining on her fingers, staining the dirty glass as she pushed it.

Inside, the reception was shuttered.

A sign was taped to the wall. ANYONE FOUND TO BE DEALING DRUGS WILL BE REMOVED FROM THE PREMISES.

Fine. No drug dealing. OK.

A fish bowl bubbled in the yellow light. No one seemed to be around. A restaurant adjoined the main hall, but it was either under renovation or else abandoned, sofas piled up as if in the aftermath of some long-forgotten raid. Dirty mattresses leant against the back wall.

'Can I help you?'

Cooper turned to see an old balding man. She gave her information and got her key. He wanted to photocopy her passport, but it wasn't necessary, not if you were from the UK, and she had to argue with him about it, get the proof up on her phone.

'Have you just been copying people's passports this whole time?'

'No,' he mumbled, and seemed eager to go away.

Hm.

He left, and Cooper went to find her room. The elevator was one of those old pull-shut ones. There were warnings everywhere not to put too many people inside. Not that this was a problem. When she arrived at her floor, there were no signs of anyone else, but that was the twilight of any place like this, busy or not, an emptiness of strangers. The kind of solitude that bothered her more than being watched. She needed people, even if she didn't need to talk to them.

She didn't bother unpacking her clothes, having brought just enough for the four days for which she had been booked. She dumped her toiletries near the sink in the shower room. In her backpack she had a few bottles of water, a can of lemonade, some gum. She took off her purple coat, her green top, her blue jeans, her black watch with the red trim. She stepped through and tested the pressure. She left the door to the bedroom open a little as she washed.

She was done in five minutes. She found a hairdryer under the bed. She didn't like how long her hair had grown, and hated it falling in front of her face. She only wore it loose if she felt some special occasion demanded it.

She'd had no real special occasions, at least recently.

She pulled on a red sweater and the same jeans she'd already been wearing.

She went to the window and parted the curtains. The world outside was all as it had been before.

The sea throbbed in the silence past the thin windows. If people grew noisy out there at night, she wouldn't sleep through it. She remained there for a few moments, crossing her arms. She could see her own reflection in the night, like anyone looking out in the dark. It made everything more than it was. It seemed to infect her. Dark hair, dark eyes, almost sunken in the distortion.

She turned the main light off. She could see better. It was calmer now.

Out in the distant waters, there was a blinking. Flashing. A boat signalling, maybe. She didn't know much about that kind of thing.

Mass horse mutilations, though – that was another matter entirely.

When he'd called her, the inspector had wanted to know if she'd seen anything like this before. If there was much precedent, if they were looking at the work of a madman or something else.

Revenge *could* be a motive, but from Cooper's understanding, the horses had belonged to disparate owners without much of a sense of relationship or community.

Sometimes these kinds of killings were used as a smokescreen for other motives, staging crimes in such a way that the authorities would focus on their gruesome nature at the expense of more mundane possibilities.

'Like what?' the inspector had asked, his voice crackling in the bad signal.

Like insurance fraud.

It was an easier kind of madness, at least superficially. Throughout the seventies, eighties and nineties, a hundred horses had been killed across the USA, taking an eventual human murder, and so the involvement of the FBI, to bring the insurance scam to an end.

The inspector had said they'd look into Ilmarsh's horse owners. He'd said the team was looking forward to working with her.

Alone now, watching the emptiness of this night and this sea, Cooper's sickness began to ease once more.

She needed a drink. She needed to find something to eat. She took her key and left, locking the room behind her.

CHAPTER THREE

There had been only a few reports the day before. A car's windows had been smashed near the market. A fight had broken out in a pub after closing time. There had been calls about shouts and crashes from a home with three young children and angry parents. When asked, they had said everything was fine.

The old hotels had been silent.

Homeless people were tidied away from the park and barred re-entry.

Trucks had arrived. Wooden pallets, laden with food and drink.

The town told this story to those who asked.

※

On the nearest Saturday to 5 November itself, the people of Ilmarsh would set off fireworks in King's Park further down the shore, the whole beachfront buzzing with people, with sparklers, with glow-sticks. Every cafe and every shop and every pub would come alive once more. This year, 7 November.

It was Bonfire Night.

At 3.05 a.m., the owner of Well Farm had set out west in a van containing thirty sheep. The farmer would arrive at the live-stock market shortly before six. He would not return until early evening, most likely exhausted from the day's driving and lifting and wrangling. He would be seen unloading sheep by those passers-by who knew him, those on their way to the show. One would mention that a sheep was loose on the road a little further down, but this was nothing strange, not for them.

ॐ

In town, the people had walked to the park.

Some had paid five pounds to enter and received a short programme for their trouble. Others had stood outside, content with an unsanctioned view.

There had been hot-dog stands, candy floss, light-up games, even a cart dragging along representatives of the county's radio station. Some years they had music, big classical theme tunes from films and television, all echoing out over the big speakers as fireworks took off through the sky.

Later, they would set fire to a giant effigy of a man who had once tried to blow up parliament.

ॐ

Everyone had then started to go home. Some went to pubs.

And that was that.

Few could remember anything else but that which had felt normal. Vans had moved throughout the evening, dismantling the celebration, bringing supplies and people home. One more would not have been remarked upon. There was such noise, such light. The owners of the horses had been far enough away that their animals' abduction could have gone unnoticed, absorbed into waves of cheers, of fire.

Many of the horses had been dosed with sedatives. As the police would soon discover, their owners had requested this themselves. They might panic, otherwise, they might quiver at each burst of light through the sky, each roar of distant thunder.

They were made sleepy, docile.

They would not have felt afraid, not at first.

ॐ

Just as Alec finished up at the farm, the sky electric dark, thick grey rain seeping through his only coat, a call came from the station. An old man was waiting to speak with him – he claimed to have seen the whole thing, to have been there the night of the deaths. A vagrant, sleeping on the edge of the farm, seeking refuge within a stone ruin. No fixed abode. No electoral registration. No friends. No connection to anyone beyond his walking into a police station and sharing a story about animals and torchlight.

'Do you think he was actually there?'

'I don't know,' the inspector said. 'Ask him yourself.' The call ended.

So Alec went, driving to the centre of town, his trousers squelching in his seat. The police station had long since been merged with the town's library, much of the county's budget spent on electronic helpdesks in place of a normal reception or waiting area. The library – itself almost empty and ransacked since the merger – had a lift round the back in the loading bay, but they only used that when they had to. The security system was a pain. The entrance to the station was around the side of the building, up a zigzag of metal stairs.

A dozen cameras watched Alec as he rose up, holding firmly on to the rusted rails, the old metal slick with rain.

Alec held his pass to the electric pad. The light went green and the door buzzed open.

From his glass office, the inspector waved, then pointed over to the end of the room. Alec grumbled and went straight to the interview room. Not even a fucking hello, let alone a debrief.

The hermit was inside as promised. He had a can of cola on the table in front of him. It was unopened. The whole interview, it remained unopened. Both of them sat there, wet with rain.

'Do you want a towel?'

'What?' The hermit raised an eyebrow.

'I'm going to get towels.'

Alec left and could only find stacks of blue paper towels in the bathrooms. Blue like a bedroom wall of painted clouds. A nice blue. He brought a wad back.

Both men patted their hair with it, their clothes.

The hermit told him his story.

CHAPTER FOUR

The Witness

They'd carve out vast fields of conifers, tall and thick and green and beautiful, even at night. They'd be glad of it. They'd leave them long enough to establish ecosystems, to become a part of the land in the eyes of all those who passed along the road, who lived and made their homes here. Then they'd cull it all, selling the wood for paper. The beauty was in death, in brevity. They'd move on.

These charnel fields ran amongst the farms and the forests, the river and the ponds. There was water, there were trees, and there were places the conifers had once stood, side by side in the endless flatness, this place without curvature or motion.

The hermit knew the whistle of the air, the cries of birds you'd hear in land like this. He knew each sound, though he didn't know the names of the actual species. He'd planned to use the library computer, whenever he went to town again. See if there was an answer there. He'd remember them all. He wanted to, truly he did. He'd do his best. He had his card, worn and faded though it was.

A few hours before the horses were killed, he'd walked among the trees, the sun low, mostly hidden behind a carpet of clouds. There were leaves everywhere, crumpled, desiccated. Each step crumpled more. It was satisfying. It calmed him. He looked up and around as he went. They were mostly skeletons around this place, though there were animals, still, squirrels and hedgehogs, badgers even. He'd heard stories of wild boar closer to town.

He'd found a life where living was the only purpose. He'd left everyone he had ever loved, ever cared about. He had found peace.

At the lake, half an hour past the treeline, near the rusted burned-out wreck of a car, he washed.

He dried himself with a rag from his bag, metal pans and cups clanking as he pulled it out. He'd make some coffee when he got back. He looked at the sky, wondering what day it was.

He got dressed and doubled back to the woods. He needed to gather kindling. Half-dry moss, peeled from the tree trunks. Sticks and wood both short and not so short. A few inches, thin for the beginning. Longer and thicker for the flame proper, to lay on it afterwards. It was the water that kept it going, the impurities and imperfections. He gathered what he needed and left. The day was growing darker.

By nightfall, he had fire. He fashioned the moss and the twigs – the small ones, the thin ones – all into a ball, cupping his hands round them and forging a shallow well with his fingers. He lit his match and sparked the fire in the centre of the ball, blowing into the orb, giving his own air to help the flame spread. He started it outside the little stone house he'd called home these past few nights, stacking the longer sticks in cross-hatch around the kindling. It kept him warm and gave him light for his book. He heated his beans in a can above it. He heated coffee. He'd killed a bird the day before, had stripped it of its feathers and meat. It had a tag attached to its leg.

Fireworks burst in the darkness, far away.

A small whistle, a stuttered 'pop' of stars in the long black. The rockets had been going off for weeks, though tonight was worse. He wasn't sure when the fifth was, when the bonfire and fireworks would be. Imagine an effigy of yourself being burned alive for hundreds of years. He did not want to imagine or see.

He closed the book covers and let his fire die. He went into the stone house and lit his candle. His blankets and bedding were still stretched out from the night before. They were enough to keep him warm. This place was a small ruin; it had holes in the ceiling and flooded when it rained. It was not large. He had worked out the best place to sleep. It was close to the woods and the lake. He had been left alone here. He'd stay, if he could.

He'd seen the farmer a few times, the one who lived adjacent. WELL FARM. Most people didn't know why it was called that. A good name for a farm. Hopeful, they thought. But it was nothing to do with goodness. There was a water-well in the woods, on land that had once been a part of this place.

So people thought 'Well Farm' was a nice name.

He hadn't spoken to the farmer, he'd just seen him and tried not to be seen, in case the man laid claim to this land, or knew who might. He'd watched him in his fields, spraying nettles. He'd watched him walking a dog. Something about the farmer seemed lonely.

Like a prisoner.

The hermit went to sleep.

He was awoken before light.

It was still dark. The candle wax had set, though. He relit it. Something was outside.

He heard the running of an engine, a car or a small truck, over almost as soon as it had begun. But the hermit saw nothing when he looked out through the window. The noise had come from the farm, or closer to it. There was nothing, until there was something. It made him breathe.

A torch. Two torches.

They danced in the dark, further down the fields. They moved back and forth, until they rested against the ground, illuminating vast horizontals.

The hermit pulled his coat around him and left the stone house. He wanted to see.

There were hands in that earth, patting down soil around lifeless shapes.

The strangers moved back and forth.

One of them was crying.

ॐ

The hermit left the next morning, gathering his things before first light. Before the policeman arrived at the farm. Before the eyes in the earth. Before all of it began.

ॐ

'I came back,' he told Alec, shaking. 'I came back. I – I didn't want to be alone, not after that. I wanted to get new books. I wanted to – I wanted to be with people. And I heard what had happened . . . I heard what they did.'

Alec stared at him from across the table, piles of blue paper towels all around them.

'Did I help?' the hermit asked, staring back.

Alec asked the man if he could identify the people who had done this. If he had seen their faces, if he knew their gender, or any identifiable characteristic at all.

'They – they were crying. One of them was crying,' the man said.

Of all else, he was not sure.

He was sorry. He—

'You've been helpful,' Alec said, trying to smile. 'Of course you've been helpful.'

This made the hermit beam and nod his head, his tired eyes glistening.

He had nowhere to go that night.

Alec helped him down the metal stairs.

He never saw the man again.

CHAPTER FIVE

The CD player sang a song about the end of the world. It could be heard through the glass, it was that loud, the curtains drawn at the front of the house, the fire burning – a real fire, wood and all – casting the living room in a golden glow.

Inside, visible through the hallway's end, a child could be seen playing with paper clips in the kitchen corner, stringing them together and tying them round wooden chairs, hanging his toys and action figures from various hoops.

Alec tried his best with the child, which was all anyone could do. He didn't know how to talk to him.

His wife stood near the stove and stirred minced beef into tomato, tomato into minced beef.

The smells hit him as he came in through the front door. The track changed.

He shouted, 'I'm back,' but it felt a little pointless. His wife was still busy with dinner, his son was busy with . . . well, whatever the whole paper clip thing was about. Alec tussled Simon's hair as he walked past and the boy grumbled.

'How was your day?' Elizabeth asked, not turning around.

He put his hands round his wife's waist, and she shifted away. 'Not while I'm cooking.'

'My day was great,' Alec lied, putting his hands round her waist again.

She turned from the saucepan, thrusting the wooden spoon into her husband's hands. 'Stir,' she said.

So he stirred.

'I'm sorry I'm so late,' Alec lied.

'It's fine,' his wife also lied, moving along to take the boiling spaghetti off the heat.

'It's just this case . . . You wouldn't believe what we're dealing with.'

He waited. The music kept playing. The kid kept playing.

He continued. 'I said, you wouldn't believe what we're dealing with.'

'I heard you.'

'You're clearly angry about something,' Alec said. 'What is it?'

'*You're clearly angry about something,*' she repeated, her tone all silly, mocking, ridiculous.

'Oh, great.'

'*Oh, great.*' She reclaimed the spoon and took over stirring, tasting, preparing. He caught the beginning of a smile in the corner of her mouth, and he smiled too.

'You're just copying me.'

'*You're just copying me.*'

'I think Alec Nichols is very sorry for whatever bad thing he did.'

'*I think Alec Nichols is bla bla bla blah.*'

The little boy laughed at this. Alec smiled too, in spite of himself.

'Hey,' he said, touching his wife's arm, gentler than before. She turned, clearly tired. 'I think Alec Nichols doesn't know how lucky he is.'

She didn't repeat this, only frowned.

'Hey,' he said again, his eyes staring into her eyes, both of their expressions fading into light smiles.

'Let's . . . let's just get dinner on the table, OK?' she said, after a pause. 'We can talk later, when he's in bed.'

Alec took a moment to move, but when he did, he scooped his son up off the floor onto his feet, and told the seven-year-old to tidy his things away.

He went back to the hall and took off his coat while his wife served dinner at the table. There was still snow on his sleeves; it had probably fallen on Elizabeth when he'd grabbed her.

He was tired. He rubbed his eyes, a headache brewing at his temples.

He wondered if—

ॐ

Alec stopped. He needed to stop.

Standing outside his house, his clothes still crusted with horse-mud, there was no fire inside, no music playing, no warm kitchen.

It was empty. It was a different building, in a different place, in a different time. Though Simon was still with him, he was out camping with a friend tonight. The boy was eighteen now, bigger every day. He was almost ready to leave school, and it had been years since he'd hung his toys across the seats. He went swimming in the sea, despite Alec's protestations about safety, about tides. He spent most of his time at home reading. He played games on screens. He sat with Alec a lot of nights, and neither of them said a thing, neither one knowing what they wanted the future to be. He'd come up with all sorts of jobs. Police officer, briefly, surprisingly. Doctor. A vet, maybe, if he couldn't get the grades to be a doctor. Alec didn't know if one path was harder than the other, but it had to be, hadn't it? It had to be more difficult to save the life of a human than a dog.

And Alec had tried to explain the potential problems his boy might face with university applications – that from his brief searches, so many difficult futures lay ahead, but still, Simon didn't know.

It was strange, what we asked of eighteen-year-olds.

The sky was dark now. The sun had set on the horses. Caught in an early November battle between autumn and winter, the next couple of days were supposed to be getting warmer and warmer.

It was hard to imagine after the rain of today. It was hard to imagine the weather at any time, these days.

He opened his door.

He flicked on the light and pulled off his dirty boots. He threw them back into the porch and locked it shut. The house was cold inside. The heating had been off.

He was smeared with mud and half-dried splashes of marsh water, all six feet of him. His black trousers and jacket stank. The muck had even seeped into the white shirt beneath. He had thrown his coat on when the rain had started in earnest, but maybe he should have left it off. Maybe he should have let the sky rinse him clean.

Alec undressed right down to his baggy boxers. He looked in the hallway mirror, cracked, damaged.

He needed to throw it out. Get something new.

But it felt like bad luck to let it shatter. And it still worked, sort of. He could still see his reflection. There was dirt across his dark stubble, even a hint of blood on his cheek. He must have scratched himself.

He blinked, his head hurting a little. He was dehydrated, too.

He went over to the kitchen.

Normally, the television would be blaring from the lounge at this time.

Alec sighed. He paced to the kitchen, put the kettle on, grabbed all his muddy clothes and threw them into the washing machine. He went to the shower and remained there for ten minutes, heat searing against skin and muscle. He'd had long baths as a teenager. It had given him space where he'd had no space.

He thought about how this investigation would go.

As much as the scene had distressed him, it had fascinated him, too. They'd have their four days to look into all this – the inspector wasn't one to waste money – but there would be a deterioration, wouldn't there? As fresh bad news replaced the old, as the week brought new horrors here and far away, people would soon care less than they did now. He expected to have the initial statements and records of each of the horse owners by the morning; the department was keen on the insurance angle, and even if that turned out to be a blind alley, the questions they were asking as a result might benefit them. Whoever they were, these people knew about horses; they knew where they were kept and how to handle them and how to kill them.

An owner was not out of the question.

Alec tried to stop thinking about it. He knew he shouldn't bring work home with him.

They'd protected the crime scene as best they could.

He hoped the rain wouldn't wash it all away.

He turned the shower off.

He dried off with a towel he should have cleaned weeks ago, musty with constant use. When he was done he got dressed, went downstairs, and realized that he'd now have to boil the kettle a second time. He wondered why he'd bothered putting it on before.

He flicked it on again with a sigh. Water began to churn.

As he waited for the boil, he stared at the photo next to the calendar. It had been taken back when Simon was six, when Alec had had a thicker beard, not just stubble.

Elizabeth stood beside them both, arm round Alec, Alec's arm round her. She was smiling, he was smiling. Her blonde hair was cut short, and his dark hair was longer at the time; he'd been going through a phase. A phase before the arguments. A phase before all that had happened to them, all they had learnt about each other, all they had done to themselves in the learning.

Now his hair was short and scruffy.

Alec wondered why he was thinking about her so much today. Was it because Simon wasn't here? Was it the day Alec had been through? Being with the farmer and that family, that empty place out in the fields?

He'd walked past this picture a hundred times and had not felt like this. He didn't know what had got into him.

The kettle continued to boil.

He left it, moving swiftly to the bin. It needed emptying. Why hadn't he emptied it already?

He grabbed the black plastic rubbish bag in his fist and stormed out into the night, eager to keep busy.

He thought about his day again, about the farmer, about the hermit. He'd made the man smile. He felt good about this. He'd seemed so sad.

⚭

The moon was thinning. The night was getting worse. He opened the wet lid of the wheelie bin, pushed the sack down, and began to drag the bin along the garden, wet uncut grass bleeding into his shoes.

Tree leaves shook about him, the wind picking up a little. The garden fence swayed. He opened the gate and pulled the bin through to the alley. Ilmarsh was a town of alleys, even its streets, even its main roads. So much was so narrow, so restrictive. The suburbs had more grazing room, granted, though Alec still felt it out here. A cloying kind of emptiness, south of the centre, right on the edge of the fields.

This area had been bog-land, once. A house extension three streets over had unearthed some old coins with faded faces, a few broken shards of Norse pottery. There had been a story about it in the local paper last year, before the paper had shut for good.

This whole area, the marshes and wetlands that had given the town its name, it had been a place for those exiled from other places.

The country had needed more fish. It had needed homes for the fishermen, so they'd reclaimed the wetlands and drained the last remnants of all those who had lived and died among the reeds.

Then they found oil, out in the sea.

In this rain Alec could barely see a thing and his T-shirt was getting soaked, sticking to his body. But he dragged the rubbish along all the same, downpour be damned.

After fifteen feet, he turned around.

It was nothing. There was nothing there.

The alley was empty. Of course it was empty.

On his way back in, he slammed the door so hard that the frame shook.

He walked through the kitchen, eyes catching on the stupid, repeatedly boiled kettle for the third time.

His phone vibrated against his keys, further along the counter.

Pint. At the Stag.

It was a message from George.

He always sent him these messages when the others were going to the pub. Well, maybe not always, but enough that they'd mounted up on his phone. Alec used to make excuses about why he couldn't go, about casework and his son, about needing to be at home.

He didn't know what was wrong with him.

He didn't want to feel like this.

It takes four years to know a place, someone had told him once. Alec didn't feel even halfway there. He thought about the advice for a moment and got annoyed at it. Why were four years good for anything? Four years went by just like that. Four years were nothing.

He missed her. After all that he had done, and all she had done to him, he missed her.

He changed his shirt and put his coat on.

He thought of a world where she was still alive, a world where he was not alone. He went out into the night.

CHAPTER SIX

The tents shook in the storm, barely holding up against the onslaught of rain. Already water leaked into them, coalescing near the head of a young mare, a chestnut-coloured horse who had been called Sally. She had been her owner's best friend.

It was hard to see any of this. There were no street lights, not this far from town.

If you stood in those fields that night, you would not have been able to see anyone, even if they were standing right next to you.

Even if they were looking right at you.

You wouldn't see their grey-hooded gas mask.

You wouldn't see their tight rubber gloves.

It is a beautiful thing to be seen.

Stars, dead for millennia, kept faith.

They walked out into the night.

CHAPTER SEVEN

There were stag heads mounted on every wall.

'Do . . .' Alec paused. 'Do you think people like me?'

George stared for a moment. Suddenly, his tired face broke into a mass of wrinkles, his chapped lips curling into a great big smile. 'Do people *like* you? Jesus . . .' He shook his head and drank some more of his pint. 'Where'd that come from?'

A baseball-capped twenty-something sat at the slot machine. He sniffed and scratched his neck. A middle-aged stranger talked quietly on his phone with his wife. He'd been denied disability allowance. It was going to be OK, though. They'd make it work. They'd find a way. A few tables away, five balding men huddled in the corner, laughing uproariously at some shared joke about Argentina. Old couples lined the brick wall like waxworks. The pub was surprisingly full, given the weather.

Alec hesitated, a little defensive. 'People don't talk to me the same way they talk to you. That's all.'

'What people?'

'People here. I don't know.'

'And in what way do they talk to *you*?'

'They're . . . quiet. They stare a lot, they don't care if I notice, they just stare at me. They don't seem to want to know me or want me to be around. I don't know if it's my job or the way I talk or . . .'

'Why do you care if people *like* you?'

'Because . . . I don't know.' Alec screwed up his face. 'That's what we're supposed to want, right?'

George laughed and finished his drink, calling over for another one. 'Not enough time in life to worry about anything like that. You need some perspective, that's all.'

'I just don't like to be judged.'

❧

They talked about the case for a while, about the witness, about the possible involvement of two people. Eventually the conversation turned to their boss.

More officers had left the department a few weeks earlier – Alec had barely known them, but to George they had been old friends, old partners all.

'Harry did what he had to do, didn't he?'

George shook his head. 'No one has to do a thing they don't want to do.'

'They'll be OK.'

'Will we be OK, when they kick us out?'

Alec shook his head, putting his glass down on the table. 'They can't.'

'Why can't they?'

'We barely have anyone left – how could—'

'We barely had anyone before,' said George.

'I didn't come here to be . . .'

'Be what?'

'Pessimistic,' Alec said, and George laughed.

'You just spent ten minutes talking about how nobody likes you.'

Alec frowned.

'You're going to come into work one day and kill us all, aren't you?'

'What the fuck kind of thing is that to say?'

'You're like a postman.' George laughed again. 'You're like that guy . . . what was his name? Lived off the coast, didn't he?'

But Alec didn't smile. 'He wasn't a postman. And that's not funny. You shouldn't—'

George put his finger to his lips, looking around, mock *shushing* him. 'No one's listening. Don't worry.' He drank some of his drink, and his smile had changed, somehow.

And they moved on to other topics.

Old cases – cases like that – no one talked about them, but on nights like these.

Nights where you forgot what you were supposed to be.

Where you had nothing else to do.

Where you wondered if people liked you.

They came back to the question, before the end.

ॐ

Before George left, he decided to give his partner some advice after all.

He decided to tell him the secret of all life.

'Try to help others. Focus on the happiness of other people, not just your own. Not just on what you think is right and proper. That'll stop all,' he said, gesturing to Alec's head, and then his own, '*this*.'

Alec scoffed. 'That's selfish.'

'How is it selfish? Why else did you become a police officer?'

'If I try to get people to like me by *helping* them, then I'm just doing it to—'

'No, no, no.' George pulled on his coat. 'You do it right? You won't even *care* if people like you. It won't be important to you. Their happiness will be yours.' He looked down at the empty glasses on the table, their mouth-prints almost like lipstick. Alec remained where he was. 'Just relax, OK?'

'Because *that's* always a helpful thing to say . . .'

'Didn't your dad teach you any of this stuff?'

Alec didn't answer this. He just looked at his drink.

George sighed. 'You be you, then.'

'I will.' Alec drank more of his drink, and his friend lingered. 'I'll just finish this,' he said. 'Then I'll go.'

George sighed.

'I'll be fine, really . . .'

'No, you won't.'

'Goodnight, George.'

After hesitating, the other man left, sighing again. Alec sat there for a while longer, staring at his drink before suddenly downing the rest and going to the bar for another.

'Whisky, please,' he said, leaning on the wood.

The bartender nodded, a little bored, maybe. 'Double or single, mate?'

'Double.' Alec waited for a moment as the bartender took the bottle and poured. He stared into the mirror ahead of him.

He blinked, pained, and reached into his pocket for some paracetamol.

He turned. He couldn't bear sitting down, not now. He looked through the dirty window at the beer garden, the false bamboo fences adorned with fairy lights.

He needed fresh air, even if it was raining.

He needed to get out of here.

He went outside, his passage marked by the jingle of door-bells. It took him a few moments, a few sips, to realize he wasn't alone.

🐎

The woman was leaning against one of the wooden posts at the edge of the garden, still protected from the downpour by the awning above. She wore a dark red sweater with black floral patterns like ink blots. Blue jeans ran into brown boots. She was staring intently at her phone. She hadn't looked up. On the table near her was a small plastic folder full of paper, a notebook, and a drink on top to hold them down from the growing wind, a purple coat hanging from the back of a chair.

Her dark hair was rain-speckled, partially illuminated by the glow. She was biting her lip a little, agitated, thinking about whatever was on the screen. And suddenly her mouth curled at whatever message she had been sent, and Alec smiled too, and the woman looked up to see him.

Shit. Alec looked away, focusing on his drink.

He went inside and paused. He looked back.

He put his drink down on the table and left. He pulled on his coat as he went through the door.

⚶

Alec took the long way back by the seafront. He'd had too much to drink, he knew. He needed to clear his head.

The storm raged, but the amusement arcades were still open, even at ten o'clock in the evening, even on a night like this.

A caravan shook near the waves further down, perched in a car park near a brick cafe.

The lights were on, and a stranger stood outside, his hood up.

The stranger looked at Alec, his face full of water, and Alec looked back, the same.

They paused for a moment, thirty feet away from each other, the only sound the heavy rain hitting the roads, neon swaying through the drops. Static filled the world until there was no picture left.

The man's lips moved. Alec did not know what he was saying, or if he was talking to him. God help him, he did not care.

Alec turned, angry, broken, making his way towards a house that was not a home, towards an empty, lonely bed.

Tomorrow, he would go and dig up the horses. He'd meet the forensics expert, they'd find who did this, and the expert would leave and he would stay. His life – his shitty, broken husk of a life – would continue on.

He'd do what he had to do until he could do nothing else.

'She asked me a question, once.'
The van slowed down for the turning.
'She asked me if I knew what God wants.'
The noise of rockets pulsed through the air.
'What kind of a person asks a thing like that?'
The driver did not answer.
'Are you religious? Do you believe in anything?'
The driver shrugged.
Everything was silent now.
The sound of screams had ended.

Day Two

CHAPTER EIGHT

The next morning, Alec hit a pedestrian with water from a puddle.

Technically speaking it was an illegal act, worthy of a thousand-pound fine and three points on his licence. He grimaced. He'd let himself off. The jogger was on his side of the road. He shouldn't have been running away from the direction of oncoming traffic, especially considering how dark it was.

Alec hadn't even seen the man.

He slowed down a hundred yards away and briefly considered honking his horn in apology, but this might seem like taunting, so he didn't. He just sped up again, off to the farm.

He'd awoken to emails containing files and witness statements from all the horse owners, compiled from phone calls at the station and a couple of in-person interviews.

It was a varied group. Three of the horses had been owned directly by the local riding school and livery; four more by a former town councillor, Joanne Marsh; most of the rest by farmers and local kids. Two of the horse owners they had not yet traced, no identification chips being present in their animals' necks.

One of the owners had a criminal record: Michael Stafford, forty-three, lived by the sea. He had used his horse for work, driving kids up and down along the shore in his carriage. Alec looked at the file.

Aggravated assault. Possession with intent to supply. All when Michael had been a younger man. But mistakes were like arrows fired through time. They kept going, on and on, unable to find a target, unable to stop.

Two other names stood out on the list: the stable owners Charles and Louise Elton, the only joint owners of horses and therefore a ready-made fit for the mysterious couple spotted by the hermit on Well Farm. Judging by their age, however, it felt difficult to imagine the pair hacking off skulls.

George would look into what he could; today, he was needed on other cases.

Alec would follow up the rest.

He had a couple of hours before he was due at the crime scene. He planned to talk with the farmer again. Among the horse owners, several had not only heard of Albert Cole, but spoke of a troubled past. There were rumours about his wife Grace and why she had left him; his daughter Rebecca had been pulled out of school around the same time.

Alec wanted to speak to the girl, too. He'd tried to do so the day before – she'd been the first person to find the animals, after all. But her father was protective, evasive, kept claiming that she was busy with her work or that she had some urgent chore to perform at the farm. Alec did not know what was or was not urgent in a place like this.

He thought of the stag heads on the wall of the pub.

He kept driving. He kept his eyes on the road. The specialist would know more. He knew so little.

CHAPTER NINE

The teenager angled away from the rising sun. Her whole face convulsed, forcing a sneeze out onto the damp mossy rock beside her. In the early light, droplets dribbled down into the miscoloured marsh below. The void behind her nose ached.

She was alone.

Sat here as she was, hunched up on as natural a throne as anyone might ever find, Rebecca didn't need to hold her hands before her face. She didn't need politeness. To sneeze and not care, that was freedom.

Far off, the tents had survived the storm. Even now, one of the policemen was over there, Mr Nichols. He'd arrived at first light, just like the day before. He'd spoken to her, her father at her side.

How did you find the horses? Why were you out so early?

Why did you touch one?

Did you see or hear anything strange?

Do you know why someone would want to do this?

She was walking the dog, she'd had problems sleeping.

She wasn't sure what she was looking at.

No, apart from the sight itself.

No.

She looked out at the lonely lights of nearby farms, far enough away that they seemed like campfires now.

Something moved beneath her dangling feet.

There was no sound but the cricking of crickets, of tree leaves rippling like rain.

She peered down. Her heart beat a little faster. Just a little. It was like music switching on by itself. Like a voice mumbling in another room.

The thing below her feet . . . it was coiled, thin, flat . . .

The hair of horses, the clotted pile of tails from two fields over . . . for a moment, it looked just like them.

It tilted. It was breathing, pulsing. She pulled her legs up instantly, bracing with her hands on the rock side. She blinked, the thing in shadow. She shone her phone's torch down, and it stared back, unmoving now.

It was only a snake.

Black ran like pixels along its body, all mingled with leathered grey. A single V crowned its face.

The adder had risen at the fast movement of her feet, letting out a sharp hiss. The camera light still shone down upon it in the dark. She stared at the snake, and the snake stared back.

The sky grew brighter until at long last the girl sneezed again. The adder reared its head back, baring its fangs in response to her sudden noise. She wondered what it would feel like to be bitten.

She got up, dusted her jeans, and looked down to see the snake had vanished.

It felt like a dream. It felt like she was living in a dream.

And a car was pulling up, slowing down on its route from town.

Rebecca didn't recognize it. It wasn't one of her dad's friends, few as they were. It wasn't more police. It wasn't anyone she knew.

The noise frightened her, somehow.

She clambered along from her perch. Later, when the police had gone, her father would have to come out here to kill that thing. There were sheep nearby.

CHAPTER TEN

Cooper accelerated. She always accelerated on big verses, ABBA's 'Waterloo' ringing out from the speakers and from her own lips.

The roads were empty and long. Little broke the world but itself, the edges of the forest, the car.

She was going to be forty minutes late to the crime scene and she'd slept terribly, the bed of her shitty hotel room seemingly made of granite. She had stayed out too late, probably, and had been up too late when she'd got back. But she'd felt better this morning, waking to the sight of waves, of their brief almost-blue in the fresh sunlight. What was it they'd said? Try to be positive?

She swigged black coffee from her flask. She sang about winning, about love, about a war.

It was the only CD in the hire car, forgotten by some previous driver. Her phone signal was poor, and the radio, the radio was just full of static out here. And this, it was the kind of song that made you push your foot down on the accelerator. The kind of sound that woke you up.

She made up five minutes in the end. Just thirty-five minutes late now, not the forty she would have been. Yay.

A police car was parked by the side of the road, thirty feet or so from a farmhouse, and there was an open gate nearby, tyre tracks running into the fields.

Cooper parked further down. She got out and hurried to the

boot after taking a final slurp of caffeine. She stuffed her dead phone into her jeans pocket. She opened her boot bag and hopped as she made the change from driving shoes to waterproof overalls and boots. She grabbed her kit last of all. Her lenses, tissue-sampling pots, forceps, flea brush, needles and syringes, biopsy punch, a packet of mints, and scalpels. She almost always carried a scalpel, or a pathology knife, if the mood struck. You never knew when you might need one.

Sixteen horses dead, their heads and tails severed from their bodies, each buried with a single eye facing the sun.

They'd sent her all they'd found.

She slammed the boot shut.

Over near the farmhouse, she saw a police officer scratching at his arm, his sleeve rolled up. There was a red rash along it.

Cooper walked on.

句

She'd once seen a sergeant put his fingers into a bullet hole in a sheep's skull, no gloves. They had stopped on an unrelated call about poaching. The accused man had just stood idly by, nodding as the sergeant suggested that the sheep's wound might have been caused by a bird or something. A bird who could somehow peck through living bone, apparently.

She crossed the bank, the hum of flies and crickets all about her. Everywhere was saturated with the rain of the night before, and she could only thank God there did not seem to have been much flooding. She let out a sigh of relief when she saw the white arc of tents in the distance, waving like the sails of a ship. The bodies had been covered.

Her boots squelched slightly, sinking in the mud, the noise of the insects ever louder. She swatted midges away from her face.

She thought about the photos she had seen.

The eyes in the soil. The rat-king of tails in the dark.

There was something different about a horse, wasn't there?

Cooper had gone on about it once, sitting in a bar with some colleagues after a long day. How when people crashed a car, they said 'I crashed' or 'I got hit', not 'my car crashed, my car got hit'. They extended their concept of selfhood to their vehicle. If they thought about it, they'd see it's just the same with a horse and a rider.

She blinked, listening to the sounds of the reeds as her boots clipped through them. She briefly thought someone was looking at her, but there was no one.

The crime scene had been staged in a ritualistic manner, the heads placed carefully on their sides so that one eye was exposed to the sky. The tails were left in a pile nearby. It was theatrical and showy. It was intended to cause fear and anger and outrage. This much the photographs had suggested. She'd need to look at the scene to know more.

Dying places produced desperate people. Desperate people were not, as a rule, careful or subtle in their actions.

She did not imagine the case would be difficult.

৪৫

Nearer the tents, around twenty feet away, a police officer had stooped down, examining something on the ground.

The man was tall and stocky, his face full of cowboy stubble. Whatever he was looking at, it had his full attention. Cooper was just a few paces away when he looked up.

His expression changed immediately.

'I'm Dr Allen,' she said. She always led with the 'doctor'. It had weight where weight was needed.

He didn't say anything. He looked like she'd just stepped on his shoe.

Something felt odd to her too. 'Have we met?' she asked. 'You seem familiar.'

'No,' the man said, blinking. His face grew calmer. 'I'm sorry – no, I don't think we have.' He scratched his neck before suddenly trying to smile, extending his hand. 'I'm Detective Sergeant Alec Nichols – nice to meet you.'

His handshake was firm, but she was ready for that, and gripped back firmer. His eyes were shot red. He was clearly a strong man, but he didn't exactly look well.

She looked down past him.

There was a crow on the ground. It had dried blood speckled across its body. Most likely something had mauled it.

'Sorry if I'm a little out of it,' he began, and then hesitated, wiping his eyes. 'I was out all night on a job . . . didn't get much sleep . . .'

'I can imagine.'

She looked back down at the bird, and so did Alec.

'Not sure if it's relevant, but it wasn't here yesterday.' He paused. 'I was the one who found the horses. Well, after Mr Cole and his daughter, of course.' He paused again. She looked up at him. He was a hard one to read. He seemed nervous, almost, at first. But that wasn't it at all, was it?

◈

Cooper bent down and picked up the crow in her gloved hands, holding it at a distance. She tried not to grip it too tight, lest she hurt it.

She felt along the keel of its body, gently examining its ruined wings and legs.

Wordlessly, it opened and closed its beak.

The crow had ventral swelling and was in considerable pain. It was emaciated and utterly infested with parasites, as she'd expected.

It was going to die. Even if they nursed it back to stability, it wouldn't last more than a week in the wild.

Holding its midsection with one hand, she snapped its neck with the other. She placed it down to the ground and looked back at Alec. He blinked, clearly a little surprised, but remained silent.

CHAPTER ELEVEN

In the tents, large buckets and troughs had been placed where the water had collected and dripped through. Torches punctuated the gloom. Thin lights had been set up along the ground. Coloured string had been tied to pegs, marking the boundaries of each point of interest.

Alec assured her that the scene was already fully photographed. Cooper took a few of her own regardless. From afar, on approach, up close. Proper photographic documentation was essential for any criminal proceedings that might follow, even with animals – *especially* with animals.

Only images sold the potential for pain, for the discovery of malice.

Cooper's life had been an education in this, in more, but the world had a way of surprising you.

§♥

The horse heads had been buried on their side. For each, the soil had been manipulated to cover everything but the region around the one open eye.

There were five in this tent, the heads all arranged a few feet from each other.

Cooper knelt down, her knees digging into the soil as she

reached into her bag. She found her brush. She chose the nearest head and began her work.

She scraped some of the soil away from the horse's eye, careful to look for anything caught within, gentle in her movements. She found nothing at first. After scraping a little more, she found another layer of soil, impacted below.

The killer had secured the horses in the ground by digging holes, dropping the heads within these holes, caking soil around the flesh, then spreading loose dirt to help the skin blend in with the surrounding earth.

The purpose was to delay them being found, but not indefinitely. To make the realization itself a moment of power.

She kept going. Next, she looked at the site of decapitation. She had to move carefully, gently displacing foreign matter from the base of the stump while trying not to affect the tissue below.

'This one was beheaded with something sharp,' Cooper said. 'But . . .' She hesitated. 'It took multiple cuts. Possibly with different tools.'

'Slashes?' Alec croaked. Something seemed wrong with his voice.

'More like some of the head was sawn off,' she said, looking back at the horse. 'We'll know more when we get to the lab.'

The horse appeared to have been a healthy weight before death, based on the amount of fat around the crest of its neck, at least. She felt its skin, cold and almost limp.

Around its nose, there were traces of dried blood. Rigor mortis was fading and the eyes were cloudy, more than Cooper would expect for November deaths. Decomposition was proceeding unusually rapidly, but at least there was not much insect activity. There were more things in the air outside than in the dead.

She pulled the horse's mouth open a little, the weight heavy against her hands. A small section of tongue poked through the teeth. She checked the gums. The mucous membranes were pale on both sides. She palpated the submandibular lymph nodes, but these were unremarkable.

She rose to her feet.

'Where are the tails?'

৳ⓒ৲

They went through to the second tent.

Alec kept looking at her as they walked, shifting his torch each time he turned. A tell-tale wobble of the light.

He seemed uneasy in her presence. He acted like he was responsible for every piece of contamination.

'I picked one of them up,' he said, 'but I didn't know what it was at the time.' He shuddered. Moments passed, and then, suddenly, his voice slightly higher, he asked her if she'd ever seen anything like this before.

'Mutilations, sure,' Cooper replied, stepping over the string boundary around the tails. They were located in the corner of another head-circle, away from the others, like the tip of a Q.

She knelt down and placed her gloved hands into the hair pile.

She felt along for a bony stump. She found it and pulled one tail up and away from the others.

'The cut's similar to the heads. A sawing motion, back and forth.'

She felt along the hair of the tail, holding her breath as she did so. It was coarse, and towards the top there were clumps of more bloody discharge and soft once-liquid faecal matter. Diarrhoea, perhaps? It was difficult to say.

Looking around, not all the horse tails had the same signs as this one. The blood was slightly older here, suggesting that the tails had not dried together, but separately.

'They were probably killed in different locations,' she said. 'Rather than at the same time.'

'We've got nine confirmed owners accounting for fourteen of the horses,' Alec said. 'The last two horses have no microchips, though, and no one's claimed them.' Alec's torch shone down upon the tails and around.

'When were they called in?'

'What do you mean?'

'When did the owners notice they were gone?'

Alec grimaced. 'Some of them didn't, not until we told them . . . most, early yesterday morning. Soon after I saw the heads for myself.'

Cooper looked over the tail for a moment longer before putting it down.

'You think you'll find something?' Alec asked. 'At the lab, I mean . . .'

'The only way not to find something is not to look.'

The morning progressed. Cooper went into each of the other tents and performed similar examinations with similar results. There was no evidence any of the eyes had been pecked. They hadn't been out there for more than a few hours before their discovery, and it had still been night, then, if the farm's testimony was to be believed.

Before they left, Alec asked her if the horses had been alive when it all happened.

'What do you mean?'

He asked her if their heads had been taken after death or during.

If they'd felt pain.

Cooper said she didn't know.

But that wasn't true.

☙

There were traces of tyre tracks through the field from the road. Alec showed her photos. A large van. They didn't know the make or model, not yet.

'CCTV?'

He shook his head.

Further on, within sight of the horses, there lay a small stone ruin. Their witness had slept there, had reported seeing two people burying the heads, one of them crying. The land was littered with these lost structures.

Standing there in the clear light of day, they had an uninterrupted view of the rest. Of the silhouettes of abandoned tractors and cars. Green, seething, desolate. Sheep cried somewhere behind them, bleating for food.

The sun had come out a little more. The air started to get warmer.

'You know . . .'

'What?' He turned his head to her.

'You asked me if I'd seen anything like this before.' She hesitated. Sheep grazed in the field over the road, one of them staring at her. She turned ahead. 'There was this man once . . . it was a big case down south. It started in Croydon but spread all around the M25.'

Animals bleated. An unseen dog barked far away.

'This man . . .' Cooper continued. 'He'd lure cats away from their homes, he'd bludgeon them, he'd cut them and he'd leave them on owners' cars and in their front gardens, all laid out to see. The tails, the limbs, the heads, all spaced out.'

'That's horrible,' Alec said, his lip twisted.

Cooper nodded. 'The investigators thought it wasn't about the animal. It was about the owner discovering it. It was about the absolute power the killer had in that moment, the triumph over the owner's relationship with something they loved. It was thought that he waited around to watch the owners wake up and go outside. It was about the finding, not about the dead.'

Alec sighed. The farmhouse was in sight.

'Who did it?' he asked.

'It's too early to say.'

'The cats, I mean. Who killed the cats?'

Cooper was silent for a moment.

'Did you catch him?'

'The police closed the investigation. They decided that it was just foxes. That all the clean cuts, all the staging, all the arranging of limbs about car roofs, even the flesh found in plastic knotted bags . . . all of it was just a coincidence.'

'How many were killed?'

'Four hundred,' Cooper said. 'There were four hundred cats.'

CHAPTER TWELVE

Cooper ate her lunch near her car, sitting by the side of the road. Beef coated in a thin anonymous red sauce, the bread white and tasteless.

Meat – mourning the meat of another.

She smiled to herself, faintly. Then she grimaced as she swallowed another bite, before downing some coffee from her flask, still hot from a few hours ago.

There were thin fences all around her. Holes in everything. The subsidies, they were mostly gone now. She wondered how much of a loss Well Farm had made these past few years. If they had thought of selling up, if there had even been anyone out there willing to buy. Parts of the world grew worthless, abandoned. Here this father and daughter continued on, alone.

The mother had fled. The girl had been pulled out of school around the same time, taught only by her father. Alec had told Cooper all about it.

They'd had a look in the house, the different officers, nosing around where they could. The mother had taken warfarin for a clotting disorder, GRACE COLE on the label.

Elsewhere, clothes, jewellery, all left behind. Recent letters still sent here in her name, unanswered. This Grace had wanted absolutely nothing to do with her own flesh and blood. She had abandoned them a year ago. No contact since.

The sun fell through the sky.

Cooper finished her sandwich and stood up, stretching. The heads were almost all loaded up.

Soon, dissection would begin.

CHAPTER THIRTEEN

Later that day, Michael Stafford sat up in bed and stared out of his window. The carriage driver had told the police all he knew. But they kept asking him questions all the same. They wanted to know where he lived. What he'd been doing. Why was he being treated like this?

There were no bingo calls that morning, no snatches of music through the walls of his caravan. He'd slept badly through the rain of the night before.

Across the bay, islands sat, squat black smears across the horizon.

He looked for a drink. He needed to open the windows, he needed to air and clean this place. There were empty bottles everywhere, vodka and rum.

He walked out, the salt air smacking into his face. He shut and locked the door, and headed down to the Local.

On the way he got a phone call. Joe wanted to speak to him. He wanted to say he was sorry.

'For what?'

The man croaked something inaudible. Then he told him to go to the arcade at 3 p.m.

Michael had grown up nearby, had remained in this town by the sea while all of his friends had departed. Mistakes had forced him to leave when he hit twenty. Paying for them allowed him to return.

He still remembered the butchers, the moustache of one, the dirty beard of another, the red faces all around, the soap-meat smell of the drains outside, the suds on the steps, the red cuts in the windows, as pleasurable and tasty-looking as good food can be in films.

But it was not there any more.

Now, there was a small supermarket in its place.

The automatic doors hissed aside from his steps.

He headed for the spirits.

He found them near ice and frozen food. He found a great bottle of rum on offer and clutched it in his right hand as he felt around for his money, as he headed down the long aisle.

There were other people here, though not many.

He wondered, briefly, if he recognized one of the strangers, an older woman trying to find cereal. He did not know how he would have known her. There were children, too, on their phones near the magazines and newspapers.

He thought maybe one of them had taken a ride with him and Annie, once. He didn't know.

As he went to join a short queue at the checkout, he felt fingers touch his neck.

He spun around, the bottle slipping from his hand and shattering on the hard plastic floor, shards of glass and spirit skipping along the ground like stones upon a sea.

There was no one behind him. At this realization, he began to feel cold. He began to shake.

He heard the sound of amusement arcades again, the door open at the Local's front, the horror of their music manifest once more.

An assistant came to help. He had a roll of blue tissue paper and a dustpan. He began to gather the spilt mess.

'It's OK—' Michael began.

'I just need to clean it up.' The man set up a yellow sign to warn of a wet slippery floor.

'I only had—' Michael looked around and stopped.

Other people were near him now. Everyone looked back at him. As if there was something to see. The older woman from down the aisle, she was behind them both, and she looked at him with awful pity.

He was shaking. He looked at his hands and saw he was shaking. He looked at the open door of the Local, he listened for the music, and it was louder, now.

'If you see my colleague at the till, you can pay for the bottle,' the assistant said.

'I can't buy two.' Michael stared down at the man. 'I can't afford two.'

'Then just pay for this one.'

'But I didn't drink it.'

'You broke it.' The assistant stood up. 'You're on CCTV. We're recording you.'

'What does that mean?' Michael's face began to twist. 'What does that mean?'

'Don't get upset. Just pay.'

'I'm not getting upset! I just asked you what you mean – that you're recording me. Why are you recording me?'

'We – we record everyone.' The assistant looked slightly nervous, now. 'It's what everyone does.'

'Why?' Michael felt like he might cry. He felt ashamed.

'In case you do anything wrong.'

'Someone touched me on the neck,' Michael said, 'I – I didn't do anything wrong. They made me turn.'

The assistant stared at him.

'I just want *what I paid for*.' Michael grew more agitated. 'What is wrong with that? I just want—'

The older woman came up behind the assistant and placed her shopping basket on the conveyor belt.

'It's OK,' she said, nodding to herself, unloading a tin of coffee, a box of oat cereal, and a large bottle of rum. 'I'll pay for him. He can pay for the broken one, I can buy the new one.'

'Why?' The assistant stood, shaking his head.

But she did not answer.

The checkout assistant asked her the same question. He told her that she thought she was being kind, but she wasn't. That a man like him didn't need more of what he was having.

The woman said nothing.

Outside, she handed Michael his bottle.

'Thank you,' he mumbled, taking it, his hands still shaking. She seemed like she wanted to talk, but Michael turned away.

'Don't you want to talk?'

He left, hurrying down the street.

'I guess that's the thanks I get,' the woman said, but he kept going.

He kept going.

෪෯

He tried not to have too much before the arcade. He had a coffee to wake himself up. He walked back out into the light, minutes drifting into hours. It felt like days had passed since the morning.

The arcade was blue-carpeted, dark but for the flashing lights of machines. There was a boy playing an arcade light-gun game, firing madly at aliens rushing towards him on the screen. Old men stood by the gambling machines at the back, an area called REEL, eighteen and over only.

It was through there Joe disappeared, week after week. He had heard a rumour once that Joe owned all of this. He had heard another rumour that the man didn't own anything at all, that it was just in his name, that it was a scam, it was all one big scam.

That was all. Those small plates moving back and forth, back and forth. The glittered lights and the copyrighted music. Realistic-looking ducklings moving up and down in a cabinet. An emptiness of gum and scattered coin.

The amusement arcades were open all the time, even though no one came.

The problem of how they possibly survived as businesses when all else failed had used to bother Michael, until he'd had a drink one day, until someone had told him the secret.

The arcades, they weren't what they seemed.

'People put coins in them all the time. They don't get anything back,' the man had said. 'Don't you understand?'

Michael hadn't understood. A stranger had come up to the two of them, had begged, and his friend had told the stranger to fuck off.

'The arcades clean the money. They clean everything. All the filth right off it, it's like detergent, those games.' The man had stubbed out his cigarette in the tray, smiling then roughly tousling Michael's hair. Michael hadn't liked that. 'Where do you think the money goes, Mikey? Where do you think that fucker's money goes?'

So Michael sat there now, all those months later.

He sat waiting for Joe, who might have owned this place, might have owned nothing.

A stranger came and hovered near the chair. 'This seat taken?'

Michael shook his head.

The stranger sat down, scratching his neck. It was an old guy, grey hair, thick arms. Michael thought he'd seen him around, somehow. He'd seen him driving.

'You lose much?' the man asked.

Michael stared at him, and paused. 'Yes,' he said.

'I don't gamble much myself. Not with money.'

'Then this is a strange place to be,' Michael said, looking around. Joe wasn't there yet. 'Unless you like the kid games.'

'Heh.' The man grinned at him. 'Can I ask you a question?'

Michael didn't answer. Something about the stranger was starting to bother him. 'Do I know you?'

'Answer me first. Humour me.' George smiled. 'Where were you the night of the seventh?'

CHAPTER FOURTEEN

Clouds drifted across the fields as the moments passed. There were no towers to break them, no city to conceal the wake of the sky.

To be accused of something you didn't do, it might not be character-building.

But it did something, didn't it? It was half of Alec's business, potentially laying blame upon innocent people. You just didn't know who might be right or wrong at the beginning, who might be lying. You had to do your job.

He listened to his friend, a small sheen of sweat along his dirty cheek. The phone had cut against it, resting now against his ear.

'Michael claims he was at the fireworks show, the night of the killings,' George said, his voice slightly robotic from the weak signal. 'No names of anyone he was with, but . . . he says he was there. Claims he went alone. What can I say?'

'And his heavy goods licence?'

'Apparently he hasn't driven a truck in years. Just a horse and carriage for our ex-con.' George hesitated. 'Had a look through his caravan windows before we spoke. He's drinking pretty heavily, maybe some drugs too, it was hard to tell.'

'How was he to speak to?'

'Sad, I think. I don't know . . . All he had was that animal. It was his business. It was his friend, I guess, his pet. I don't buy that he'd hurt it.'

'He's been violent before,' Alec said.

'So have I. We can all make mistakes.' George sighed. 'I don't know, like I said. If we're on this much longer, I'll see if we can pull some CCTV from the shore. Must be a camera that points his way. Might help with the alibi, what time he got back, what time he left. I wouldn't rule out some of his associates being involved, I suppose. But him personally? I doubt it.'

'OK,' Alec said. 'We got all the heads to the vet surgery. The consultant is looking over them now.'

There was a pause in the line.

Over near the Coles' farmhouse, he heard the noise of a rattling door.

'Do you think she'll find much?' George's voice was muted.

'She said the heads might have been sawn off . . . Seemed to be promising.'

'Strange kind of job she does,' George said, and then, after a pause: 'You seemed to be getting on well earlier.'

'What?'

'Just what I said. You seemed to be talking a lot.'

'About four hundred cats.' Alec scowled.

'I don't understand.'

'They were – they were sliced up in people's . . . You know what? Never mind. It's—'

'Why would people slice up cats?' George sounded genuinely hurt, mystified, his voice grown quieter. 'That's horrible.'

'It *is* horrible,' Alec admitted. 'Talk later, OK?'

'OK. Sure.'

Alec put the phone back in his pocket.

He sneezed. For a moment he thought he had sneezed blood, but it was only a trick of the falling light.

When Cooper had asked him if they'd met, Alec had lied, or he'd told a half-truth, anyway.

The vet had looked different in the morning light, especially in the green boiler suit, the black wellingtons, the tired eyes. But it was her. The night before – the dark-haired woman in the dark red sweater, the one he had been caught smiling at in the beer garden. It had been Cooper.

He couldn't tell her that was their first meeting, that he was the silent weirdo at the pub. He didn't know what had been wrong with him, why his thoughts had been so strange. He wondered if she'd even registered it. A woman like that, she probably had guys fawning over her all the time.

He thought about the way she had snapped the crow's neck.

He stared at the road. The land was so flat out here. There were no hills in sight, no escalation or fall. It was a vast blankness, punctuated only by a few barns, a few tractors, and the curve of the Earth itself hiding all else from view. Only Ilmarsh was visible to the east, its low buildings sprawling. You couldn't even see the sea.

There was a skip nearby, just outside the corner of the barn. Rusted farm tools and machines stuck out of the top. Alec saw something fluttering within.

He approached the skip, the shiny plastic cluttering his eye. He did not know what it could be.

He had to move a wheelbarrow a little, but he found the source soon enough.

Metallic, half deflated, rising with a passing breeze, then falling once more.

It was a balloon.

'Happy 16th Birthday,' it said.

LOST CAT:
PLEASE HELP US FIND OUR JAKE.

JAKE IS A TABBY CAT.
LAST SEEN BEFORE FIREWORKS NIGHT IN LOWER
GRENWOOD, ILMARSH.
HE HAS A RED COLLAR SAYING 'DO NOT FEED'.
DIABETIC.
PLEASE HELP US FIND HIM.
SMALL REWARD.

CHAPTER FIFTEEN

There was a drain at the centre of things. It dipped in the middle of the yellow-painted concrete. There was blood within it, or there had been recently. Most large animal sheds possessed such a drain.

The shed was cold and lonely, even with the other vets standing around outside its open entrance. It was a quality of the place, just as much a part of its existence as the great straw-lined bays that kept animals during the day, or the yellow floor. Cooper had never seen such a yellow floor. One wall was stacked with shelves and containers, rope and suturing material.

There were no windows. There was a single red door for people to enter through, stuck right in the corner near the sink. Next to it stood a rolled-up corrugated metal shutter through which they'd brought in the animals.

The heads were now laid on chrome tables beneath white fluorescent lights, all spaced out in a five-five-six configuration. A trolley held the tails.

৩৩

The vets took their gloves off and washed their hands. They had cups of tea on the threshold, out in the gentle breeze – the old greying director of the vet practice, Frank, and a younger mousey vet named Kate. No others had stayed late to help her.

'I like your mug.' Cooper smiled.

'Oh!' Kate looked down at it and then up. Her mug read *I'm not sheepish about doing a good job*. 'My friend gave it to me.' Her cheeks went a little red. 'It's just a bit of fun.'

'My best mug was *Crazy for Ewe*. E – W – E.' Cooper shrugged. 'From an ex.'

'How'd you let him get away?'

Cooper smiled again but did not answer, and in the silence she asked about her temporary colleagues.

Kate was a relatively recent graduate – two years in practice now. She'd made this surgery her home base during her extramural studies; she'd lived nearby as a kid, before her parents had moved away.

Frank had been at the practice for years. He co-owned it and did a lot of the large animal work himself. He'd worked in France and Belgium for a while, as a younger man. He talked about that quite a bit.

'How about you?' he asked. 'How'd you get into your line of work?'

Cooper tried to smile. 'It's not that interesting a story, really.'

'Try us,' Kate said.

'Watched too much TV,' Frank added with a smile.

Steam rose from Cooper's teacup, bleeding into the air before the yellow floor.

'It's a living.'

৯৯

They talked about the things they had seen.

They told her of the worst.

The history of their community's infections.

BSE, three decades ago.

Foot and Mouth, closer now.

'Three farms were culled, movement restrictions placed on the rest.' Frank grimaced. 'They got compensation, but . . . some of those cattle, the bloodlines went back decades. How do you make up for all that breeding? I was around during the outbreak, the first time, I mean – when was that? 2000? 2001? You should have seen what it did to this place.' He put the kettle on again, pausing. 'You been into town much yet?'

'I stayed here last night,' Cooper said.

'Then you *have* seen. All we had left was farming, after the fish and the oil and the tourists left. It was all we had. Those farms . . . you think those horses are bad, imagine standing in the middle of dozens dead, a hundred. Imagine watching them all burn, a grown man breaking down in tears right next to you. All that pain.'

'There was a human death, too,' Kate said.

'One of the farmers offed himself,' Frank said. 'Shotgun to the mouth. Contagion hit him twice. First 2001, then last year. And there was the business off the coast . . .'

'What business?'

'There was a fire at a farm, an island a couple of miles out. No one knew them, not properly, but there were rumours . . . Maybe it wasn't an accident. Maybe the farmer started it himself. Hard to know the truth of it, though. Hard to know the truth of any of this.' He shook his head. 'These are bad times, Miss Allen. Bad times.'

He poured more tea into his cup, offering none for anyone else.

'What about the Cole farm?' Cooper glanced at the clock. She needed to get started.

'What about it?' Kate asked.

'Where were they in all this? I saw mainly sheep when I was out there, just wondered if they used to keep any other animals.'

'As far as I know, yes, just sheep,' Frank scoffed. 'And I wouldn't call it a farm, not a proper one, anyway.' He seemed annoyed.

'You had trouble with them before?'

'Not trouble exactly,' he said. 'Not with their livestock, at least. The truth of it is, the man owes us thousands.'

As they spoke, the horse heads watched through the open shutter. The rainwater had spiked their forelocks, their hair in peaks.

Their eyes just stared ahead.

❦

The other vets went home before 10 p.m. Cooper remained, the shed now sealed.

She wiped her eyes clean of sleep.

The overhead lights were in the wrong places for her work. The shed was fluorescent and cold. They'd brought in lamps to help her see better, though there were not enough. She had to unplug them and replug them as she moved along.

She began her work.

It started with cleaning, enough to expose likely evidence without destroying it, which was always a losing battle, especially with bodies buried and left to the elements. It was a trade-off, like most things.

She looked at each of the horse heads in turn to see whether there were any inconsistencies in their degradation, any differences. This might not mean much, ultimately – water may have leaked through in different amounts and locations throughout the various tents – but the process itself was like solving a puzzle.

You didn't know what was or wasn't relevant until you had more of the picture. Neither could you make assumptions. Evidence could lie.

She'd strung the police photos above each head.

One taken when they were mostly buried, back when they were dry and fresh.

One from the morning, taken when she'd first seen them, still unexcavated.

One from when they had been dug up, but still not moved from the scene. Alec had already numbered each of the horses, so Cooper numbered the photos accordingly.

The lack of waterlogging was reasonably consistent with what she would expect – the heads had not been there long enough to take on much water. Only one of them was worse than the others. The photographs helped explain the abnormality. This particular specimen had been placed to the side of a small mound, that was all. Water had doubtless pooled on the uneven ground.

She went through the tails. It was not possible to definitively match most of them without DNA testing, but for three or four where the hair colour was unique and similar enough between tail and head to support an educated guess.

As she moved from horse to horse, she followed an identical procedure, logging the results on her tablet then backing them up. She looked, first of all, for signs of trauma or disease that might lead to potentially distracting lesions on the skin.

There was some bruising on a few of the necks, very light.

A few nicks in the skin, probably made with a knife. For the most part, these were only found on the larger horses.

There was scuffing above some of the eyes, suggesting they had been dragged across a hard surface.

The majority of the damage had come after death, beyond the severing of the heads themselves.

ॐ

Next, as best as she was able, Cooper completed identification.

Strangers became individuals. There were chips in most of their necks.

She could access identity and owner via these microchips and cross-reference them with the vet practice's intranet, detailing age and treatment history. They had given her a temporary login.

For almost all the horses, the only reported problems in the past year had been various degrees of lameness, and that was to be expected – not because there had been an absence of other conditions, but because few other problems would affect the primary value of the horse for most people: their ability to ride it.

Only two horses were unknown and, chipless, unclaimed by any owner. The only way to determine their age was via their teeth. Both of them had Galvayne's groove, an indentation on horse incisors that was found to appear shortly after a horse turns ten, and extends with age, only to disappear as they grow older. It ran halfway down for one, slightly less for the other. Based on the condition of the other teeth and the head itself, she'd place the first around seventeen to nineteen years old, the other perhaps early to mid-twenties. An old girl for a horse. The thought came, strange and discarded. There was no way of knowing the sex.

She cleaned herself up at the sink in the corner. Her throat was dry, even a little sore, but she didn't want to call it a night yet.

She looked at each stump with a black-rimmed loupe, its high-power glass lens magnifying the flesh below, its ridges and its furrows. She shone light at the dead. Each decapitated stump bore signatures, both in the flesh and in the bone. The deaths had begun with the slitting of the necks, ventral soft tissues cut smoothly in a curve. The skin, the trachea, the major blood vessels were all severed in two. In some cases the bone and cartilage itself had been nicked in the same motion, but whatever blade had done this could not contest against the skeleton beneath. In most, decapitation had occurred through the vertebrae.

There were abrasion ridges in the dirty white bones. The bone cut ends were slightly charred, the soft tissues dorsal and lateral to the vertebrae frayed and singed. She found small wire fragments when she looked at a few of them, confirming her initial hypothesis that the heads might have been sawn off. But she doubted, based on the thread and the presence of knife cuts above, that all this had been accomplished with a power tool. It almost looked like what you'd see with a fetotomy wire, or something like it, at least. Old-school vets used to use – and sometimes still *did* use – this kind of wire to dismember dead calves within the birth canal, hacking off heads and limbs so they could be safely removed from their mothers. Nowadays such wires were also utilized for dehorning, or sometimes to amputate cow toes.

The overall effect and cleanness of the decapitation varied across the sixteen. The killers had, perhaps, became more and more practised as they went along, or more and more frantic.

Or one had known what they were doing, and the other had not.

A knife to slit the throat of a standing, partially sedated horse.

The animal's legs slowly crumple.

It bleeds, barely able to breathe, until it falls to the floor.

A wire to remove the head as it dies. A knife in case it is needed.

She'd read the witness statement.

They – they were crying. One of them was crying, the hermit had said.

Cooper made a note to look for abuse cases in the area. Whether there had been any spikes in missing or mistreated animals.

She went on.

Cooper began to skin them. It was harder than with some other species; some you could cut into the skin and pull the face right off. With horse heads, the skin stuck closer to the skull bones beneath. You had to remove it in patches, in fragments, though she tried to do as much in one go as she could. She worked on the best-preserved specimens first, double-checking her initial work as she went. She was curious to see if there were any puncture marks where a needle might have entered the skin, particularly on the neck – perhaps focal pooling of blood at the site. She knew some of them had been given sedatives by the vets themselves; but what of the others?

She laid the pieces of skin on boards, marking where she found lesions and abrasions that might turn out to be significant at a later point. She labelled each with a paper note; she took photographs – hair side and underside – from different angles; she logged them on her tablet.

Autolysis was underway. The digestion of the self had begun.

CHAPTER SIXTEEN

When Alec had first moved to Ilmarsh, he had seen his neighbours only briefly. It had surprised him, how much these people kept to themselves, how few said 'hello' as he passed them by.

He could only imagine what went on behind the curtains and blinds of each adjoining home. They stood in a curve all around, a crescent grin of bricks and electricity. One light was red, another blue, another almost white. It was just the curtain fabric that made them so.

He began to unzip his coat as he approached his house. It was going to be warm tomorrow, he'd heard. Almost twenty degrees Celsius, somehow, anyhow. It terrified him. George had been going on about trying to have a barbecue if he could, a final fire for dark November.

He reached his front door.

It hung loose, already open.

Someone was inside.

He thought Simon was already home – he assumed the muddy footprints on the stairs belonged to his boy, that his son had forgotten to shut the door, that maybe he'd just got home himself.

The possibility of anything else would not occur to Alec for one minute and forty-three seconds.

He locked the front door behind him and went to the kitchen to make some coffee.

He shouted into the hallway, asking if Simon would like anything. Nothing.

ॐ

Alec heard a key turning in the front door as the rumbling of the kettle came to an end, soft steam clouds moistening the blue ceramic wall tiles.

He came out to find Simon coming in, his backpack already dropping to the hallway floor, his brown hair speckled with rain. People had said they looked alike, but all Alec could see was the ghost of his wife. Her bright eyes, her nose – her features were all different in the eighteen-year-old, but still, all were there if you knew what to look for.

'You got mud all over the stairs,' Alec said, frowning.

'What?'

'When you came in before – you left the door open, you—'

'I just got back,' Simon said.

'You were home,' Alec repeated.

'What?' His son seemed confused.

'The mud.' Alec felt incredibly angry all of a sudden, and tried to hide it.

Again, Simon seemed confused, even more so as his eyes lit upon the dark stairs. 'That wasn't me. I just got back.'

The footprints were still wet. They led above. No second set led down.

The father told his son to wait there.

ॐ

He searched each and every room, his frame trembling, his eyes blinking. He found no one and nothing. The footprints ended on the landing after doubling round slightly near the light-switch – maybe the intruder had realized they were making things muddy? Beyond the dirt, all lay apparently undisturbed, no lights on, nothing missing, no windows left ajar.

When he came downstairs, his heart beating fast, he found Simon watching television.

'You weren't home, then? That wasn't you on the stairs?'

His son shook his head, not turning round.

'You'd tell me if you were lying?'

'You saw me come in,' the boy said. 'I don't know what you want from me.'

ॐ

Alec shook as he boiled the kettle again. Something in him felt like it was ending, like it was breaking. He'd left notes in his home, photos from the scene, from others, too. He'd left his laptop. He didn't know if someone had been on it, if they could have accessed the files within.

He saw more and more as he walked through the house.

He saw all he'd left for anyone to see.

Half-filled reports from the station.

The note on the table, the phone number of the farm's absent mother scrawled down upon it. He still had to phone her.

He wondered what Simon would say if he saw it. If Alec had written the name *Grace* next to the digits, which, thank God, he had not. Would a woman's name make his son think his father was dating again? How would that make the boy feel, if that were true?

In the kitchen that photo still stood, right next to the calendar.

His boy, twelve years ago, only six. His wife.

Love was terrifying. What you lost to other people. What parts they held of you, and you of—

He'd – he'd had this thought before. Lately. He didn't know when.

He felt like he was losing his mind.

He sat at his computer in the almost-dark, waiting for a locksmith to come. He didn't know if it was too much, even as he tried to put these events out of his head, to live in wilful ignorance of all that might have happened, all that still could.

He took the hallway mirror down, its surface cracked. That, at least, had been his fault. He'd kept meaning to do something about it.

He wrapped each fragment in old newspaper so they could hurt no one. He put them in the rubbish bin out back, but he was careless in the final moments of the task. He cut one of his knuckles as he pushed the glass down.

He went back inside.

There was just a shadow on the wall where the frame had once stood.

He looked up a number on the internet.

He wanted to find out what it could mean, even if it was crazy, even if it turned out to be useless.

He tried to find the meaning of sixteen.

One Month Ago

CHAPTER SEVENTEEN

Miles on from the bay, where the sea had begun to take the coastline, there were a few rows of abandoned bungalows.

Sea water seethed around them. Their floors were flooded.

No one came here.

Up the bank, the forest watched.

A car drove along the road.

Inside the car there were a few tins of pet food. There were some packets of crisps, supermarket own-brand, inexpensive. There was sticky tape, duct tape too. There was a phone with a scratched screen. There were keys.

The car stopped in the middle of that road, the engine running for a little while, nothing happening. Then the ignition died. A wave hit one of the homes, the structure's walls strangely pastel-coloured.

The car door opened.

The driver walked towards a clearing further inland, past the edge of the tall trees on the other side of the road.

In the clearing, there were twelve wooden crates. All of the crates had originally been laid out on their sides. They had stood – and some of them still stood – like miniature doorways. Two of them, far away from the others, were sealed, nailed shut, two large rocks resting on each.

The sun and the shadows danced their rays and reflections across time.

The driver opened tins of food and emptied them into each of the open boxes.

Then the driver sat back down and stared. The driver waited.

After an hour, the driver took out a book and began to read.

When the fourth hour came, the sky had started to grow red. It was dust, the news had said. Blown in from the Sahara desert, changing the light across the northern world. It looked so strange. The red light would remain with them for the better part of a week.

§©

Something moved.

A dog stood across the clearing, right at the edge of the treeline. It was scared, malnourished, mangy, its grey-brown hair all in patches.

'Here, boy,' the driver said.

The dog seemed to respond, but only tentatively.

The driver took a treat from the bag and held it out, even with the dog all that distance away, even though it was frightened, even with its teeth so sharp.

After a few minutes the dog limped to one of the two crates and stared at the driver some more. The driver sat unchanged, staring back, still holding the treat. The dog turned and ate out of the crate.

The driver spoke again. 'Who's a good boy?'

The dog kept eating. It did not look back when it left.

§©

The next day, later in the afternoon as the red sky grew dark, the car returned. Within half an hour, the same set-up of actions had been completed, and the dog emerged once more.

This time the dog wandered to those crates closer to the driver. These boxes held objects of different kinds. In some of them, treats. In one, a ball that squeaked as the dog took it in its mouth and let go, as if it couldn't quite remember what toys were for. Its tail began to wag, even so.

The driver talked all the while – gentle, rhythmic.

The dog grew calmer.

The dog limped round sniffing all the crates. It took a last pause, waiting beyond the reach of the stranger, before bravely approaching and sniffing the treat in the still-outstretched hand.

The dog took the treat in a lick that made the driver smile. The driver let out a 'heh'. The dog's tail wagged more and more. The driver stroked its head and patted it. 'Who's a good boy, you're a good boy.' The dog shivered in its happiness.

৬৩

The third day, the dog was already there when the driver returned. The day was warmer. This time, the dog approached the treat first. There was no food remaining in the crates, of course. The ball had long since vanished in the distant ditches of the forest.

Eventually, the dog fell asleep at the driver's feet. The driver watched the creature for a while before lifting it like a sleeping baby and placing it in one of the crates.

The driver took an electric screwdriver and some screws. The driver inserted them into the corners, sealing it all around with the dog inside, a single air hole poked through in the side, large enough for the animal to breathe but not for it to see through.

Still the dog slept.

The driver picked the crate up and brought it to the far edge of the clearing, weighing its top down with a large rock.

The driver waited in that place until the dog awoke. Waited until the noise began.

The driver went back to the car.

Back to Ilmarsh, past the sunken homes.

One day the driver would stare Alec in the face.

One day the driver would think back to those weeks of wooden boxes, far from town.

One day the driver would smile, and then cry, and then smile again.

All things died.

One day, the driver would try to die, too.

But not yet.

Day Three

CHAPTER EIGHTEEN

The phone rang. Alec heard it before he opened his eyes. He didn't like phone calls, not least when he had to handle them at 6 a.m. Even less so when he'd barely slept.

He was in his car. He'd left the house early, had driven to the bay, had parked right out by the diner, waiting for it to open.

He'd just closed his eyes for a while, and no dreams had come.

'You're awake,' George's voice crackled down the line.

'I'm awake.'

'The pills not work?'

'They work just fine,' Alec said, watching the lights start to flicker on along the dark shore. 'I just didn't take them.'

'I don't—' George broke into a fit of coughing.

'You OK?'

George ignored the question. 'Harry called. Wants us to go out to the riding school.'

'I thought you'd taken a statement already?'

'Something new,' George croaked. 'The stable owners made their insurance claim.'

'So?'

'They tried making it a couple of hours before we'd even spoken to them. We hadn't even told them where the horses had been found, but still, they knew . . . they mentioned Well Farm in their call. It's all in the transcript.'

'We were quite visible in those fields,' Alec said. 'News travels fast.'

'Even so. They knew a lot about the case. The wife didn't seem too upset, either.'

'I'll meet you there?'

'I'm sick. Not going in.'

'You're sick?' Alec raised an eyebrow. No one could see.

'Fuck you. I'm sick.'

'. . . OK, fine. You're sick.' The row of amusement arcades juddered to life as they spoke, lights beginning to blink, music beginning to reach out towards the sea.

'You still coming to my barbecue?'

'I thought you were sick.'

'That's why I need rest.' George yawned. 'Don't be an idiot.'

'You've got flu and you're going to handle food for a barbecue you're doing in November?'

'I don't have to explain myself to you.'

Alec sighed, stretching in his car seat. His whole body ached from poor sleep. 'Want me to bring anything?'

'A personality.'

CHAPTER NINETEEN

An hour passed. Their little empty world lurched to life.

Alec sipped his chocolate milkshake and waited for his coffee. He stared out at the islands and watched the sun rise over the sea.

Beyond breakfast, there was not much reason for Alec to come here. The call-outs were few. The odd couple having sex in the dark. Addicts leaving needles in the sand. Nothing that need concern the police, stretched thin as they were.

He wondered if a place could remember.

A boat moved across the water.

He'd ordered for Cooper already. She'd messaged to say she'd be late. How, when her hotel was ten minutes' walk away, he did not know. Overslept, maybe.

'How d'you want your eggs?' the waitress called over.

'Fried.' He paused, tapping his fingers against the table. He tilted his head. 'No, wait . . . scrambled.'

The waitress relayed the instruction to the cook, who seemed never to be allowed to leave his small vent at the back. She then got back to setting up, getting out menus from behind the counter. An ornamental dog, a great red, white and blue cash register, and a toy sports car sat as landmarks upon the long blue surface, punctuated by cutlery holders and ketchup bottles. The diner was American themed, in the loosest way possible.

'You working on the horses?' the waitress asked, three tables away.

Alec nodded. He was the only customer in the room. She didn't normally ask about work. 'Why?'

'People are talking about it.' She put a ketchup bottle on his table and kept moving.

'How?'

'With their mouths.'

Alec rolled his eyes. 'Anything specific?'

'I heard . . .'

'What?'

'One of the heads was, you know . . . human.'

He scowled. 'No.'

⁊☉

He'd woken up earlier and earlier lately, taking any morning calls he could. He'd been finding it hard to get to sleep, and to stay asleep.

Waiting for Simon to wake up, to watch the boy eat his cereal, to see him out the front door, it wasn't needed any more, and coming to realize that, it was a sign of the end. Soon he'd move out, he'd be off to university and more. Soon Alec could just be himself again, he'd have his own space again. Life would be life once more. Maybe that was terrible to think. He didn't know.

Maybe other parents felt that way, too.

Maybe everyone felt that way about everyone they loved, on some level.

Maybe he was utterly, profoundly alone.

And when he ate these breakfasts by himself, he'd read a newspaper, sometimes. He'd eat each bit of the meal together, stuffing egg fragments onto clumps of sausage, then spearing a tiny bit of bacon beneath, topping it off with flakes of black pudding.

This is what he was doing as the bell rang on the door, as Cooper hurried in. She almost crashed into the waitress.

'Sorry!' Cooper said, her eyes glancing fleetingly at both of them as she sat down. Her breakfast followed.

'How'd you sleep?'

Cooper took her purple coat off and unwound her grey scarf. 'Rough. Think I twisted my neck – slept on it funny, I don't know.' She picked up the mug of coffee from the table and before Alec could say anything, she drank it, pulling a face as she did so. 'Ugh. Not very warm.'

'It was mine,' Alec said, quietly. 'I was waiting for it to get colder . . .'

'Oh.' She grimaced. 'Er . . .'

'It's OK.' He turned to the waitress and asked for more.

৪৩

They talked through Cooper's findings. Decapitation had been performed with a combination of a knife and wire – most likely a fetotomy wire. The theory that two or more people were involved was supported by the different proficiencies with which the heads had been severed.

'Why both?'

'The knife wouldn't get through the bone. But it could cut their throats. It could immobilize them, it could give you enough grip into the skin and soft tissue for the wire to work. And what we're talking about, it's a veterinary tool.'

Alec paused. 'So whoever did this might have had a farming background, or worked with animals, maybe.'

Cooper hesitated. 'Possibly. I—'

'Likely they'd know the horses were sedated,' he carried on, cutting her off. 'They would know how to handle them, and where all the horses were.' He sipped his coffee. 'Someone local then, involved in local life. How hard would it have been to use these tools?'

'It would have taken whoever did it around ten minutes per head, if they were strong enough, and if they managed to keep the horses still, which would have been a feat enough in itself . . .' Cooper finished her beans. She ate each part of her breakfast in methodical sequence, not mixing anything at all. 'Maybe more than ten minutes, then. I don't know.'

The waitress came and collected their plates, obviously taking her time and trying to listen. They sat in silence until she left.

'So we're not looking at an axe-wielding, frothing-from-the-mouth psychopath. Someone more deliberate than that.' Alec finished his coffee. 'How were the vets, when you spoke to them?'

'Fine,' she said. 'The director, Frank, he was a little . . . well, he was abrasive, but a lot of partners are. The only other vet I spoke to there was Kate – she was a bit timid, worked with a few of the animals. Neither came across strangely.'

'Hm.' Alec watched as the waitress left through the kitchen door. 'We should speak to them again later, maybe. See if any of their supplies have been taken, which farms or properties they've brought these phot – photeto – what was it?'

'Fetotomy wires.'

'Could anyone else have had access to these tools? Anyone likely to have used them on a frequent basis?'

'Like who?'

'Like stable owners.'

Cooper shook her head. 'Even if they bred animals, you wouldn't risk doing a fetotomy in a mare by yourself. You'd call the vet.'

He nodded. 'Anything else?'

'One thing . . .' She opened her bag and pulled out a folder. Inside there were print-outs of message boards, missing animal posters, and more.

'What's this supposed to be?'

'Cats and dogs,' she said. 'I—'

'I can see that. How's it relevant?'

'I wanted to see if there were any heightened abuse cases in the last few months, any evidence of other animal attacks,' she said. She took a final gulp of her coffee. 'I didn't find much – they don't always come to the notice of vets, let alone cross police desks. They're voiceless.' She wiped sleep away from one of her eyes. 'So I decided to look for reports of missing animals – both in the local database and online. And it was mostly normal: cats who never came home, dogs who ran off in parks, et cetera et cetera. But if you look at the frequency compared to other months . . .' She pushed some of the papers in front of Alec. 'You'll see they've been rising. And fewer of the missing have been found, whether at shelters or otherwise.'

'So let's say there's a connection. What would it be? The killer is graduating to larger prey?'

She did not know.

Alec kept on pushing for explanations she could not give. She didn't know who would do a thing like this, but at the same time, everyone knew, didn't they?

Everyone spoke to hollow people every day.

People who made you want to say goodbye.

People you wanted to run from or hurt.

CHAPTER TWENTY

There were twenty, maybe thirty deer out in the fields.

They looked like they might flee at any moment, all caught on the edge of some final stampede.

They watched the car until it left. Alec looked back at them in his mirror.

He drove on. He tried to make sense of his temporary partner.

Cooper's eyes were sharp, almost glaring, no matter her mood. She had a slight unintended intensity to every smile, every frown. He had only rarely known people like this. Sometimes he found it hard to talk to her, just like he found it with everyone else. Sometimes she felt like an old friend, like he'd always known her.

She had agreed to come with Alec to this interview, to assess the way the stable owners had run their business, to help him understand whatever truths, lies and evasions they might offer.

They talked about the case for a while, about the area, about the community. Cooper asked about the island fire – she told him the vets had mentioned it.

Alec just nodded. He told her he hadn't been on the case, that he didn't know much about it.

He told her it wasn't all as dramatic as she'd heard, though. It had been an accident.

He moved off the topic quickly.

He wanted to know how she'd entered this line of work, and

so they talked about their jobs for a while instead, about why they did what they did. She had not been a vet for very long before she had turned towards crime scenes and forensics. He did not get to hear much about why or how this change had occurred, or whether she missed her old career.

She shifted the subject towards Alec, wanting to know how he had started on his own path.

There was no tragic backstory. Nothing he tried to avenge, no wrong the world had done to him, no grand excuse for all he had done in turn. It was just one of those jobs that children think they'll do – fireman, doctor, policeman. Everyone thinks they will save people. That's why they like stories. In Alec's case, he just kept going with his. He was good at it. He vanished into the role.

He asked Cooper if she'd ever considered becoming a doctor instead. She just laughed without explanation or elaboration.

'Did you ever think about joining the police?'

She shook her head, putting her phone back in her pocket. She had a faintly amused look.

'Why?' he asked. 'I'd have imagined you'd be valuable.'

'I like travelling to new places. Choosing what I do.' She opened her window slightly. 'Working by myself.'

He raised his eyebrows. 'You can do a lot of that in the police.'

'You can choose where you go? What you want to do?'

'You can transfer, yes.'

'And you wanted to transfer here? That was your choice?'

'Fresh start.' He tried a big broad grin he didn't really believe in. 'I always wanted to live by the sea.'

'Why?' She twisted round to adjust her headrest.

'Doesn't everyone?'

They were around eight minutes from the stables. It was a little after one in the afternoon. The air was almost humid. It felt like more than twenty Celsius, more than they said it would be.

'What's the worst thing you've ever done?' he asked, suddenly.

'What?' She turned to him.

He looked ahead. 'Just . . . just small talk.' He paused, sheepish. 'I'm not very good at it.'

Cooper looked back at the road. 'I scratched up a car once.'

'Why?'

'I was thirteen, on a paper round. I saw a man kick his dog. I wanted to teach him a lesson. I took my house key – I'd just been given it, my dad had picked me up from school before he moved away, but now, you know, I was walking myself back, so my mum gave me one. I took the key and I dragged it along the dog-kicker's paintwork.'

'How did it feel?'

'Great.'

'Did you get in trouble?'

'Not really.' Cooper frowned. 'But . . .'

'But what?'

'It turned out I got the wrong car.'

They both laughed at that, and caught each other in a smile.

'Is that really the worst thing you've done?'

'No,' she said.

‽

The sign was a faded green, a wooden rectangle arched at the top in a light curve. It looked to Cooper like it had, at some point, been repainted badly and quickly. She could still see the drip smears, frozen throughout the numbers of a year.

ELTON RIDING SCHOOL AND LIVERY.
EST. 2001.

The stable curved back round from the path's end, shielded by tall conifers and hedgerows, all bound by ivy running up and down and in and out, crested by the roofs of the buildings and the sheds. The road was the only entry point large enough for a van, and even then, not by much. The horses could have been led elsewhere first, perhaps. There was a public footpath cutting through the land, marked by a post.

The Eltons' house stood across the fields. It was the closest thing to a hill Cooper had seen in this place, a light slope followed by a ridge, a set of steps leading down the miniature hillside. The house felt alien to her, somehow, standing against the sky when nothing else could.

CHAPTER TWENTY-ONE

'We woke up, we had breakfast. It was a . . . it was a normal morning.' The stable owner tried to smile, but her eyes couldn't follow. 'We went out to feed them.'

Atop the red-brick fireplace, there was a single image – of a long-forgotten nephew, maybe – and a clock next to it, a silver clock with two bells that never rang. It ticked in the silence. Dust seemed to catch in the light beams from the window. The room was full of horses.

Little figurines, pictures, photos, place mats. Alec wondered who it was all for. Whether you wouldn't grow sick of it, given enough time, given enough proximity. He thought perhaps this room was more for guests, for parents of students, rather than for those who lived here. It felt like it was supposed to give an impression. A takeaway box from an Indian restaurant, just lying in the hallway – that had been the only clue of a messy, human life.

They sat with a coffee table between them, the stable owner in her gown and fresh slippers on one sofa, Cooper and Alec bunched together on the other, three cups of tea steaming in the middle. It was barely big enough for the both of them.

'They were empty,' the stable owner said, her voice soft, almost broken. 'The stable bays, I mean.'

'And then?' Alec asked, pen in hand. It was a fountain pen, a birthday present from his son.

'And then we made our statement,' she answered, picking up her tea. Her hand shook slightly as she did so, the saucer clinking against the white china cup.

'What do you remember from Bonfire Night?'

'We were in town.' She sipped her tea. 'We always go. Did you go?'

'I was working, yes. At the right entrance for a while, then on patrol.'

'Much trouble?' she asked.

'No, no.' He smiled. 'People were surprisingly well-behaved, all things considered. Some kids were acting out near the seafront, but – nothing major.'

'We don't have many nights like this.' She nodded. 'We get to see all our friends. People used to go to the pub more, used to do the farmer's market on Sundays. It's all stopping.'

'They don't do the farmer's market any more?' Alec frowned, and she nodded. 'I liked going to that.'

'They haven't done it for a year.' She smiled. 'You can't have liked it that much.'

'So . . .' He looked at the window, just briefly. He thought he'd seen movement, but there was nothing. He turned back. 'So you were at the fireworks show. Are there people who will verify you being there?'

She nodded.

'What happened earlier in the day? Anything out of the ordinary?'

'No. Just, just lessons.'

'For who?'

'Kids,' she said. 'We don't get many adults wanting them.'

'You have a lovely home,' Cooper said, and Louise smiled at that, surprised at the compliment, grateful for the escape it provided. More tea was poured for everyone. 'How did you get into this line of work?'

'The old owner moved,' Louise said. 'We couldn't bear to see it shut down. It hadn't been used like this for years—'

'Used like how?' Alec took his cup.

'Like a riding school.' There was a noise in the hall, a little slam as someone came in. The husband, probably. She continued. 'We . . . we wanted to give the kids around here the same opportunities we had.'

'You rode when you were younger?' Cooper asked, and Louise nodded happily.

'Charlie did. I was, well, I was scared.'

'Of horses?' Alec raised an eyebrow.

Louise hesitated. 'No, the animals themselves, they're lovely. It's the riding I don't like – they're too tall for me, too strong. Moving on something that was alive, it . . .' She shrugged, smiling. 'I like helping the children, but it's – it's not for me. Though Charlie . . . you should have seen him, seventeen, trotting along to me in the field. We were friends before that. We grew up together and we liked each other and nothing more, but when he came to me out here, I saw that I *loved* him. And this place, it was . . . it . . .' She seemed to struggle to find the right words. 'It was important to us.'

'How were the horses, before all this?' Alec asked.

'They were *lovely*.' Louise came alive. 'They—'

'I mean their health. Were they healthy?'

She deflated a little. 'We did our best.'

'Customers ever complain?'

'Sometimes,' she said. She sighed. 'But it's . . . it's something you have to get used to. I was, you know, I was a teacher before I retired, at the school. Right up until last year. You . . .' She tried to smile. 'I bet people aren't happy with you, sometimes. People work for the public, they find a reason to be unhappy with us.'

'You cared about them,' Cooper said. 'It's why you dosed them.'

'Dosed?'

'You arranged for the horses to be sedated, didn't you?'

Louise nodded, after a brief delay. 'Yes. Yes, I did.'

'What does that mean, exactly, Mrs Elton?' Alec asked. 'It knocked them out, or . . . ?'

'It made them docile,' she answered. 'They get scared, with fireworks, and . . . it's – it's safe. It calms them.'

'And you did this yourself?'

'The vet did it,' she said. 'I – I'm not good with needles.'

'Which one?' he asked.

'Kate. I . . . I don't know her surname, though . . .'

Alec felt her eyes on him as he wrote in his notebook. 'You said you didn't know they were gone until morning.'

'Yes . . .'

'So you didn't check on them the night you came back?'

'We don't normally,' she said.

'They're kept right by the entrance. It wouldn't have been difficult?'

'We've never had problems before.' She hesitated. Her nails, long, chipped, dirty light blue, dug into the soft white fabric on her arms. 'Why are you—'

Cooper put her cup down. 'He's asking because he's wondering why someone who cared enough about her animals' fear to pay for intravenous drugs wouldn't take a minute to see if they were OK.'

'You tried to make your insurance claim before you'd even spoken to the police,' Alec said, calmly. 'Why?'

CHAPTER TWENTY-TWO

Louise Elton said she had not tried to make an insurance claim, no matter what the company had reported, no matter how the transcript sounded. She'd just been enquiring about their position. It had been a precautionary measure – she'd wanted to know if they'd be OK. Other owners had already messaged her. What did it matter, raising the alarm? Their animals were gone. But they still needed a roof over their heads.

'The thing about my – my family,' she tried to say, 'we always try to do our best. We always try.'

'Which family?' Cooper asked, and Alec turned.

The stable owner did not understand. Neither did he.

'The one you married into or the one you were born into?' Cooper went on.

'The one I made.'

Louise explained and explained, a bird moving along the rotten windowsill outside, the sky bluer than her nails. Neither colour felt real. Neither colour felt right.

She kept trying to explain.

The last few years had been difficult, for both of them.

෫෨

Most lies are mundane. Most people don't even know they're doing it, and if they're caught, they rationalize their deceit. Cooper understood this. She did not like it.

She was up for some minor rule-breaking as much as the next person – she'd been *quite* the illegal downloader at university, and there'd been some weed sometimes, too, and an almost-expulsion, and a little attempted suicide, but who *didn't* try to kill themselves when they were twenty, you know? There was a difference between living in pain and living in lies.

And this man – this temporary partner – this Alec, he was a man who lived in lies.

Not in his work. Not in his job, or what people might think were the important things. Not like a criminal.

It was something in his voice, the movement of his eyes, the hidden fire of each impulse, cut off.

He was not a man who lived authentically. He was not honest with himself about who he was, about how he really wanted to be.

She felt sorry for Alec, the more she watched him. The more he spoke, needy, endlessly deviating from protocol. Wanting to be liked, and disliking in return.

'I need to go,' Cooper said. 'I—'

'What?' Alec seemed surprised.

'Where's your bathroom?' She turned to their host.

Mrs Elton told her it was through the kitchen.

'Can't it wait?' Alec asked.

She shook her head. It was a real tragedy.

She shut the door behind her as she left the hall. She heard their muted talking, Alec's deeper grumbles, Louise's half-shrill croaks.

Unwashed plates were scattered throughout the kitchen. Cooper took her time as she moved towards the next door. The calendar didn't have much on it, a circled *visit Danny* crossed out, the date of a film further down. They hadn't even changed it from October, yet. There was nothing in November.

There were letters near the kettle, sorted into two piles. Cooper picked some of them up.

FINAL NOTICE.

Overdue balance.

The fee will be applied to your account on 28 December.

Your application has been refused.

Overdue payments may affect your credit rating

for a period of six years.

County court judgements may affect credit availability.

Card declined.

FINAL NOTICE.

Balance: -£15,468

Credit cards: -£89,421

FINAL NOTICE.

Please contact us to discuss a voluntary credit arrangement.

The direct debit has been cancelled.

Beneath the letters, there was something glossy, almost plastic in its edge. Cooper looked over her shoulder. No one was there. The house was still and quiet, but for the noise of Louise's breakdown in the lounge.

Cooper pulled the letters away from what lay beneath.

There on the counter sat a photo of a brown Labrador, a polaroid. The light was dark in the image, the camera struggling to catch it.

The dog's eyes were not open.

Its paws had been separated from its body, a small three-inch-long section laid out next to each leg.

ॐ

Cooper returned to the lounge.

Alec turned to her as she sat down, and then he quickly looked away again.

He had done that a few times.

Louise Elton was going through the names.

There were no strangers who had taken an interest in horses, no weirdos lurking in the woods.

Louise's concerns were those of hate.

She told them about everyone.

It might have been one of them.

Every client who might hold a grudge. Everything people had said to her. Everyone who had not paid, who had complained about their animals, about their kids, about cancellation fees, about anything and everything. Everyone who had not been kind to her.

'I never had any children,' Louise said, shaking her head. 'I loved those horses. I did. I loved them. I loved . . . I love Charlie. But this . . . all of this . . .'

She was silent for a moment.

'It might have been someone who knew us,' she said, quietly.

Cooper opened her bag and removed one of the missing animal posters she'd shown Alec at the diner.

Louise froze when she saw it.

Cooper made sure it was on her lap for a few moments before she put it in her notebook and shut it away.

Louise opened the table drawer and pulled out a small plastic bottle, trying to empty pills into her hand, but there were none. Her eyes clenched shut. 'I'm sorry. I—'

She got up and left the room.

MISSING DOG.

CHOCOLATE LAB.
RAN AWAY IN DENTON PARK AUGUST 2ND.
VERY FRIENDLY. ANSWERS TO LIZZIE.
PLEASE HELP US FIND HER.
£50 REWARD.

CHAPTER TWENTY-THREE

Cooper had told Alec what she'd found in the kitchen. A minute later and he'd seen it for himself. Then, shouting from the base of the stairs, 'Mrs Elton? Are you OK?', no answer had come.

A few minutes later, looking around the lounge, finding nothing, they went up regardless.

The light, it spilled through the dark hallway of the landing.

౬౧

They found a door, slightly ajar.

This door was an oak-wood door. This place had been a nursery, once, though not for decades. A tree was carved into the wood, its surface painted a mottled, flaking blue. The paint had not been right for a door like this. In the dark places of the hall, damp ran riot across the walls.

The door was slightly open.

Their feet made the floorboards creak; of course they did.

A fly buzzed past them.

And they could see Louise Elton right on the other side, crying at her desk, shaking.

Before her on the table, there were dozens of photographs, black and blue and green, all catching the red sun.

'Mrs Elton, are you—'

She wheeled round, mouth agape. She tried covering the photos, snatching them up in her shaking hands, suddenly aware of where she was, of who she was with.

Alec pushed the door fully open. She turned back to the desk.

'They keep sending them,' she croaked. She dropped the pictures down as if her soul had left her body. She kept holding on to an envelope, her blue nails curled around it.

The images were of animals, of wooden boxes, of a shore, of an island far away.

'We keep *finding them*, we—'

'Mrs—'

'They know,' she just whispered, shaking her head.

'Pick up the phone.'
'Just talk to me.'
'Listen.'
'Please.'
'I didn't do anything wrong.'

CHAPTER TWENTY-FOUR

The water buckets were almost full to the brim from the storm two nights earlier. Hay floated in the muck. Nearby, outside one of the stable doors, bales of haylage had been bound in plastic. One was half torn open, most likely unused for weeks.

Cooper felt strange being out here alone. A car was coming, at least. The silence was easing.

The stables were capable of holding at least twenty animals. The only boarding place for miles apparently, but there had been only six occupants. Whoever had taken these horses had taken all they could. The old quarters were full of grime, some faeces, too. Most likely they had only been mucked out a couple of weeks before. There had been no grand erasure of evidence, no attempt to hide how they had lived, at least so much as Cooper could see.

'Hi!'

She turned. Kate, the mousey vet from the surgery, had arrived, her rusty green car parked just beyond Alec's own.

Alec had remained back in the house with two other officers, searching the building while Cooper looked over the grounds. They hadn't been able to get much more out of Mrs Elton; she had refused to say anything else until her husband came home. The man appeared to have fled the premises sometime during their interview. His tractor lay abandoned in the fields, red and vast against the hill. His car was gone from the driveway. Attempts to reach him by phone had failed.

'I'm glad you called,' Kate said. 'I wanted to help yesterday but—'

'Just need some background,' Cooper said, turning to lean over one of the stable doors. 'You were the one who sedated these horses?'

'Yep.' Kate nodded, awkward, sharp. 'These and a few others. Mostly those closest to town, those who might have problems with the fireworks.'

'What's your opinion of the Eltons?'

'As in . . . ?'

'Were they good owners? Good people?'

'They were OK,' Kate said. 'Left some problems untreated, but . . . what business doesn't?'

'What kind of problems?'

Cooper knew her manner was somehow upsetting the other vet, but knowing this didn't change her actions. She'd once thought her speech compulsive, unhinged from social conventions. She'd thought that other people – like her family, like her schoolfriends – simply didn't understand her. But the older she got, the more Cooper felt that the opposite might be true. That there was some secret for knowing how to act that she'd never learnt. Sometimes she had no idea how to imitate, and the vague instinct to do so just seemed to push her further and further away into her own head.

So she'd asked Kate what kind of problems the Eltons might have left untreated.

'Possibly some signs of lameness. A few of their horses were shifting their weight, the older ones, mostly. The Eltons started avoiding contact as soon as I pushed the issue. They probably couldn't afford any treatment or surgery.'

'But they could afford sedatives?'

Kate shrugged.

Cooper disappeared into one of the stable bays.

'You have any suspects yet?' Kate's voice grew slightly high. Cooper didn't answer, and so she went on. 'Hopefully you'll have time to enjoy the town once you're done, anyway. Let me know if you want any recommendations or anything.'

The tentative pleas for warmth made Cooper feel bad. She tried to focus on the task.

'Help me lift this.'

They moved a wooden crate from the corner of one of the unused bays.

'What are you looking for?' the vet asked.

'Photographs,' Cooper said.

౫⬭

The first image had been sent in the summer, just a few months past if the Eltons were to be believed. Louise claimed to have found the photograph in one of the empty stable bays, lying flat against the dark.

It had shown a wooden box in the woods.

The couple hadn't thought anything of it.

More and more photos had arrived over time. And then there would be no thinking of anything else.

Images of their students riding through the fields, taken from far away.

Images of mutilated animals, of pets long missing.

౫⬭

They had been blackmailed, Louise Elton claimed. They'd done none of this.

Alec held the evidence of it in his gloved hands, cut-up newspaper print pasted to old white paper.

The threat was simple, the same words Louise had uttered after their confrontation.

WE KNOW.

The demand, from whoever had sent all this, was unclear.

Alec's own demand was not.

If the husband did not present himself for an interview at the police station by the next morning, they would find him and they would arrest him.

To that, Louise did not even look up.

The police took all the images and letters they could locate.

They left her home alone, a horse mat beneath her cup, a horse painting on the wall, a horse statue by the clock.

She was supposed to talk it over.

She had no one to talk to, no one at all.

The clock ticked on the red-brick mantelpiece. A fly buzzed through the kitchen. All the visitors began to leave. It was a place of children, not a place for men.

ॐ

As they moved through the stables and the grounds, Kate and Cooper talked about their careers. Cooper tried to smile more, tried to force ease.

'I had this idea,' Kate said. 'I was going to change it all. Everything I saw during uni – the animals who didn't need to be put down, the money that could be saved if owners knew how to do some things themselves, when to call us, when not to call us . . . I pitched it, in my interview. I was going to do animal management classes for the community. We'd all be working together.'

Even if life was harder than she thought it would be, she'd tried to make a difference in her own way.

People weren't bad. No one was bad, not really.

They could be taught. They could be made better.

But there was no time, no funding. Her bosses kept saying 'no'.

'I've got to get back to the practice,' Kate said, removing her phone from her jeans pocket. 'Got consults at 2 p.m.'

'And you'll have a look at your supplies?' Cooper asked. 'See if any fetotomy wires are missing, ask around about them?'

Kate nodded, as nervous, as smiley as ever.

CHAPTER TWENTY-FIVE

Cooper opened the car window to let some air in. Alec shut it using his own controls just a few seconds later, then apologized – he just didn't like the window being open.

He didn't want to get sick from all the fumes. 'It's not safe with other vehicles around, you know. People have them open and—'

They didn't pass another moving car the entire drive.

They drove towards the water.

Several of the torture photographs found at the Eltons' property had shown a stretch of sea, a small row of crumbling homes visible on the shoreline through the edges of the trees. Alec and Cooper spent their lunch hour driving along the coast, trying to find this place.

'There are twelve distinct animals in the images,' Cooper said quietly. She felt a little car-sick, looking through the photos on her screen. 'Six cats, four dogs. I can't identify the other two animals, not in the condition they were left.'

Alec nodded.

There were teenagers in the photographs, too. Other officers had been assigned to match and trace each of the kids in case they'd seen or noticed anything those weeks prior.

'We should find out if they know Rebecca Cole,' Alec suggested. 'They're about the right age. And, she *was* the one who found the heads. Kids talk.'

Their planning eventually fell into silence.

Whatever warmth there had been between them in the morning had chilled at the sight on Louise's desk. Cooper did not even feel smug about her lead any more. There was no victory to be had.

There was an awful potential, lurking in every case, every investigation. Some answers could not survive being found. Even if converted into words, even if the perpetrator stood in front of you and told you honestly all they knew, all they had done and thought they had meant – some actions could never be understood, not truly. Not unless you were capable of doing them too.

Gravity pulled Cooper a little in her seat as Alec took some corners a little fast, a little haphazardly. He was not a careful man, not when he had somewhere to be, not when he thought he was right. It only made her car sickness worse.

Half an hour down the coast, islands visible on the horizon, they finally arrived at the location shown in the photos.

'Whoever left these must have known we'd find this place. Must have wanted us to come here.' Alec stopped the car.

෪

Beyond the car, the outgoing tides barely touched the wrecked homes in the water. They had begun to fall apart already, the sea having reached them some weeks ago.

There was no reason for most people to drive this route, so far off the main road as it was. Further yet, the track rose and rose, elevating to small cliffs full of green.

'There's a path into the trees. Fits the photo's angle.'

So they went towards it.

Alec wondered, briefly, if they should have brought other officers, but Cooper was already ahead. She looked at everything, everything in the world. She tried to imagine what it was like to do a thing like this.

They followed invisible footsteps.

There stood twelve wooden crates, some of them open, some nailed shut.

They stood like doorways, displayed at different angles, fallen.

What Alec thought were children's toys, balls, rattles, they lay all around.

The earth – woodchipped and moist and vast and small all the same – crawled with an invisible world of insects, flickering like static in the soil.

There was a smell of distant smoke. They'd never find its source.

They opened the box.

ॐ

'What—'

Cooper didn't answer.

'What *is* that – what—'

The smell from beneath reached Alec's nose.

ॐ

Alec could not breathe.

They stood in the open air, in the middle of beautiful woods so far from any inhabited place, and he could not breathe. He covered his nose and mouth, he staggered up and away.

His head rolled back as he moved, looking around at all the leafless trees, how the sky pierced through their thin branches.

Even with the mutilation of the horses, their burial, the eyes in the soil, there was something beautiful there. Something that

could inspire awe, even as Alec imagined the pain of those creatures, even as he feared the reason why.

The crates . . . what had been left here . . . what had been
done to those poor animals . . . all of them drugged, all of them
poisoned and trapped until their deaths . . .

There was nothing beautiful here.

Nothing of ritual or symbolism, either. Nothing that made Alec
run to research numbers and esoteric systems of meaning. Nothing
that kept him up at night, theorizing as to the motivation of those
who had committed such an act.

In those boxes, in those woods, Alec saw nothing that invited
wonder.

He saw pain and suffering prolonged.

Regardless of law or definition, he saw murder at last.

Spread across the empty crates, freshly painted to the touch,
he saw letters on their sides. He moved them, rotating them into
position. Cooper called out for him to stop, for him to stop
touching it all, but he couldn't. He had to know.

He saw the letters, red against the wood.

W

A

T

C

H

they said.

Watch.

CHAPTER TWENTY-SIX

They left before evening came, heading back to their car by the shore.

'I'm not sure this was about insurance,' Alec said.

The sun was low above the distant islands. Nearby, water lapped around the edge of the abandoned homes.

'Were they watching us today?' Alec leant against the car's bonnet. Cooper sat beside him, coffee thermos in hand. 'What was it you said about the Croydon cat killer? How all those animals were found chopped up, mutilated . . .'

'Yeah?'

'You said it was all about the moment of discovery. The moment of seeing the owners' faces, of knowing how they felt . . .'

'That's what some thought, anyway.' Cooper finished her coffee. 'We don't know for sure. Maybe it was foxes after all, like the police said.'

'Maybe foxes put them in the crates, too,' Alec said, shaking his head. 'Maybe they took the photographs.'

'They're pretty wily.'

'They have sex outside my house every other night.' He sniffed. 'They make the most awful – awful—'

His nose wrinkled, and he caught himself, stifling a sneeze. 'Bless you,' Cooper said.

'Have you come across many other cases like these?'

'Foxes having sex, or, taking photographs?'

'Serial animal abuse.' His tone was serious, and Cooper stiffened a little.

'Well, there's Macdonald's triad,' she said. 'You know that one?'

His expression was blank. He shook his head.

In the weeks to come, he would think of this – that he didn't know the name. That she'd even asked him, a police officer, a detective. What had she thought of him to ask?

He found himself disarmed, asking question upon question to quell the feeling.

He listened to her talk. He'd learn later that Cooper had gained a master's degree in Forensic Science a few years after qualifying as a vet. She'd put in the time. Her choices, whatever they had been, had let her rise so far.

Alec leant against the car and listened to Cooper talk about the conditions needed to create a predator.

Abuse.

Arson, vandalism.

Cruelty to animals.

'But all these theories, they're based on trusting the words of the killers themselves – people who are often trying to get sympathy for appeals or stays of execution . . . Blaming childhood like newspapers blame video games.' Cooper shrugged. 'Maybe psychopaths have no idea why they do what they do.'

Alec nodded, getting up from the car, wincing as he did so. He seemed like he might be about to speak, but he didn't.

A boat moved across the waters, the sea almost red in the evening light.

᠀

They came back to animals before the end.

'Some think it might be practice. That dangerous men might

be too afraid or constrained by social norms to progress to killing human beings immediately. That it's not about the animal at all.'

'And what do you think?'

'I think cruel people rarely need a reason to be cruel, but . . . I don't know. There's certainly a lower risk factor to hurting animals. Maximum penalties are only a few months, and often, even in major abuse cases, courts are loath to ban people from keeping pets forever. There isn't much justice when it comes to animals, not if they don't walk and talk. And little of the kind of notoriety these people seek as a result.'

'So you don't think it's like . . .' Alec hesitated.

'I don't think what?'

'Inevitable, that one thing would lead to another.'

Cooper raised an eyebrow. 'You're not being clear.'

'That someone who hurt animals would hurt people.'

'Nothing's inevitable,' Cooper said.

꙳

They arranged for the corpses from the crates to be transported to the vet practice for further analysis.

Before they parted ways, Alec asked about the coincidence of two people having such broken personalities that they'd want to hurt animals, that they would collaborate on a crime like this. He suggested one of them might have been led into it all . . . the hermit had mentioned crying, after all. Maybe there were even more than two people involved, maybe—

'You look tired,' Cooper said, smiling, and something about the smile made Alec blush, before suddenly looking at his watch.

'Shit.'

'What?'

'I'm supposed to pick up my son soon. Can I drop you back?'

'I thought everyone drove in places like these.'

'He still hasn't passed his test.' The way Alec said it made him look annoyed.

'It took me four times to pass mine.' Cooper shrugged, opening the car door. 'I'm sure he'll get there.'

⚮

Waiting for the crate corpses to be brought to the vet practice, Cooper headed back to her hotel for a quick nap. She wasn't as bad as Alec, but she *was* surprised how much the day had taken out of her, how her hands shook, ever so slightly.

She thought about it all as she went up the steps.

The photos from the stables. The crates in the woods. Victims within and without.

Louise Elton, buried in debt and silence.

Albert Cole, a farmer who had wanted a new life, who had come so far to live so alone, who had lost everyone but his daughter Rebecca, and how long would she even stay? A year or two? Who knew?

And Alec . . . Alec who'd nearly had a panic attack at the uncovering of the crates. Alec, who kept looking to her for answers.

⚮

Four days, they'd said.

Four days to solve this case, and two were almost over.

There would be no other help, no second chances.

Alec had gone to pick up his son after they'd taken the bodies to the vet.

He kept saying he was sorry for how he'd acted, he—

She'd told him she'd see him in the morning. She'd try to be on time for breakfast.

He'd looked like shit, a pale sheen of sweat visible upon his neck as he went. Cooper imagined she also looked terrible. She didn't even bother to turn on the lights as she shut her hotel room door, as she stripped off her clothes and collapsed into bed.

She set an alarm for an hour's time.

She did not dream.

CHAPTER TWENTY-SEVEN

Down the hallway at Ilmarsh Vet Surgery, there were consultation rooms with old computers, scales outside for weighing animals. An office and a kitchen lay beyond. They still had a few old Halloween decorations up, some witch and broomstick fairy lights, a pumpkin leaning out the top of one of the bins. Papers sat on desks, forms, files, printers.

A vet sat there alone, coffee steaming in her mug.

Crazy for Ewe, Kate had written on a blank white mug in permanent marker.

A week ago, she had given one of the horses an apple. He was called Bruce. He had been showing signs of pain as he walked, avoiding the use of one leg – favouring, vets called it. It was all Kate could think about as she drank her coffee, as she tried to calm down. The way he'd come bobbing over, friendly, affectionate.

She thought about the sound of his scream.

In the mid-afternoon, a child came into the practice with a bleeding cat in a plastic bag. It was his pet. He'd remained home, sick from school, and had heard the screech of tyres and brakes outside. He'd walked all the way here with the eleven-year-old black tabby, barely breathing, barely struggling.

She stabilized it, but only first aid was free.

More would cost money. More always cost money.

The end was not inevitable, not even now, not with her help. She could save it, if they could only get consent. If the owners only did what was right.

And that was the problem, the conundrum at the heart of her profession. How to save the animal from the owner.

&⌒

Four consults, one outcall to the stables with Cooper, and two surgeries.

That was Kate's day. It ended in a slow ride to the tower she called home. She was tired, already on the cusp of lost consciousness.

The lobby of Kate's building had an old discarded fridge in the corner that had been there for three months, a distant mould within now spread to the facade. The old elevator was a pull-shut, pull-open, old-fashioned machine you wouldn't trust to keep you alive. It had a sign saying it was out of order, defaced with graffiti, boxes of anonymous building supplies making up the remainder of its freight. The lobby smelt faintly of urine, though it had been cleaned a week ago. Kate knew it had, she'd seen the man with his mop.

She walked up the stairs of the converted hotel, more graffiti smeared along its walls, some of it bright and beautiful, some of it just initials, manifested for the sake of it. A couple sat and kissed near the sixth-floor doors, the boyfriend's face wet with tears. Kate tried not to look, and they did not look back at her, but something about the encounter made her want to cry too.

She found her door, painted blue for some reason. She turned her key in the lock and jiggled it so that it would turn. She pushed it open.

She went inside and clicked the light switch on. She walked past plastic-wrapped cat food tins, past the climbing tower, the scratching post she had not yet taken to the dump. She opened her fridge, took out some leftover soup, and heated it up in the microwave. She poured a glass of water to drink with it. She sat and she ate on a small table by the window, looking out onto the small fields, the tyre place below, the light fading.

When she was done, she drank more water, went to her bedroom – the only other room – and took off her clothes, put on her pyjamas. It was humid, hot. There were mountains of clothes in need of cleaning, toiletries spread across every surface. A book she had meant to read, that she had bought months ago, abandoned by her bedside table, the bookmark – bought for the same optimistic purpose – still held between pages six and seven.

Kate thought of Cooper, of the way the other vet had looked at her. She opened the bedside drawer and removed some anaesthetic she had taken from the practice several months ago, pretending that the vial had broken. She injected the ketamine into herself.

That was a ritual, too.

She switched on the little television at the end of the bed.

She counted gently in her mind as she rolled back, wondering how long it would take until there was nothing.

One. Two. Three. Four. Five.

'Once I caught a fish alive,' she murmured, trying to get comfortable.

Six, seven, eight, nine, ten.

'Then I let it—'

Two Years Ago

CHAPTER TWENTY-EIGHT

The first sick or abandoned lamb, the first creature to be rejected by its mother, he or she had it the hardest. The old stables on the Coles' farm had eventually been repurposed for the storage of sick sheep. The owners used this space to keep animals isolated. They hand-reared them. Hours in between, left in the cold and in the dark with no noise but the distant bleats of the flock.

That first lamb, they'd often find it suckling the edges of the old fridge in the corner, cuddling round tools and abandoned troughs.

The first pet lamb rarely survived. The others, they had a chance.

Rebecca would heat up some milk for them, even as a child. She would mix up the powder, go out, and she would sit with the newborns for hours, morning and night. She would rear them and they would bleat for her and she would name them many names and most would die. Those who survived eventually went back to their flock, but there were some who remembered her always. There were some who ran over at the sound of the shaking bucket, ahead of the rest, a spring in their steps, a head bent for stroking and a bite of a carrot or two. There were those who were never sent for slaughter, not on purpose.

There were three overarching barns and a house at Well Farm, a mess of byres and anonymous corridors in between. These halls were full of plastic boxes. Some held objects that could have been memories, had they been protected from the winds that seeped through the old bricks in winter, from the flies that swarmed the living and the dead. There were old journals and diaries, some from when the farmer had been young, when Albert Cole had dreamt of being a fireman, or a doctor, or any number of things. Some belonged to his daughter, a collection of miscellaneous cards representing birthdays, Valentine's, Christmas as seen through the eyes of Rebecca's five-year-old self. And some objects, no one would know where they came from.

These were the things that made land more than just land. There were places that were the only places Rebecca had ever called home.

There was the ditch she'd played in as a kid, accompanied by the dogs and her toys.

There was the broken swing in the garden, put up for one glorious summer, out near her mother's office.

There was the front garden where she'd tried growing her own plants, until that garden had been destroyed.

There was the second barn where one day, fourteen years old, she had gone to feed the sheep.

ॐ

It had been so cold. It had been March, and it had snowed every day of the month, a full two feet accumulating over the fields just as they'd been preparing for lambing. They had brought as many of the sheep inside as they could, stuffing three barns with the entire flock and allowing the rest to spill over into a run they had set up outside, with temporary steel fences and gates erected to keep them within. At night, all of them were squeezed inside. Snow was not really a problem in the outside run – the heat of the sheep, the small amount of protection provided by the looming barns between them, it stopped much of the snow from settling. But deaths were inevitable in that cold, as were spontaneous abortions. The flock thinned.

Her mother had never had another child. There was no brother or sister.

One morning, Rebecca had come outside expecting the outer barn doors to have been opened already. She was going to smash up the buckets full of ice water. She was going to throw down feed into the troughs. She was going to stay outside for a while. She didn't want to be in the house.

The barn doors were not open. It was still a little dark. Inside, a small world of annexed structures, of old, collapsing halls, stood housed within a rusted metal shell.

Her father stood at the edge of the byre within, quietly watching the sheep on the other side of the gate. He turned and put a finger to his lips when Rebecca approached. He looked enchanted.

She came up beside him and leant on the metal gate. It took her a few moments to see it.

Between the clustered sheep – a hundred or more squeezed against each other, all hemmed into a pen – there was something else. Just a bit taller.

The sheep around it kept trying to move away, uncomfortable with its presence. The creature stood frozen, staring right back at the humans all the way across the barn.

It was a fawn, twin swellings on its head where one day antlers might spring.

'Won't be more than about six months old,' her father whispered.

'What . . .' She paused, her voice kept low. 'What are we going to do?'

'Its mum can't be far away. If she's still around.'

A block of snow slid off a panel near Rebecca's head. She did not jump, though she did shudder.

'What are we—'

'Already asked that. Don't repeat yourself, Becca.'

'You . . .'

'What?' He turned, his eyebrows slightly raised. 'You what?'

'You didn't answer my question,' she mumbled. 'That's why I asked it again.'

He turned back to the deer, grimacing. 'How'd it get in here, you think?'

Rebecca paused, looking first at the deer, then the barn door. 'Did we shut it in? Did it get in when we were closing up?'

Her father shook his head without looking at her.

'Was it already there? Maybe it had hidden round the—'

'No,' her father said.

There was a long silence then. Frustrated, peering back and forth in every direction around the barn, Rebecca turned away from the metal. She walked back through the byre towards the house, but paused before the exit, looking either side at possible entry points. She turned towards the main outer door – the same one through which she had entered. A flimsy wooden door she had been supposed to lock the night before. Which she was sure she had locked.

She turned back to her father.

He was staring at her.

'It came in just like we did?' She walked back over to the gate. 'It came in through the door.'

He nodded.

'But . . . why? It would have had to jump over the gate into the crush. Why squeeze in with all the sheep? Why not just stay in the byre? And why wasn't it afraid?'

She looked ahead at the deer. It had calmed down a bit, though it kept staring at them, even so.

'It was cold and lonely,' her father said. 'That's reason enough to do most things.'

'What are you going to do with it?'

'It can't stay here,' he said.

'Why?'

'Don't know what it's carrying. Wild animals, they will have all sorts.' He sighed, looking down at her. 'Come on, let's get back into the house and have some tea.'

'We haven't fed the sheep yet . . .'

'They'll keep.'

⛥

Two days ago, Rebecca's mother had asked her to strip. Rebecca had forgotten to take the dog in overnight. She kept forgetting things.

I found him cold, Becca.

Take off your top, Becca.

Take off your top.

'Mum, please—'

Take off your trousers.

'Mum, please don't—'

It's cold, isn't it? This is how it felt for the dog.

'I'm sorry—'

You can't be sorry. You can't be.

This is empathy.

Stand here.

Her mum had left to go into the byre.

A few moments later, water started spilling from the hose end, the whole thing still coiled on the floor.

The breeze bit into Rebecca, standing there without her top or her trousers.

She started to shake, and her mother didn't come back.

The water trickled along the ground and began to creep towards her bare toes.

'No no no no no—' she began to murmur. 'No no—'

She shook, her cry a little louder.

Still, her mother did not come back.

Across the road, an occasional car passed and did not stop. The fields rolled on and on, the clouds spreading darkness as they drifted, replaced by light just as soon.

The water touched her feet and she wet herself from the cold and wet, shaking, uncontrollably now.

Still, no one came to switch the hose off, no one came to point it at her, either. It just lay there, unspooling itself against the stone. Rebecca shivered, clutching her arms to her body, crying, unable to move, and she would think about that in the months to come, why she did not move, what she had allowed.

§☉

They had not spoken about it since. Rebecca didn't even know if her father knew, if he'd agreed with it, if he'd been part of it.

Her mother would be nice to her for a while now.

She was always nice to her, after the worst of it.

After they found the baby deer in the barn, Rebecca's mother made tea in the kitchen and they watched some boring Sunday documentary of the kind made solely for boring Sundays. Rebecca's father told her to stay inside; he'd take care of the sheep today. She should rest. Looked like she was coming down with a cold. Her mother protested that she looked perfectly fine, but that was that. Rebecca stayed inside for a while, even though she didn't want to.

Her mother took her own medicine, heart pills.

She wanted Rebecca to eat better, to exercise better, so she wouldn't end up like her mum. The girl would later learn her mother's condition was nothing to do with what she ate. Blood-clotting disorders didn't work like that.

Later that day, Rebecca was sent to the byre to get some garden peas from the freezer.

The sheep were inside and outside, the sky starting to grow darker. There was no sign of the baby deer. The troughs were full of water. Sheep ate what they could as fast as they could, so the empty troughs were not surprising.

She returned to the freezer and took the peas.

Halfway back to the house she heard a scratching sound.

She turned around.

There was no one there. There was nothing there.

She kept going, until she heard it again, louder this time. Now she recognized the sound. It was a tool. Her father was in the workshop.

She went back, walking past plastic and metal. Buckets for making sandcastles. An old lawnmower, collapsed into three pieces. A woman's suitcase.

She moved towards the open door.

Her father had his back to her. He was working at the table with his apron on, the whole surface draped in tarp. He hadn't heard her arrival, or he didn't care about her arrival. Either possibility might have been true.

He put his tool down. There was a body on the table in front of him. Four hoofed legs, two either side of her father, curling round him like a magnet. They dangled off the table, pink and moist.

Rebecca stepped closer.

'Dad, what—'

He became very still, very quickly.

'What are you doing?' She couldn't tell what it was.

'Why are you out?' He didn't turn around.

'Mum told me to get peas.' She held the peas higher as proof, despite the fact he wasn't looking. Her cheeks grew slightly red and she lowered the peas to her side.

Her eyes flicked to the creature on the table. It had been skinned.
'Dad?'

He turned, and as he did, she saw it.

The neck of the creature ended in a stump.

There was nothing beyond that stump.

Her father had cut off the head. Of course he'd cut off the head.

It's what you do when you kill a deer.

Day Three

CHAPTER TWENTY-NINE

It was night. The door to the mud room was open when Rebecca got back. The police had left the farm. The horse heads were gone at last.

There were muddy boots, wax jackets, half-finished cat litter bags and hamster feed, and boxes for things broken or forgotten years ago. A leaflet from the council, a few unopened letters.

'You left the front door open!' she shouted, but her father did not answer.

She pulled her wellingtons off, hopping one leg onto the straw thatch mat as she did so. Through the dirty window she saw a truck zoom past. There were no street lights to mark its path.

Pulling off her outdoor fleece, the movement caused her pain. There was a rash all along her right arm, down to the back of her hand. It was a nasty thing, black scabs over portions of welted skin. She'd put cream on it earlier. She got inflammation sometimes, from lambing and milk-replacement powder. She once had a great big brown tick attach itself to her eyelid. A rash was nothing.

She walked straight to the bathroom and locked the door. She peeled off her dirty clothes and finally, stepping into the plastic tub, showered. Her whole body ached. She felt light-headed, too, but the water helped with that at least.

She looked in the mirror when she was done. She was sweating from the cold. She could see her ribs just a little. She'd first seen them a few days ago, and it was so strange each time. She'd felt overweight for so long – she'd been told she wasn't, of course, but telling never helped, not when you didn't feel it, not when you didn't see the evidence with your own eyes. And now a miracle was here – skin stretched over bone. She'd been dieting for months, the only exception being her birthday. But the ribs were still there.

She'd forgotten her clean clothes. Shit. She peeked out into the hallway and, seeing a clear coast but for their stupid cat Toby, ran across to her bedroom and locked the door again. She dried her mouse-brown hair and wondered how it might look if she dyed it sometime. She thought about the new vet's hair colour – a kind of dark chestnut, maybe, almost black. Or something different, she didn't know. She worried she might look weird. As if she didn't already.

As she pulled her clothes on, she thought about the snake she'd seen earlier.

She thought about the noise of the cars throughout the day. The wheels, turning and turning against the soil.

She sat down at her computer – an old and slow device, even by the outmoded standards of her family – and played a game for a while. She tried to settle herself.

In the game her character fell in love. She'd made all the correct choices, following a guide on another website. It was her tenth time playing it. Peter said he'd played it, once at least. But Peter mostly watched recordings of games, he didn't actually buy them or play them himself. So did a lot of people. Rebecca hadn't seen her friend for months, now, not face to face. If they'd ever even earned that term, if he and the others had ever even cared about her. She didn't know.

You didn't have to be yourself. You didn't have to hold close all the things you had suffered and still suffered, all the things you had done to others and that were still done to you. You could just pretend or forget. You could think however you wanted to; they were just thoughts, weren't they, and what were thoughts but made up? What was consciousness but a form of fiction? You could make your life a life of stories. This was her mother's gift to her.

Her life as it was now, in these games without people, in messages without faces – Rebecca lost her head in machines. She lost her body in thoughts.

She'd felt overweight for so long. Like there was too much of her. Others had said so. She'd asked Peter what he thought, once, trying to seek another opinion, some kind of escape. He'd just looked embarrassed. He'd just said he didn't know.

There was a knock on the door. It was time for dinner.

⅌

The hall was empty again, but for the white ball of cat, licking the fluff off its own belly. Rebecca walked towards the lounge, and the cat leapt round and ran away down the hall. She pushed the door open.

They ate venison steak for dinner, blood practically seeping from the barely cooked cuts. Her father liked to claim he was a vegetarian, sometimes; he said it to strangers, he told it to friends, then ate meat all the same. He thought it was funny, this secret violence, though the joke was never clear to her.

She didn't eat much of anything.

Her father wiped bloody gravy from his moustache with a flick of his tongue. Half-forgotten greens lay steaming to the side. They watched the news in silence but for the scrapes of knives against plates. A politician was being interviewed.

'Should this just be a case of "put up, shut up"?'

'Well, first of all, I'd say it's rather oxymoronic, even dangerous to throw around phrases like "put up, shut up" when we're talking about the expression of democratic values – the casting *of a vote doesn't have to mean the end of a debate. Laws change, governments lie, and sometimes people don't know what they want, or worse – groups pervert our institutions to oppress others for their own gain. The history of democracy is littered with tyrants and demagogues who gained power through perfectly legitimate means, and we shouldn't forget this—'*

Her father abruptly changed the channel. He always did it without asking, even when her mother had still lived here.

This flu was something else. She was still sweating from the shower. The meat hadn't helped.

She tried to forget about it, sipping her water.

On the TV screen, a man in a black suit sat across a table from a dishevelled wreck of a human being. The room was dark. It looked like a detective drama, but it wasn't, not really. Something was off.

'I need to get home.'

Rebecca watched as the man in the black suit just stared at his captive.

'Is this going to take very long?'

The man in the black suit took out a cigarette packet and placed it on the table, quite deliberately. *'Can I smoke? Do you smoke?'*

The prisoner nodded. The man removed a cigarette, lit it, and took a puff.

'Why am I here?'

'Why don't you tell me about your day?'

'No.'

'Excuse me?'

'I want to know why I'm here.'

The man stared at him. *'You play chess?'* He tapped his cigarette in the tray.

'No. Once or twice. You?'

'No.'

They sat in silence for a few moments.

'*Why do you want to get home so badly?*' the man asked.

'*Doesn't everyone?*'

Rebecca felt light-headed again, so she finished her drink. She touched her forehead. It felt cold, clammy, somehow.

There was meowing from the hall.

'Did you feed him?'

Her father nodded, not taking his eyes off the screen. He hadn't spoken to her all day, but for pleasantries and grunts.

The cat began to move towards their dirty plates. He tried to be coy and stealthy and above it all in that way only cats can be, but Rebecca was wise to the tactic. She got up and collected the plates.

The television flickered.

Rebecca lingered in the doorway, smiling faintly at the cat. He stared back, upset that his scraps were being taken away. She thought about her life.

She thought about the horses' eyes buried in the earth.

She stepped through to the kitchen and her heart stopped.

CHAPTER THIRTY

George could smell the smoke all the way up to the third storey, his suit jacket and trousers piled in a ragged heap in the corner of his room from the night before, his nose running.

He was exhausted, had barely got out of his pyjamas all day. He was hungry. All he could think about was dead things.

Pig offal burning in the sun, burgers, pork, sausages. That, and having a drink. A bottle of beer. Some wine.

It was just about warm enough to sit outside. Warmer than the weather had promised.

And all this in November. What a time to be alive.

Downstairs, his wife, his friends, the plus-ones and the tolerated we-have-to-invite-them-or-it-will-look-bad remnants, sat and stood and drank and smoked and chatted and ate.

He had planned to cook those sausages. He *always* cooked them. And it wasn't like many of these sods invited him to *their* houses, or if they did, that he'd be served anything but salmonella.

'Are you sure you're up to it?' Shelly had asked, just an hour or two after they had woken up. She'd been very concerned about his cold. She'd bought him medicine, made him tea. He'd taken a sick day, hadn't he? Why had he taken a day off if he was capable of running a barbecue? He'd tried to explain the finer points of exaggerating a situation to work colleagues, but still, she would not believe or trust him. He was expelled from the whole event.

His wife and brother-in-law had then oven-cooked the meat inside, just to be safe. It was November, however warm it seemed, and you didn't barbecue things in November. They finished it all in the fire to give it an extra crispy finish.

George kept telling her his cold was nothing, but still she kept fretting.

'What about your hands?' she'd asked.

'What about them?' George had grimaced at her from the kitchen table, from the low light.

'They're all red.'

'It's called work, Shelly.'

'Don't tell me something's not wrong with those hands.'

'They're fine.' They weren't. They were rough and sore. The business on the farm had been difficult, even with the gloves Alec had forced him to put on. 'Go on. Have it all without me, then. I'll rest upstairs.'

'Are you sure?'

'Positive.'

She frowned.

'What?' He raised an eyebrow.

'Nothing,' she said softly. 'It's just I don't want you to be annoyed at me.'

'Why would I be annoyed?' His voice was flat and strained, as passively aggressive as he could make it.

'OK.' She turned to smile. 'If you're sure.'

So here he was in a room full of piles of unwashed but neatly organized clothes. He'd seen cairns like these. Little piles of rocks in heaths and moors and fields, dedications to the dead that you could crawl inside.

His hands burned. His head began to split.

He had no water. He knew he should go to the bathroom and pour more from the tap but his body and mind and will would not cooperate.

He drew the curtains and lay down, hoping it would all go away. He checked his phone, setting an alarm for a few hours' time on the off-chance he fell asleep.

His phone background showed his wedding day. Fifteen years since then and he'd never changed it, not on a single phone he'd had since.

They'd been happiest without friends.

An email had arrived. They'd got the CCTV footage from the shore, the night of the fireworks and the killings.

He'd go in to see it tomorrow, if he was better.

He rolled over and closed his eyes, already stinging.

He'd cut himself in places – he didn't know how exactly, but it had been a long day at that rusty farm. He'd put ointment on the nasty scabs and he'd hidden them from his wife by wearing long-sleeved pyjamas.

He just needed a good rest. She would only worry and fret.

He fell asleep, trying to ignore the sun streaming through the window.

⁂

Outside George's house, the barbecue was coming to an end, and with it the last heat of the year. Around a dozen or so guests remained, chatting, poking skewers of marshmallow into the campfire's flames. Midges danced around their heads and arms, pulling blood from beneath the surface of their skin. No one noticed the theft. Globules of O-positive, AB, and insulin-rich B floated around their laughter and smiles. Someone opened a cold beer in the dark, preferring to keep away from the heat.

One guest was showing everyone photos of her new home. Fiona was moving much nearer London. She wanted to be near her family. It was the reason everyone moving on gave, as if leaving this place represented some fundamental human failure.

'Empty nest,' she said. 'The house is filled with ghosts, now they've all gone. Now Richard's gone.'

Her husband had died the year before. A stroke after a long bout of emphysema. He'd been older than her, they hadn't entirely loved each other, but she was alone now, no underlying conditions, no anything.

'It feels like my kids are gone too, sometimes,' she said. 'I know where they are . . . one of them only lives half an hour away, but . . . it . . . it feels like they're lost, all the same. Like they're waiting for me.' She picked up her drink, smiling. 'Sorry. Too much wine.'

'I want you to keep in touch,' Shelly said. 'I don't want you to forget me.'

Fiona smiled back, gently, half dismissive. She didn't say anything.

'We've thought of downsizing ourselves, but, well. We like it here.'

Fiona nodded. And then, after a moment, after staring into the fire, said, 'I always said I'd move closer to my children if he died first. Do you know what Richard said he'd do if *I* died first?'

'What?'

'He said if I died first, he was going to travel the world.' She sighed, trying to smile. 'He had an Irish passport.'

Out on the road, they heard a car speed past towards the town centre. Must have been breaking the limit.

'Where did he want to go? Any place in particular?'

'Ireland, for sure.' Fiona's face quivered a bit.

'Why?'

'He'd never been,' Fiona said, and the back door opened.

Shelly turned when she saw the faces of her guests. Concerned. Upset.

It was George.

'What are you doing out of bed?' she said, rushing towards him.

He was covered in sweat.

'George?'

He moved a step forwards and fell, dizzy, his head hitting the wall of the extension.

'George?!'

His head was bleeding where it had hit the brick. He didn't say a thing. His eyes were shut.

CHAPTER THIRTY-ONE

'I love you,' the farmer whispered, those eyes that looked back up at him so much like those horses in the earth, so much like what had happened to his land, his life.

Rebecca's head was still bloodied where she'd fallen in the kitchen, that same blood still slick against the counter.

He drove her to the hospital.

She had awoken briefly on the journey, had tried speaking, but her words had not made much sense.

Memories ran through her mind.

She talked about a black carriage.

Her father didn't understand.

৳֍

The horse's breathing was laboured, her nostrils flared, her neck moist with sweat.

She dipped her head into a bucket of water next to the sign. It seemed narrow for her. Rebecca thought about her eyes, how the world must look to a creature like that, being either side of her head rather than the front. It was thirty degrees Celsius. The horse had been bringing people up and down the beachfront all day, a black carriage harnessed to her back, her driver an old man.

Michael brushed the sides of the horse's neck, her black mane, too.

'We'll be ready to go soon,' he said.

Rebecca nodded.

'We don't get many people wanting to do this by themselves.'

Rebecca didn't answer.

Soon she was inside, seated on the stale starched candy-stripe seats, watching the waves pull in and out at sea.

The driver did not turn around as they went. She watched the way the horse moved forwards, the way he called her 'Annie'.

'It's my birthday present,' she mumbled.

'Oh, right.' Michael kept his eyes ahead. 'Well, happy birthday.'

Rebecca nodded.

ঙ৩

What do you want most in the world?

'You.'

You've already got me.

'Still.'

Tell me what you actually want. What do you actually want?

ঙ৩

They kept moving and moving. The ride took them past the arcades, past the cafes, past even the abandoned hotels. Down here there were rows of old white houses that had once been expensive, other buildings, wrecks of places no one visited, no one kept.

The old cinema, one of the first in the whole country.

Four false Corinthian columns stood along the front like faded tree trunks. Above, where in an ancient temple you might have seen beautiful marble friezes depicting wars and gods and the history of human suffering, there were just letters. This frieze was not triangular, but flat like the roof itself. There were only letters, bound to the front of weathered stone, several now missing.

EM—R, it read.

The doors and the windows below had been boarded up and bolted.

Outside, someone waited far away.

He had a camcorder in his hand. He was filming her ride. It was hot and sunny enough that she could barely make him out, heat-fog rising from the pavement. Rebecca wondered, briefly, thinking of this, if the horse's feet were OK on this concrete. She'd heard something about dogs on paths, how their paws could be burned. Maybe the horse was made of sterner stuff.

She looked at the camcorder, and waved to him.

He didn't wave back.

The driver's head changed angle briefly, looking at the stranger too.

'Who's that?'

'He paid for this,' Rebecca said. 'It's his gift.'

'He didn't want to come and ride with you?'

'He's afraid,' Rebecca said, trying to smile.

'Of horses?' Michael scoffed.

'Maybe.'

They went on and on.

Later, her father would pick her up from town. She'd told him she'd gone to town with friends. Her mother had been supposed to pick her up, but she was in bed again. Still she refused to see the doctor. She'd always been like that.

'Happy birthday,' he said. 'You had a good one?'

They had a cake for her back at home. He'd made it himself. It was a surprise, but she'd seen it in the byre fridge. It was full of mini edible sheep.

Rebecca thought about the horse, on and on.

'Can I go riding?' she asked.

'What do you mean?'

'Riding lessons.'

Her father sighed. 'Why?'

'I don't—'

'Ask your mother,' he said, and that was the end of it.

Rebecca wouldn't ask. Of course she wouldn't ask.

The sky grew dark.

The world passed by.

Rebecca stopped having these memories.

She stopped seeing anything, even in her mind.

She had started to cough once they got inside the front doors of the hospital.

Her father drove back by himself, not telling anyone he was leaving his little girl alone, or that he was returning. He thought about the farm, about those early days. He thought about walking the fields, about the policeman, about the marshes.

There could be lovely days out here, there could be sunsets that made him cry for joy. There could be moments when the world assembled itself in his eyes, puzzle pieces of reflected light, echoes of distant bleats in the wind, the blossoming of wildflowers in colours he had no names for. He'd watch birds dance in the air, he'd listen to them call to each other through the reeds. He'd take antlers and place them all around his home.

His wife had been sick for years, in her mind and in her heart. No one had understood her, no one had understood *him*, what he had tried to do for all of them.

He imagined everyone thought he was just a fool, but he knew the secret of all life. He knew that thoughts were no one's fault, not in the end. They are just things that happen to you.

They are just like everything else, like weather, like the sun, like frost.

He was crying, now. He accelerated along the road.

He was going to go to his fields.

He was going to be alone, now, too.

He wondered if he might see his wife again, somehow, some day.

She had been Grace, in her name, in meaning, in smiles and in tears.

He wondered if they would forgive all they had done to each other.

He wandered, walking out into the reeds, into the awful dark.

CHAPTER THIRTY-TWO

The sun had set on Ilmarsh, the sky a faint red. On earth as flat as this, there was nothing to stop the spread of light along the horizon, not the low buildings, not the hedges, not the abandoned tractors, not people. The light changed the world, if light was all you could see.

The radio played in the car. It was dark, now.

'Can you turn it off?' Simon asked.

Alec began to sing along, exaggerating each syllable.

'Dad . . .'

'Fine, fine.' He turned it off. They drove in silence for a while, but for the rumble of wheels on the road. Simon's rucksack sat on the seat next to him in the back. He'd gone to a friend's house after school, a hamlet far from the centre.

'You hungry yet?' Alec asked.

'A bit.'

'We'll get something on the way back, yeah?'

His son didn't say anything.

'Something on your mind?'

The boy was eighteen. Everything was strange with him, like it is with everyone's teenaged child. He was sort of almost an adult but he wasn't. Simon was his boy, but he was a man, too, old enough and big enough to have a life his father didn't know.

Alec didn't know how to talk to him. The boy had been asking questions, and Alec had no idea how to answer, no idea what he thought himself.

'I had a dream last night,' Simon finally said.

'You have dreams every night. We all do. It's how the brain works.' Alec grinned at his son in the rear-view mirror, but the boy wasn't smiling.

'I don't,' he said.

'You do. You just don't remember them.'

'Can I say what my dream was?' There was something in Simon's voice.

'Sure.' Alec looked in the mirror again. 'I was just saying you have more dreams than you think. It's interesting, we don't actually know what—'

'Dad.'

'Sorry. Go on.'

'No.'

'You're going to sulk?'

Simon looked away.

'Come on, tell me about your dream. I was just having fun.'

'No. It was stupid, anyway.'

ILMARSH, 25 MILES, the sign read. Everything was so spread out here, so isolated, even this thirty-minute drive felt like a quick journey. It was nothing like London.

They soon passed back by Well Farm itself, the white tents fluttering in the slight breeze, reflecting the headlights. They were going to take them down in a couple of days, once they were certain there was nothing else in the soil.

'How was school?' Alec asked.

'Can we turn the radio on again?'

He did so.

Silence, but for low voices talking about traffic in a distant town. Outside, the view seemed to remain the same no matter how far they travelled.

'Simon?'

'Yeah?'

Are you sure you're OK?

I'm sorry if I've been distant.

'What do you want for dinner?'

His son was staring out of the window, lost in some thought. After a pause, after Alec repeated the question: 'Sorry?'

'We could get fish and chips, a kebab, anything you want . . .'

'Chips would be good.'

The road was rougher here, potholes that had not been repaired for over a year.

'I know what's wrong,' Alec said suddenly, trying to be cheerful. 'It's a girl, isn't it?'

'Dad . . .'

'Hah, I knew it was a girl. What's her name?'

'There's no girl.'

'Of course there isn't.' He looked in the mirror. His son's cheeks had grown red, if he wasn't mistaken. 'Was she . . . was she on your trip?' He paused. His son said nothing. 'Well, I hope I get to meet her sometime.'

If there's anything you want to talk about, just let me know, OK? I'm here. I'll always be here.

'My dream . . . it was about Mum. Mum was in it.'

Alec dreamt about her too, sometimes. And he thought about that a lot. He had ideas about it.

It's what people don't tell you, when you lose someone. Your dreams don't know. They'll appear just like they always were, as if they'd never gone. But some part of you knows it, and seeing them, it . . . it doesn't know what it's doing to you, your brain. It's showing you the part of that person who lives inside your mind.

That's all people are to each other in the end, Alec thought. All our experiences, the good times and the bad, everything we've ever done or had done to us by a person, it forms an impression in our heads. It takes much longer for that to die than any body.

He stared ahead at the road.

'I dream about her too.' That was all he said.

'I know.'

There had been silence after that. They kept on.

Ten miles to town, now.

'You know, I used to have this one really bad dream when I was a kid,' Alec said.

'A nightmare?'

'Kind of. I don't know.'

'What happened in it?'

'It was one of the only ones I had more than once, that I remember at least. It's funny, isn't it? That we have all these things happen to us and we don't know half of them . . .'

He took the exit, turning left.

'I didn't know what it was at the time, not at first.'

He felt down for his water bottle, and took a sip.

'The way this thing looked, in my dream I mean . . . it was this place, this black building on a hill, it was dirty. I think I had a thing about that . . . I still do, kind of, though it's better . . . like I always washed my hands too much. You ever notice that?'

Simon didn't say anything.

'I used to be worse. As a kid I'd wash my hands for two minutes – for three, even – just scrubbing till I was sure, digging under my nails, sometimes. I grew out of it, but I still don't like mess.'

The moon came and went beneath the clouds.

'Your gran and me, we'd be driving through town – we'd be coming back from a friend's house, or the beach, sometimes . . .' He paused. There were signs above the road. 'It was cold and dark – colder than anywhere had ever been, in real life at least. And the wind, it blew down newsagent signs and restaurant menus and even dog walkers, it was just silly, really . . . I'd try to look at the sea, but there'd be nothing there, just noise. It was a town a little like this one, but bigger – in better condition, I guess.'

He paused, feeling an itch in his nose. He sneezed a great big sneeze.

'Bless you,' Simon said.

Alec smiled. Simon smiled too.

'It's so silly that we say "bless you",' Alec said.

'Why do we even say it?'

'We'll look it up when we get back.'

He yawned.

'What happened in the dream then? You just walk around with Gran?'

'Well, in my dream . . . it was one of the only dreams I ever had more than once, like I said. We'd be in the car, and I'd see this black building . . . this ruin . . . and it looked at us from the hill. I couldn't make out anything but for some letters – great big dirty white letters, the others all missing. It was tall. And I wasn't myself.'

He scratched his head.

'I'd see this building and I'd—'

☙

Simon came to, something wet on his cheek. He touched his face, barely able to see, his sight blurred. Then he saw red. His hand had blood on it.

He struggled to straighten himself, one of his fingers crunching in pain.

'What—' he croaked, starting to focus on the trees in front of the car, illuminated only by the headlights.

They weren't moving. He turned. The car was at an angle.

The driver-side door was open. His dad wasn't there. The airbags had inflated in the front, engulfing the seats. He didn't know the windscreen had been cracked. He didn't see the blood.

Simon immediately shifted upright in his seat, eyes darting across the land before them. It was night. They were not on the road. He undid his belt and tried to open the door. Every bone hurt. His belt had worked, but he'd slammed forward nonetheless.

They'd hit something.

He swung the door open and staggered out.

There was a noise in the distance. Faint.

'Dad?'

They had driven into a field, somewhere, somehow, tyre marks on the ground where they'd spun round. There was no road before him, just the mud the car tyres had churned up, just the filth and the trees and all those things an eye can't see.

He stepped forward uncertainly, head bobbing as he lurched, adrenaline spiking through the groggy wake, the world moving up and down with his vision.

There was something wheezing on the ground in front of the car.

'Dad, where . . .'

The noise, it was clearer now. It was sirens.

He moved closer to the body.

It had its back to him. It was long and brown, broken antlers springing back from its head as it coughed.

They'd hit a stag.

It was only a stag.

The sirens got louder. They were almost there. Ambulances. Something else, too.

His dad must have called them. Why wasn't his dad answering?

What if he never answered?

Simon turned, looking behind him at the lights. The ambulances were coming down the road.

He looked back down at the stag. It could barely move, let alone stand. He bent down at its side and sat with it.

The ambulances drove past them.

There was silence, but for the croaking of the stag.

'Ph—' it coughed. 'Ph—'

Simon blinked, his vision hazy with blood and tears. He'd not cried for so long.

He knelt in the dark. His father's radio crackled out from the car.

All—

CHAPTER THIRTY-THREE

When Cooper woke up, it was still dark. There were no voices outside, neither in the hall nor in the street. The sea sighed through the thin window. She tried to make out the clock on the wall, but it was too dark. Her alarm hadn't sounded yet. She felt terrible.

She reached for her phone, arm aching, and found it was ringing, silent, no sound, no vibration. There was an incoming call from an unknown number.

She'd been asleep for six hours. It was just past midnight.

She'd missed her alarm – she'd—

Shit. *Shit shit shit*, she'd been supposed to go to the vet's, she—

She answered the phone, sitting up in the dark, her neck and back stiff.

'Have you—' There was static.

It took Cooper a while to recognize the voice, and even then, she was not sure.

'Hello?' Cooper cleared her throat.

There was static again.

Outside their buildings miles apart, the black sea shook, ancient stars caught in rippling reflections.

'I have.' Kate's voice was thin on that line, caught close to laughter, to tears, to silence. 'They screamed as he cut them.'

Dark cars drove down dark streets.

Through shadows that had once been marshlands, the long and level world stretched its teeth around them.

They danced through the darkness, through the void.

Red and blue lights, they began to dance.

They came towards the sea.

CHAPTER THIRTY-FOUR

Kate's speech grew slower, each sentence more slurred than the last.

She had taken something, or been given something. She wouldn't answer Cooper's questions.

'Who did this to you? Who—' Cooper's voice was firm and deep across the noise, though she felt her heart beginning to race in her chest. She'd sat up, hands shaking. She remained calm on the line.

'I drove us. I thought – I thought we were just, just *taking them*, I didn't know what—'

Cooper struggled to switch on her bedside lamp.

'He cut them in the back,' Kate murmured. 'I was driving. He cut them, and they screamed, they – they screamed, they could hardly move, I'd given them – I – I—'

The woman began to cough. Cooper looked frantically for her clothes, her keys.

'Where are you, Kate?'

'Crazy for Ewe. You – you liked my mug, you—'

'Kate, what did you—'

'He told me he'd tell everyone what I'd done,' she whispered, the line croaky, full of noise. 'I'd be struck off. I'd – I'd never work again, and I – I had to help – I didn't know what he'd do, I—'

Cooper hit her head on a wooden beam as she picked up her boots.

'It's in you now, too. What's in me, it's in you. I never meant this. I never meant any of this.'

'What's in me?' Cooper asked, starting to shake, her head pounding.

Lights came through the curtains.

'I found a message . . . when I woke up, I found it,' she whispered. 'He loves you.'

The lights were red and blue.

There were men outside their homes.

'For Ewe . . .'

It was the last thing Kate would ever say.

৪৩

The men's biohazard suits were pure white, almost fluorescent in that dark.

The hotel's halls were deserted, just like they'd always been.

Outside, an ambulance waited for her. Multiple vehicles all around, a roadblock a little way along the shore keeping a smattered crowd back.

They gathered as they always gathered.

Reality began its collapse.

Boats headed out into the night.

'*We have reason to believe—*'

Cooper couldn't hear. She couldn't think.

'*Infection—*'

৪৩

She thought of the horses, of the eyes in the earth.

She thought about that number, sixteen. That strange number.

Not once had she wondered about it before; not once had she said a thing about it.

They gave her a sedative.

The world went black.

CHAPTER THIRTY-FIVE

Charles Elton woke up and found his wife gone.

He made the bed again, pulling the duvet back. It was 3 a.m., but he'd had five hours of sleep. He often found it difficult to get much more.

He shaved and showered, his face strangely red, or maybe it had been this red for a while, he didn't know. He felt like it was a new start, somehow. Like the weather had broken. Like the air was clear.

He was supposed to go to the station today, or they'd arrest him, wouldn't they? That was the threat.

He got dressed and went downstairs, calling out for a coffee from his wife.

There was no answer.

He went looking for her around the house and noticed some things.

He went outside, and her car was gone. Down the slope, the stables stood empty, too, their roofs wet. He didn't remember it raining. Perhaps it was a trick of the night. It was hard to see. The fields were empty but for the red tractor, abandoned weeks ago, not moved since then.

Sometimes, Louise went for walks.

So she'd gone for a walk, then. Taken the car somewhere to get away. Who could blame her, what with the day they'd had?

He got his phone and went to the kitchen and made a list of groceries they might need. He texted them to her on the off-chance she might still be out and about in a few hours' time.

He made himself a coffee, and a ham and cheese sandwich with brown bread. He waited and decided to tidy, to make the place nice.

He waited, and it was almost light, and still Louise had not answered. He checked his phone. She had seen his message.

It would be the last message she would ever send him, that notification, that 'seen'. He lingered over his phone in the minutes to come, holding it there, thinking of what to say, what to type. *Charlie is typing* no doubt appeared a hundred times on her phone, but he never sent a message in the end, not then.

He found it a while later.

In his wife's office, tidied now of all the photographs, there was a letter on the desk.

On the piece of paper there was a request, pasted in newspaper letters.

KILL YOURSELF.

Louise must have opened it. Must have seen it.

His name was on the front of the envelope.

The password to his encrypted hard drive lay below.

Are you coming back? he finally texted.

No reply came. He went to the bedroom, looked through his wife's cupboards, her drawers. All of her jewellery was gone. Most of her clothing, too: their suitcase, absent from the loft.

He went down to his study, letter in hand, and sat amongst the horse plates, the horse paintings on the walls.

He sent a final message.

I love you, Louise. I love you.

There were still things he needed to do outside. Rubble that had to be cleared. Things he had to move. He tried to concentrate on that.

He burned the letter in the fireplace.

He went upstairs.

He took the gun from the safe, put it into his mouth, and pulled the trigger.

GRUINARD ISLAND, 1942

Three.

Two.

One.

Five men stand in gas masks. They are of different shapes and sizes, looking almost like a family huddled for a photograph. One of them has a camera. They direct it at bleating sheep.

The air is cold. The sea around them is peaceful.

The sheep have been accumulated in tethered masses near the detonation sites. The men stand far enough away that they are at little risk.

The countdown over, Vollum 14578 manifests in a cloud of dust. The air becomes brown near the sheep. It all happens on the end of a stick, the detonation toppling it, spores inhaled by all living things within a prepared radius.

The strain had been discovered in a cow in Oxford.

The man who discovered it gave his name to it, and *Vollum* was all that remained of him in the world, the final memory of his life.

The sheep die and are incinerated within days.

Men make the world warmer.

No one ever lives here again.

PART TWO:
THE HOLE IN THE WORLD

Day Four

CHAPTER THIRTY-SIX

There was an image in Cooper's head, the last image.

The flesh of a horse's face, laid out across a board.

Numbered tags poking into each lesion, ready for examination, for recording.

That was the final thing she could remember, the last remnant before she came to.

The skin from the face stretched out against the chrome and the white lights.

Skin that had been stroked a thousand times in rain and sun, a map of trauma and love.

She woke up.

ॐ

Specialists from Public Health, police officers from surrounding areas, they had come for her on the roads.

What's in me, it's in you.

But it wasn't.

She couldn't stop thinking about Kate's voice. She couldn't stop hoping she was OK, that they were all OK.

Cooper had been given the all-clear in the early hours.

The night had felt like a dream, somehow. Like all the parts of her mind had splintered off into the waking world.

The authorities had put her up in this room, twenty miles from Ilmarsh itself, and had told her little else.

§⑥

This room in which they'd put her – it was full of mahogany bookcases, but for the bed in its centre, its impossibly white, now-ruffled sheets. She was staying in what had once been an old mansion. It was mostly used for conferences, now. The authorities had set this building up as a base of operations, an area for the press in halls on the lower floor, beds for officials to stay in on the floors above.

There were leather chairs in shadowed recesses. There were books on the shelves that could be read by anyone, that never were.

There were bright yellow curtains. It was a terrible colour scheme. Cooper thought it looked like something her sister might have come up with.

These curtains reminded her of something else, too, but what, she could not remember.

A knock came.

§⑥

When Cooper was twenty, she'd tried to die. She'd climbed onto some distant train tracks. No one had been at that station so far from any city. The vet practice where she'd been completing her extramural studies had been perfectly pleasant to her. Hardly allowing her to do a thing other than watch, of course, but their lack of petty power displays or absurd neglect made them nicer than many of the other places she'd been. On her way to her temporary accommodation, the sun was still, warm, visible – it didn't hurt her to stare right at it. She stared long enough that all sound seemed to leave the entire world.

She'd stopped right at the cusp of a railway bridge. The country fields beyond – the rolling pastures and oaks older than her parents, the distant cottages and the air so free of smog and smoke – she saw them all.

She went down the steps and slid off the platform with slow, calm movements, her mind relaxed in the same way a hot bath might have calmed her body. The loose grit of the platform dug into her palms as she pushed herself off it. Her palms were softer back then.

She walked down the track towards the sun and the hills, wondering.

She passed by people who looked at her briefly from their old homes with purple doors. She felt her legs tremble.

No train ever came. The government had decommissioned this railway line sixteen weeks before.

She never did anything like this again. She'd tried never to think about that strange hour. She hadn't even been unhappy. She hadn't had a right to feel like that, to become untethered from her walk home, from her plan for her life, from life and normal living.

What bad things had ever happened to her, to justify a stupid, selfish act like that? She rewrote it in her mind when she could – that she knew the railway line had been decommissioned, that she'd just been going for a pleasant, sunny walk in her sunny new career.

She'd left the railway track before it was dark. She overslept that night.

When at Christmas Cooper's sister talked about a suicide at her secondary school – a boy who'd gone into the sea, who'd never come back, who they thought might just have been dragged out into the great nothing after biting off more than he could chew – Cooper left the room and went to have another nap.

That was all she could do with most of the problems in her

life, other than shouting, or breaking up, or seeking a solution – any solution – no matter it be good or bad, no matter the cost to her or those she cared about. Certainty mattered more than goodness.

It was all she could do in the end: crave the certainty of sleep.

ॐ

The morning after she and Alec had discovered the crates in the woods, it was cold, or maybe it was just the hotel room.

The stranger who had knocked, who came to speak with Cooper, was just a man, no mask, no protective gear. He had serious eyes and slow, shifting movements. He wore a white shirt and red tie. It took him a few moments to smile, a practised smile, and it rarely left him after that. He held a small folder of A4 pages in his hand.

'You're awake,' he said. 'That's good.'

CHAPTER THIRTY-SEVEN

That whole morning, Cooper did not ask for their names.

They did not offer them.

They'd passed police officers on the way down and across the hall, she and the man in the red tie with the fake smile. He'd asked if she'd wanted water. She'd said yes.

'I can't live without it,' she added, and then, after a pause: 'Because it's water, and—'

'What?'

She had immediate regrets. 'Nothing.'

She was nervous, tired.

The man opened a door for her. He left to fetch her drink.

It was quieter in here, at least.

An old man and a middle-aged woman waited for her within.

This new room was like the one she had woken up in, in its colours at least. The same yellow curtains. The same dark polished wooden shelves. This had been a lounge, once.

The old man sat across the chamber with a cup of tea. His face was pitted by acne scars, his suit pinstripe black on grey. His hands were upturned, his fingers criss-crossed as if they were about to initiate prayer. His eyes were vacant. He rarely looked at Cooper. He said nothing the whole time they were there.

The woman, however – she stared right at her. The stranger's cheek was caught on the edge of a twitch, a slight tremor in her hand as she scratched her ear. She was in her forties, fifties, maybe, though it was hard to tell. She also said nothing, for a while, at least.

Documents and folders lay around the tables, some bearing the insignia of Public Health, some marked with other acronyms, other government departments and committees.

The door opened and Cooper stiffened at the surprise of the noise. She knew she needed to calm down. She—

The man in the red tie came back with Cooper's water and set it down on a table next to an empty chair.

Cooper did not sit there.

'You worked on a case for us, once,' the woman said. 'Years ago, now . . . We wouldn't have spoken.'

There was something careful about her words. As if she was processing something in her mind, some hidden disgust that wasn't about Cooper, wasn't about any of them. Something that couldn't let her go.

'What case?' Cooper asked, but even as she spoke, the doors opened once more. People came in with croissants, pastries, a covered plate of bacon.

'Feel free to help yourself,' said the man. 'And please. Sit down.'

Cooper did so.

The waiting staff left.

The woman went on, buttering a croissant. It was a long time before she was finished, before she finally spoke.

'Tell me about these horses,' she said, a knife still in her hand.

'What about them?'

'How you came here. What the locals told you. Tell me about it.'

'I mainly worked with the police,' Cooper said. 'I didn't conduct many interviews.'

The woman kept staring at her, finally eating the croissant. Cooper went on.

'The inspector – Harry Morgan – he phoned my office the afternoon the horses were found.'

'What pieces were found?' the man asked.

'Decapitated heads. Tails, also.'

'Was that all that was found?'

One of the documents on the table had a photograph of Alec on it.

'Dr Allen?' the man went on. 'I asked if all you found were the heads and tails.'

'Tyre tracks,' Cooper said, turning back to him. 'Nothing else from the body itself.' She paused. 'Someone had made a campfire nearby – a vagrant interviewed by the police the next day. He claimed to have witnessed the animals' burial.' Still they said nothing, they just waited for her to say more. 'And there was . . . well, there was a bird outside the tents.' She scratched her arm. 'It was dying.'

The man looked over at the woman.

'What happened to the bird?' he asked, turning back. 'What was wrong with it?'

'It was infested with parasites. It was having difficulty breathing. I helped it.'

'How?' the woman asked.

'I snapped its neck.'

CHAPTER THIRTY-EIGHT

The other vet – the quiet one on the phone, who'd spoken of a man and horse screams – she was dead. An overdose of ketamine, most likely stolen and written off as spillage from her surgery. The full catalogue of all those things she had taken, all those things she had ordered on her practice's behalf, would not be uncovered for weeks. Wires, certainly. Sedatives. Tools.

Personal protective equipment was missing, large size coveralls too tall for her use, masks, disinfectant.

No one had noticed.

The authorities had gone to Kate's home.

They had found evidence of blackmail there, a burner phone used around Ilmarsh for the past two months. She had been forced to do so many things. She thought she'd be helping steal the animals at first – that this was all.

Kate didn't exist any more.

Cooper thought of Kate's mug. *I'm not sheepish about doing a good job.*

She didn't know what to say.

Kate hadn't existed for a few hours now.

She didn't know what to—

The man looked through his notes, then he asked Cooper a question. 'What is your relationship with DS Alec Nichols?'

'Is he OK?'

'Answer the question first.'

Cooper hesitated. She drank some of her water. 'He's a professional. Can be a little . . .'

'A little what?'

'Nervous. Easily riled. He certainly doesn't have a good appetite for, you know . . .'

'No, I don't know.'

'He didn't cope well with the bodies.'

The man straightened his back, looking over briefly at his superior.

'Did Officer Nichols, or any other person in this place, ever discuss sickness, illness, disease, infection, or contagion?'

Cooper scratched at her nose. 'Where is he?'

'What did he discuss with you?'

The sun was rising now. The noise of people began to thicken on the floors below, like a chorus.

'I've answered every question.' Cooper turned to the woman. 'Now answer mine. You haven't even told me what—'

'It was *Bacillus anthracis*,' the woman said. 'A strain of it, anyway. Fast acting. Killed the older police officer, George Hillard. Two others critical, Alec Nichols included. The evidence suggests anthrax spores were deliberately placed around the horse heads.'

No one said a thing.

'Show her the letter.' The woman turned to her colleagues.

The man in the red tie produced a photocopy from his pile of documents.

He passed it to Cooper.

છ૭

The letter was typed. Before being photocopied by the authorities, it had been stained by some anonymous liquid.

There was anger in me once. I dreamt at times of being better. We killed to help and in helping I tasted something in me.

I have burned fires. I am awake and no one saw me and no one will. These things I did I did and no one knew until I let them. I have held the dancing plague. I blossom, now.

The smile is yours.

You could have saved him.

'A number of dead birds were discovered in the night. We found copies of this letter in their beaks. Folded down their throats, wrapped in plastic. Their necks broken, just like your broken crow.'

'Where?' Cooper asked.

The woman didn't answer the question.

The man spoke instead. 'DS Alec Nichols's fingerprints were found on the wrapping of several.'

He took the piece of paper back.

'You were vaccinated years ago, weren't you?' The woman paused. 'The full course. I read it in your file.' She smiled. 'It was like you were meant to come here. Like a hero from another hall, come to slay the monster.' Her smile had no warmth, no feeling. She sat up straight. 'I've read about you.'

Plants bloomed out in the gardens beyond.

'You were hired for four days, if I understand correctly. We'd like to extend your employment, Dr Allen.' The woman looked away at last. 'You'll be leaving within the hour.'

CHAPTER THIRTY-NINE

Their car did not stop at Well Farm. But still, Cooper heard the evidence of their work, saw it, smelt it, even through the partially opened window. The hum of the flies, the birds, the blazing fire.

How things had changed.

Men and women sifted through the grass, the reeds, the abandoned soil of the Coles' farm. They were like shadow puppets in their hazard gear, their dark silhouettes moving against the red horizon. There were thirty of them, maybe more. They had come to catalogue lives.

Cooper's new colleague, the woman who had questioned her, she looked out of the window, too. Still, no formal introduction had been made. Her coat had a nametag on it. ADA SOLARIN was printed in bold capital letters above the logo NATIONAL CRIME AGENCY. She could be anyone. She could do anything.

On the other side of the road the last great fire of November burned.

It smelt of food at first.

The black smoke rose.

৪৩

During Cooper's education, they'd sometimes gone to abattoirs. Her first visit had been by herself, back before her interview to get into vet school. It was considered impressive if you organized such a trip – a brave willingness to confront the routine and purposeful slaughter of animals whilst working in a profession dedicated to caring for them.

So, after reading this online, Cooper had gone. Being a vet had been her dream. Seventeen years old, she'd found the people working in that place to be nice – nicer than many others she would encounter in her rotations – and they'd make light jokes with her, they'd include her in their tea breaks, they'd ask about her hopes.

Chains jangled as cows were herded through one by one, pigs to follow in the afternoon. The cows did not know of those murdered before them. They were even calm in the run-up, though this turned, as the time came closer, to a slight unease. Before the end, they would understand only that this place was not a good place.

The pigs, they were different. They knew where they were, they always knew. And they screamed in their knowing, next to all those nice men.

Cooper thought of those days and other days, as they drove past the smoke of Well Farm.

She thought of it as she watched the bodies of one hundred and eighty-two sheep systematically tossed onto a pyre. Ada would tell her the number when she asked. The woman had a head for statistics.

Stack upon stack of wooden pallets stood, sourced from the same supplier who had built the town's bonfire those days past. Fallen between them, spilling from edges fused by fire and dust and wool and wind, there was a shambling mass of the young and the ewes, burned to cinder, feeding those who came after them, collapsing under the weight of all the dead and dying.

Cooper said nothing, but her face must have given her away.

'Multiple sheep were infected,' Ada explained. 'It's a precaution. It's necessary.'

Ada watched her. Cooper said nothing.

'We found a body in the fields. Too late to do anything.'

'Who?' Cooper tried to hide her feelings.

'An old man. Collapsed in the marshes. He had soil from the horses' burial site caked around his fingers. He'd brought his daughter to the hospital . . .'

Ada paused.

'Then he went back to where he had shown DS Nichols the horses, just a few days before. He sifted through their burial site. Picked at it in his final moments. Collapsed . . .'

'Suicide?'

Ada shrugged. 'He spent his final hours alone.'

He had not survived to see the sun rise.

They drove on, stopping only for a roadblock.

When Ada showed her badge, strange officers waved her through.

No one would ever live here again.

⚮

The streets were empty. Even the market was deserted. Flowers trembled in the growing breeze, red and yellow bending as they passed.

'Will Alec get better?' Cooper did not turn as she spoke. She just kept watching out of the window.

After a few moments, Ada answered.

'No one can find his son.'

The car came to a stop, up near the docks. A boat waited.

Cooper hesitated. 'What do you mean, no one can find him?'

'What I said.' Ada undid her belt. The driver turned off the ignition. 'Simon Nichols was not at home. Not at any friend's home. There's evidence someone was in the car with Alec when he crashed. Mud on one of the back seats . . . A small quantity of blood. Others are looking at that now.'

She opened her door.

'Come on. That's our boat.'

Cooper got out. They'd given her new clothes, a thick jacket. But she'd have to change soon again, anyway.

The people ahead, they wore hazard protection gear.

She thought of the letter as they walked.

She thought of crates, of heads in fields.

She thought of an abattoir, of cows, of pigs, of the nice people who had killed them.

The smile is yours.

You could have saved him.

CHAPTER FORTY

The boat cut through fog. It was everywhere, the thickening of the world and air, the collision of warmth and emptiness. The clarity of deserted Ilmarsh was lost to them.

Cooper retched within the toilet cubicle, shaken from the motion of the boat. She regretted the croissants.

She went back to the main deck.

Rust lined the edges of the blue-green metal. White bars stood at regular intervals, metal chains blocking off sections from their access. Ada stood at the end – the stern? The bow? Cooper didn't know what any of it was called. Ada had her back to all these things.

She was smoking, a slight grey mingling into the white cloud all around.

'Those things will kill you,' Cooper said.

The woman turned.

'We won't see it till it's right in front of us,' Ada said, her voice higher and gentler. 'The place we're going to . . . it had a family, once. They lived out here for years. Raised sheep and pigs. Sold their produce on the mainland.'

Ada threw her cigarette into the sea.

Cooper watched it catch in the waves. She'd had a long and complicated history with cigarettes and other toxins. She resolved to give them up, there and then. And it felt strange, the thought occurring. How unimportant, how small it seemed. But even in times like these, no one stopped being themselves. They just had to hide it better.

The cigarette disappeared in the grey water. Ada continued her story.

'Forty-five years ago, the son left his parents behind. Got a degree. Made something of himself. Did everything he was supposed to do. Got married. Had children. Served his country. I knew him.'

Still the boat hummed.

'He came back, eventually, he took them all back to meet his parents. And he never went out to the world again.'

She stared at the fog ahead.

'Fifteen months ago, fishing boats caught sight of a fire out here. By the time a response could be made, most of the family were dead or dying, the animals too. Only the youngest daughter survived.'

They must be near, now.

'What did the girl tell you?' Cooper asked.

Ada ignored the question at first, only speaking after a long hesitation, a sudden straightening that suggested she'd seen something out there. She soon relaxed. 'The marshes on the island were sewn with a novel strain of anthrax and quantities of amoeba known to assist with germination and replication. No animal vectors required. There was evidence of cultivation. Of an unsound character.' She hesitated. 'The daughter told us nothing.'

'Why?'

'She had become mute.' They were nearing the shore now. Cooper could see boats out there. There were people, moving back and forth. Shapes manifested through the thick air. 'We removed as much as we could. We committed to a clean-up operation months ago, as soon as we had the budget, a plan, at least . . . Signs were erected, warning travellers not to dock. And before you say anything . . . No one came out here, anyway. There was no risk of anything spreading, of person-to-person transmission. Other, similar sites had been left contaminated for far longer with no major incidents. They're only spores.'

ॐ

The boat drew to a stop.

'I knew the man. He worked for the government, once. He worked with me. Not at the NCA. Before . . .' Ada did not look at Cooper. 'After the fire, the few officers involved were told as little as possible. Those who already knew the truth signed the Official Secrets Act. Why should anyone know?'

They put their masks on, plastic so clear and hard it might as well have been glass.

They stepped onto the dock.

'I knew him. It's why they called me.'

Ada looked ahead, not yet moving.

'He was my friend.'

A thin, partially overgrown track led inland, the ground bulging into a slope. It was hard to see much else but the tall green conifers, and the fog that lay between them.

CHAPTER FORTY-ONE

Floodlights had been erected outside the house. The people that passed them all wore the same hazard gear, the same masks; some carried supply crates through to the camp. Cooper kept looking around as they walked, but Ada focused ahead, resolute, unfazed.

Madness had engulfed this place, once. It did so still. Rusted shells of metal littered the building edges; black shadows burned around the doorways, like the blast-echoes of a nuclear explosion. The barns' chimneys had shrivelled like crisp packets in microwaves. Empty red petrol tanks lay piled up in the overgrown grass. Plants long and thin and wide and short all thrived within the abandoned poison of a murder-suicide. Trees seethed past the cars, past the front porch.

Officers in biohazard gear conducted police grid searches, string and markers placed along the overgrown lot. Worlds superimposed themselves upon one another, morphing, merging, jostling to cement themselves in Cooper's reality. The collapse of a man's mind echoed down the years.

It led them to a tent up ahead.

A woman cried out beyond.

Others ran past them, but Ada led with a steady pace, only diverting a little from their path, the floodlights guiding their way through the numbing fog.

Up ahead, the source of the cry could be seen, had sat down

on the ground, blood welling from a rip in her hazard gear, just above her knee. They'd later discover there were tools buried in the ground near the second barn. The woman had caught her skin against some twisted hooks in the soil. The course of vaccination treatment would take months; there had not been enough time to prepare everyone. She was brought to a hospital within the hour.

Ada passed Cooper, disappearing into the tent beyond.

Tables had been set up within, dead crows spread across them. In the centre of the makeshift room, there was a pit in the soil, a thick, stiff sack beside it.

'We've provided what equipment we can,' said Ada. 'Discover what you're able to discover. How they died. Who killed them. We want any DNA you can find, especially human. We photographed the scene as we found it; fourteen birds had identical copies of the letter stuffed into their beaks. The fifteenth, we left within.'

'Fifteen?'

Outside, the work continued in near silence. Few talked. No one chatted.

Ada smiled, faintly. 'Everything consumes itself, in the end.' She turned to go. 'We found Alec Nichols's fingerprints on the letter wrappings. We need to know what else is in there.'

CHAPTER FORTY-TWO

Ada Solarin walked through the family's home.

She had done so months ago. She'd seen the wreck of her colleague's life. She'd seen what had become of her friend.

She and her past self, they went together. This place had not changed much, even across the seasons.

Bowing their heads beneath wooden beams.

Past it all, into the girl's room.

A hole lay within the girl's wall, beaten through from inside with great force, chunks of plaster and wood still on the floor below.

Through the hole she saw the treeline, close by.

ॐ

There was anger in me once. I dreamt at times of being better. We killed to help and in helping I tasted something in me.

I have burned fires. I am awake and no one saw me and no one will.

ॐ

So many were dead, now, within the space of days.

So many of them, linked by animals, by violence, by blackmail.

They'd found the answer to the Eltons just hours before. They'd sent officers round to their property after they had caught up on the case history; Charles Elton had shot himself in the head. His potential testimony had died with him. It was a waste.

His suicide note, blaming the police for their unjust attention, claiming they drove him to it – an innocent man – that was just embarrassing.

Ada knew there was no such thing as an innocent man.

He'd tried to burn a letter in his fire. KILL YOURSELF. An encryption password was found on the back of an envelope, presumably left by the blackmailer as proof of knowledge.

The idiot hadn't checked it before departing this world.

One of the computers confiscated by the police had contained a hard drive.

1,592 images and 314 videos of child sexual abuse were found within. The forensic work would take weeks – it would scar the officers who had to look at it – but the images and videos didn't appear to be created by Charles himself, at least not on initial examination.

He was evil.

Like most evil people, he was mundane, in the end. Not clever. Not bizarre or beautiful.

He was an idiot who couldn't burn a piece of paper.

Who died rather than face the truth of all he'd done, a truth manipulated by whoever had pulled his and Kate's strings. Whether that was an individual . . . a group . . . a place. In mundane Ilmarsh, too . . . there was evil.

One of Ada's subordinates came into the room. He didn't say anything. She knew he was waiting for her to turn.

'What?' she asked, not moving.

'Dr Allen's finished, ma'am. She wants to talk with you.'

Ada gave the room one final look. She stared at the hole in the wall.

She thought about all her friend had done to this place and to himself. She thought about his charred body, found hunched in prayer, one child crying in the distant sheds. The others had been found in the grass.

She'd read her uncle's books, once.

Even though he hadn't read them, she had – perhaps *because* he hadn't, she didn't know.

The act of killing your child – it was a godly act. It was Abraham and Isaac. It was fear and trembling, being willing to break all laws – even that of the divine – just because a voice in a bush told you your child was meant as a sacrifice.

Had a voice told her friend to do what he had done? Had the world, had this place? What had made him the way he was? What made anyone the way they were?

If the world was in our heads, then the end of a life was the end of the world.

The taking of a single life, it was an apocalypse.

To kill a person was to be close to God.

She went out into the poisoned air once more.

Forty per cent of homicides went unanswered, whatever stories said. At least she'd known who had killed her friend's family. At least they knew who, if not why.

She walked towards the tent, trying not to look at all the strangers stooped to the soil, trying not to listen to the silence.

Within an hour they were back on the water, and she'd never see that place again. She'd never go back, not even if they made her. She'd do anything to leave this place. Anything.

CHAPTER FORTY-THREE

'Rat poison,' Cooper said. 'Warfarin pellets were given to the crows over a few days. Based on how many were killed, it's probable whoever did this had fed the birds for a sustained period of time beforehand. They were comfortable with him. The necks were snapped post-mortem. Likely after defrosting.'

'The killer froze them?' Ada's eyebrow rose.

Their boat moved back along the surf, the fog almost faded now, but the sky itself had grown cloudy, darker. Both women stood at its stern.

Cooper nodded. 'We've not been able to locate any other sites of contamination,' Ada said. 'From what we can tell, the soil used to bury the horses' heads was taken from the same pit we found the birds in.'

'What now?' Cooper asked.

The island receded in the distance. It held Ada's gaze.

'The local police have alibis for Alec Nichols. For key times in this and more.'

Cooper said nothing.

'But it's interesting,' Ada went on, 'looking at Alec's record. There's evidence he was suffering from depression. He discontinued grief counselling. There seems to have been a shadow over his time at his previous department, though we're still working on clearing that up. There's also evidence his son was skipping school. Apparently DS Nichols told his counsellor he wished, sometimes, that he'd never even had a kid. That life would be easier once he was alone again. It's all here.'

'I thought that kind of thing was confidential.' There was a slight edge to Cooper's voice as she spoke.

Ada shrugged. 'Not in times like these. The boy's gone, blood found at the scene . . . a letter saying "you could have saved him". His son is most likely dead, of course. And if he isn't, if someone's taken him, well . . .'

Ilmarsh grew nearer.

'This is about Alec,' Ada said. 'He was part of this . . . or part of this is aimed at him. Either way, we want you to find out.'

'Find out what?'

'The truth.'

Cooper looked at her temporary home, closer and closer now. 'I'm not a detective.'

'If someone's watching Alec, they'll be watching you.' Ada hesitated. 'No one in my department has your expertise in this type of crime. I'm confident you'll—'

'I'm not right for this.'

'It has to be you,' Ada pressed. 'You've worked with him. He trusts you.'

Cooper thought of Alec lying in a hospital somewhere, not knowing what these people thought, not knowing his boy was gone, not knowing anything at all.

She thought of a farmer, lying in a field.

She thought of smoke, of carelessness, of burning sheep.

'Who else knew about the bird, the snapped neck?' Ada asked. 'Who else—'

'Alec might have told any number of people. He might be innocent, he . . .'

'Even if he didn't do it . . . someone who inspires such hate, such attention . . . a man like that is never innocent. Not of everything.'

'Alec got sick, too. He survives going out to the island, taking the samples, coming back, only to infect himself at the last minute?' Cooper shook her head. 'He's a victim.'

'Everyone's a victim.' Ada took out her cigarettes.

The lights shone along the shore.

'The letter . . . the crows . . . they were for you. They were responding to you, whether you and Alec, or you alone . . .' Ada lit the match. 'We'll clean up. We'll take care of the sick. We'll wait for more bodies. But you, Cooper . . . you'll be able to do more than wait. You'll be able to solve this. For the dead. For yourself . . .'

Ada told her that she was there for her. That her government was there for her.

She told her that we were all in this together.

'I'm not a detective,' Cooper repeated.

Ada smiled, exhaling smoke.

'You will be.'

CHAPTER FORTY-FOUR

On Ada's final night in Ilmarsh, she sat in her car out near the forest. She sat just a few yards away from the site of Alec Nichols's car crash, of a stag's death, of a boy's abduction and possible murder. She sat here in her car, the window rolled down, a cigarette in her hand, all the lights on. She was alone.

The government response had already been deemed incompetent. Ada's career would probably be over soon. Once the media had moved away from stirring up geopolitical and religious fears, once they'd realized the disaster was home-grown, the news cycle had shifted almost immediately. Many seemed to believe the horses themselves had died from anthrax, in spite of official briefings and discussions. The animals became a footnote, and even Ada's superiors seemed to adopt this strange position, as if they'd forgotten all else, and perhaps they had. The government, their society, it was meant for greater things. The clean-up was in progress. The local police could handle the finer details of horse theft, mutilation and death.

ॐ

People thought fiction was the problem – that films, television, games, comics would all desensitize the world to violence and horror.

Real things were far harder to care about.

There were so many of them.

Day after day we seemed to learn how awful the world could be, the things people could do. It's why people imagined conspiracies. It made things manageable. It made things human.

Cooper kept working. She immersed herself in every file, every report, every movement of the case that occurred.

She kept doubting she was enough. Ada kept telling her otherwise.

But of course, who knew?

Cooper would rise to the challenge or she'd serve as bait. She had little official status, her funding still ostensibly provided by the local police who were compensated in turn. If she failed to uncover anything, then she was just a vet who had got in over her head.

Ada thought about her friend.

Ada wanted to go back home, back to her office. She wanted takeaways and life and people, she even wanted family again.

Something moved within the woods. She turned immediately, dropping cigarette ash, gripping the wheel.

Someone was there. She'd seen them, she'd seen a shape move quickly, like it was dancing.

She got out of her car, gripping her pepper spray now. She stared ahead, removing her torch and shining it into the darkness.

There was nothing there.

In the hours to come, as their men searched the area, they'd find nothing but animal tracks.

Two Weeks Later

CHAPTER FORTY-FIVE

You know, I used to have this one really bad dream when I was a kid . . . It was one of the only ones I had more than once, that I remember at least.

I didn't know what it was at the time, not at first. The way this thing looked, in my dream I mean . . . it was this place, this black building on a hill, it was dirty.

Your gran and me, we'd be driving through town – we'd be coming back from a friend's house, or the beach, sometimes . . . It was cold and dark – colder than anywhere had ever been, in real life at least. And the wind, it blew down newsagent signs and restaurant menus and even dog walkers, it was just silly, really . . . I'd try to look at the sea, but there'd be nothing there, just noise. It was a town a little like this one, but bigger – in better condition, I guess. We'd be in the car, and I'd see this black building . . . this ruin . . . and it looked at us from the hill. I couldn't make out anything but for some letters – great big dirty white letters, the others all missing. It was tall. And I wasn't myself.

He scratched his head.

I'd see this building and I'd—

क़

I'd crash my car.
  I'd wake up.
  I'd be myself again.
  You'd never have been born.
  I'd be myself again.
  All the world a dream.
  I'd—

CHAPTER FORTY-SIX

When Alec Nichols woke in his hospital bed, at first he could move only a flicker of an eyelid. So no one came.

His heart took a while to beat at its former pace. He'd always been bad at winking – it had always looked like something was wrong with him.

He supposed that this was true, now.

No one came, and he faded away once more.

☠

He had spent weeks dreaming of houses and hair. Of the last days of his marriage.

In these dreams he'd be crawling onto his mattress.

Even in the past, even with sleep music – the sounds of rain, of wind, of birds lulling him to unconsciousness – he could not rest. His wife could. He'd play the big spoon and little spoon with her cold body. He'd put one arm around her, and struggle with where to put the other, whether to allow it to succumb to pins and needles.

Sometimes he'd be alone, and he'd roll towards her to stroke her hair, but she wouldn't be there. The bedsheets would be rumpled. It would be difficult to see in this light, though a bulb would be turned on in the hallway. Its strange light would seep under their door, just a bit, suddenly clicking off as he reached out.

He'd feel hair in his hands, coarse and rigid in the dark.

It would feel almost like the hair of a horse's tail.

It would be his wife's hair, made from the hair of another. He'd want to stroke it even so, but there was beeping in the cold. Years blurred into years, but the memory hung on. He lost himself in Elizabeth's time.

They'd bought the wig together, the day after her diagnosis.

It was what people did, when they prepared for the worst.

It had creeped him out, how they had made it from a real person's donated hair. But she'd wanted something real. She had wanted to feel it was real when she touched her head, she wanted to know someone had helped her, even in this.

And it would be hard, wouldn't it? She'd kept telling him how hard it would be.

She didn't want anyone to forget her. That was what she was scared of the most.

She'd known it inevitably happened to everyone.

She hadn't wanted to die, she'd told him.

They'd get through this together, he'd promised.

He—

He had the memory of hair in his hands, and even when his eye flickered, even as he came back to the world, he could still feel it, still smell a stolen smell.

※

He woke up.

He was not himself. He'd never been himself.

His eyelid would flicker, sometimes, until the end of all his days.

And he'd smell that hair.

He'd feel it, lying in the dark of his bed. Coiled on a distant farm.

The world was all nightmare, now and always. The room sang with machines. Doctors came into the room. Their mouths moved, and in his confusion Alec realized he could not speak. He had tubes in his nose, in his throat. His arms were dark with welts and scars.

His heart had stopped twenty days ago. It had been healed through the company of strangers. His wife had died once, too.

As they pulled the tubes from Alec's chest, tears fell from his eyes, but no expression of horror or dread, nothing to indicate true tears or sadness.

So it was only water. It was only skin.

His body would never be what it had once been. He couldn't breathe.

It was only horses.

He thought of their number. He grasped for their names.

⁊⑦

'We'd like to book you in for counselling.'

The doctor stood by his bed. Time had passed; he wasn't sure if it was even the same day any more, or if—

'It says in your file you previously saw a Dr Tillman for a depressive episode a few years back? What we're going to do here is more of a cognitive behavioural approach. Near-death trauma, losing a loved one, it can take a toll, but—'

What were they talking about?

'You can frame negative events in a different way,' the doctor said. 'It can really help. We may not even need drugs here.'

His eyelid still shook.

He tried to sit up, and the doctor looked away as he did so, as if the motion itself were something private, something embarrassing.

'Wh—' Alec swallowed, his throat dry. With difficulty, he went on. 'What's wrong?'

The doctor stared at him. 'Nothing's changed in your diagnosis.'

'*What* diagnosis? I don't—'

'You don't remember? We talked about this.' The doctor frowned. 'This isn't an optimal sign, you know.'

Alec tried. He was trying, but this man – this—

The sun was falling outside. How many days had he lost?

'My son . . . Where is Simon? Where is my son?'

THE HORSES

HORSE #1: Palomino colouring. Pony.
Location: Elton Riding School and Livery
Owner: Tessa Knowles (17)

HORSE #2: Piebald colouring. Horse.
Location: Elton Riding School and Livery
Owner: Charles and Louise Elton (71 and 65)

HORSE #3: Dark bay colouring. Clydesdale. Horse.
Location: Elton Riding School and Livery
Owner: Charles and Louise Elton (71 and 65)

HORSE #4: Grey colouring. Clydesdale. Horse.
Location: Elton Riding School and Livery
Owner: Charles and Louise Elton (71 and 65)

HORSE #5: Bay colouring. Horse.
Location: Elton Riding School and Livery
Owner: Leanne Hook (29)

HORSE #6: Black colouring. Horse.
Location: Elton Riding School and Livery
Owner: Eric Brown (24)

HORSE #7: Brown chestnut colouring. Horse.
Location: Elton Riding School and Livery
Owner: Jordan Hill (48)

HORSE #8: Bay colouring. Horse.
Location: Joe's Tyres
Owner: Michael Stafford (43)

HORSE #9: Dun grey colouring. Horse.
Location: Smythe Bay, Field
Owner: Nicolette Jones (32)

HORSE #10: Sorrel chestnut colouring. Icelandic. Horse.
Location: Homestead Farm
Owner: Henry Schaffer (58)

HORSE #11: Dark bay colouring. Thoroughbred. Horse.
Location: The Grove
Owner: Joanne Marsh (63)

HORSE #12: Grey dun colouring. Thoroughbred. Horse.
Location: The Grove
Owner: Joanne Marsh (63)

HORSE #13: Black. Arabian. Horse.
Location: The Grove
Owner: Joanne Marsh (63)

HORSE #14: Black colouring. Shetland pony.
Location: The Grove
Owner: Joanne Marsh (63)

HORSE #15: Chestnut colouring. Horse.
Location: ???
Owner: ???

HORSE #16: Brown colouring. Horse.
Location: ???
Owner: ???

Day Twenty-Four

CHAPTER FORTY-SEVEN

'Three weeks ago, on November eighth, the mutilated remains of sixteen horses were discovered, partially buried, on a small farm on the outskirts of Ilmarsh at around 5.10 a.m.'

The cameras snapped light all around the spokesman. His forehead creased. His face bobbed back and forth before the assembled journalists. A phalanx of microphones had been assembled in front of him. He sat in the middle of a long yellow formica table. The tent was too warm.

'An initial examination of the remains suggests multiple individuals were involved in these killings. Almost all those who have come into contact with the burial site have fallen ill, resulting in three deaths, including that of the owner of the property in question. Several individuals are in critical condition and undergoing treatment, including three police officers and a liaison officer from Public Health. The remainder of those who have visited Well Farm in recent days are under observation as a precautionary measure. I can confirm reports that anthrax spores have been found in the soil, isolated to that location. This is being treated as a major incident.'

The assembled journalists sat in the tent and listened. They were half a mile from the roadblock.

'It is believed the killings took place on November seventh, most likely during or shortly after the town's Bonfire Night celebrations. We appeal for information from anyone who may have noticed anything unusual that evening, particularly those in the vicinity of the Lynndale area.'

The room was quiet but for the snapping of cameras, the scratching of pens.

'A town-wide quarantine was established until we were able to determine there was no further risk to public health. We have now made this determination as a result of the government's diligent and swift clean-up operation. As of tomorrow, beyond certain locations, people may now come and go freely from the area. We do, however, ask that the public remain vigilant.'

Details appeared on the screen behind him.

'Thank you. We'll take two or three questions.'

CHAPTER FORTY-EIGHT

The murder of a place, of the two thousand souls within, went on.

Orders of horse chocolates, fireworks, food syringes for use in contagion-themed cocktails, came in the weeks before Christmas. The county lines started once more, children spilling out of the arcades with fresh narcotics. People were walking down the seafront again. Couples from distant places sat on benches in their coats, wondering at the sea, at what had happened here. More and more ash began to cover the streets.

One day, someone realized the street-cleaning crews were no longer coming in, a mix-up over their contract supplier, but there was more to it than that. There was somehow more waste even though fewer people went outside. Half-drunk cans and bottles stood like little funeral stones, as if whoever had been doing the drinking had just vanished into thin air.

One day, a smoker slumped against a doorway in the market, cross-legged, his sleeping bag wedged behind him. The neon signs had been switched off. The seagulls had scavenged the last of the day's discarded chips.

The joint hung firm, clenched in his split lips, his eyes shut, and he'd had to click the lighter a few times to feel it go, to smell it.

He inhaled.

The spice was like a car crash, like a hug.

It was like home.

They found new cleaning contractors but the change stuck. Abandoned poisons spread, half drunk, half smoked, half felt.

ဆၜ

On Well Farm itself, there was vandalism. People broke in and stole things belonging to the Coles. Items of Grace's make-up. Rebecca's photos. The father's tools. Someone wore the girl's clothes.

The boy was forgotten in the public horror.

The police kept looking.

Or at least they said they were. But who was left to look?

The extra support officers had dwindled after the quarantine. The volunteer searches had faded out.

This was not a little boy or girl. This was not someone with a history of vulnerability, though they stressed that Alec's son had most likely been injured, that he'd need help.

All this had done was make people think he was dead.

Sympathy passed like a fever. Christmas came closer and closer.

Cooper had gone on the walks when she could, even so.

She had gone to the volunteer centre, she had signed herself up, she had walked through marshland and scrub.

So much of the land seemed tainted, so many homes and farms now abandoned or lost.

She kept coming back to the letter. She had a photocopy with her most of the time, folded in her pocket.

There was anger in me once. I dreamt at times of being better. We killed to help and in helping I tasted something in me.

The claim to have a moral motive was key to this, somehow, Cooper knew, regardless of whether that claim was sincere. 'Anger' had led to wanting to be 'better', to 'helping', but an awakening had apparently changed everything. His actions had led to him 'tasting something' within himself – if this person *was* indeed a 'him', but this seemed right in her mind, somehow, and she wondered why it was so. Whether 'killed' referred to the slaying of the dogs and cats in the crates, or the horses, or even humans, could not for now be known.

Then there was the fact that the killer had taken a risk in placing these letters back on the island, a second ritual to mirror the burial of the horse heads.

An attempt at communication: to Cooper through the use of birds, to Alec through the presence of his fingerprints.

I have burned fires. I am awake and no one saw me and no one will. These things I did I did and no one knew until I let them.

These lines were easier to understand and typical of such letters. The boasting, self-important ego of a psychopath was recognizable anywhere.

The reference to fire was the main detail of interest – there had been few arson incidents in recent years, and the letter's discovery next to the burned-out buildings of the island had seemed conclusive enough. But Ada and her department were sure the father had acted alone in setting his fires, and with all the bodies of the family accounted for, there had been no evidence of an extra party.

Ada answered her calls less and less frequently now. Her email replies had grown more and more delayed.

Cooper wondered if she was letting this woman down. She took a breath. She read the letter again, resolving not to email more thoughts until she received a response.

I have held the dancing plague.

She looked up dancing plagues. Most incidents happened throughout Europe from the 1300s onwards. Groups of people would dance spontaneously, usually starting with a single individual, stretching out to hundreds as more and more people joined, dancing until they dropped down dead from exhaustion.

I blossom, now.

The smile is yours.

You could have saved him.

The last time Simon had gone to school had been 6 November – the day before the town's Bonfire Night. Since then, not a single soul in Ilmarsh could remember seeing him.

He was eighteen, almost out of school. He had a poor attendance record.

In his room, they'd find posters, schoolwork, notes on history.

His laptop was gone. No evidence he'd returned after the crash, and there would have been evidence, wouldn't there? There would have been blood.

CHAPTER FORTY-NINE

Trace quantities of spores had been found in the detective's hallway, on unwashed and muddy clothes sitting in a basket from the day he'd first visited Well Farm. These were then incinerated, the carpet stripped off the floors, and the whole place thoroughly cleaned after the initial search. Several of Alec's neighbours had needed to move out of their homes temporarily. They were all checked for symptoms.

The authorities concluded that the fingerprints on the crow-letter wrappings were most likely lifts from elsewhere rather than actual proof of Alec's involvement in all this. But everything else was inconclusive, wherever they went.

☙❧

On Alec's dining room table, a piece of paper had been found on its own, flotsam from another time, another life.

A phone number in his own handwriting.

They rang it and rang it, and no one ever answered.

But it had been answered once – more than once – by another.

In Simon Nichols's mobile phone records, sent through from his network, they'd found evidence of over two hundred calls to and from the number over the last four months.

Whoever the number had belonged to, they had phoned Alec's son a few minutes after the crash.

There had been no activity since.

ॐ

Alec had, for some reason, ordered an emergency locksmith the day after the horses were found. Officers had already interviewed the man. This was how Cooper followed most of the case, reading the notes of others.

The locksmith told them about his client. Alec had thought someone might have broken into his house, though there had been no signs of forced entry, nothing but dried muddy footprints on the stairs. But when the locksmith had examined the scene himself, he'd barely been able to make the prints out. And there had been mud on Alec's own shoes; the guy had been leaving trails of it along the floor.

'He seemed like he hadn't slept in a while.'

'What do you mean?' the interviewer had asked.

'He was fidgety. Had bags under his eyes, half-drunk cups of coffee all around his desk. Kept pacing, looking out of the window. You get people who need our services . . . careless people who lose their keys down drains . . . women running away from cruel exes . . . And you get people who call us out for, you know, different reasons.'

He'd paused, then, taking a drink of his lemonade.

'You get people who don't feel safe. Who've probably never felt safe a day in their lives.'

He'd put his can down, playing with the ring pull.

'And he was a policeman, you know? If he doesn't . . . who does?'

ॐ

There was something wrong with the colours in his back garden, too – Cooper was aware this most likely had little to do with anything, but she kept thinking about it all the same. Many of the gardens all around had a similar issue. A grass that was slightly too green. Winter blue flowers grown red, rare scrub and weed that had not developed in this part of the world for decades. She sent illicit samples to a botanist friend, but he did not answer her, and by the time she would push, all investigations – and their lives as they had lived them – would be over.

Nevertheless, even if nothing was ever found, something about these colours upset Cooper. Something about them always would.

In the garden bins, they'd found the usual rubbish. Alec and his son had seemed to subsist off ready meals and takeaways, mostly Chinese and pizza. He'd put a lot of cans and bottles in the main black bin instead of the recycling collection.

Beneath it all, there were glass mirror shards. Some of them had Alec's blood on them, dried. Based on the evidence, and the shadow in Alec's hallway, right at the base of the stairs, it was determined that at some point prior to the horses being found, a person-length mirror frame had been smashed. Evidence of recent scarring on his right hand suggested that Alec had fractured it a second time, intentionally or otherwise, with his own fist.

On his computer, passworded with the name 'Julia' – itself bizarre, considering no one in his life appeared to be called that – they found no evidence of wrongdoing and no explanation for the mirror. There were a few online dating profiles, a few messages sent and received, but each exchange appeared to have petered out within a few days of implementation. The descriptions Alec had posted of himself had evolved over time. He had become less and less. Where once on his dating profile he'd identified Italian food and long walks as interests, had gone into great detail about films and television series he liked (claiming he was not much of a reader), on the final profile he'd just said he was a police officer, that he was a father, that he was looking for someone nice. Many of the women he had talked to had lived miles away. Most of them were a certain type – lean, dark-haired, in colourful clothes.

All the botanist would find, when the time came to look at the samples of Alec's garden flowers, was a harmless mutation, passed down along the years.

In the home itself there were none.

֍

Cooper would walk through Alec's home, sometimes. She would sit on his sofa, pour water from his tap in the sink, boil his kettle.

She'd read folders about his life.

His father – a wife-beater – now lived in a care home six hours away, paid for by the sale of his home and some of Alec's own salary. There was no record of Alec ever visiting.

There had been a short career in a detective fast-track programme before funding was cut, most positions gone. It had taken Alec a few more years after that to get back into CID.

Arrests, but no major rogues' gallery, no one who they could find who might have some grievance against Alec in particular.

No link between Ilmarsh, between Kate Babbit or Charles Elton or Albert Cole, beyond the fact of their moving here.

Alec's wife had fallen to cancer just a few years before. There was still some of her stuff here, even though she'd never lived in this place – a box in the attic, some medications long past their use-by date, no doubt caught up in their move or else returned to the widower. Even older still, they found anti-depressants, they found some weight-loss supplements. Only a few of the supplements had ever been taken.

Cooper drank some more water, reading about what a man had lost.

The quiet life he'd had with his son. No others, beyond his

brief and lonely messages to women on the internet, beyond his closing of accounts.

She had asked him once, driving over to the Eltons' stables, why he'd come to this town.

She closed her eyes, sitting on Alec's sofa in the dark of late afternoon. For a few moments she rested.

৪৯

Cooper woke up, her phone vibrating on the table.

It was dawn outside.

She picked it up; there had been five missed calls.

She didn't know what was wrong with her lately.

It was strange, wasn't it?

The streets . . . the beachfront . . . even the people.

It had started to feel, somehow, like she'd always known them.

CHAPTER FIFTY

Everyone remembers their first decapitation.

It had been a mouse trap. Cooper had been eleven. The snap of the metal mechanism had broken the animal's neck, a little blood trickling along the wood towards the grey carpet below.

Her mother had set these traps after a post-Christmas infestation and warfarin poison had failed to produce results.

Cooper had found it. She had been allowed to bury it in the back garden. Alone, she had ended up accidentally touching the neck, the wound. Bloody fluid had come out from the nose. It wasn't even alive and it had changed. She looked at it for a while, out in the dusk light. She had then taken a knife from the garage, wanting to see the spine below.

She'd think about that, in the years to come. She'd just been a kid.

She'd just said she wanted to help.

And she had, but that hadn't stopped her. She'd been curious. She'd—

Get Well Soon.

She had a card in her bag for Alec, one she'd never give him. No message inside, no words, no signs.

Get Well Soon.

Day Twenty-Five

CHAPTER FIFTY-ONE

They were in the sea. There they had drifted.

Things came to light.

The sky was clear at last. The sun rose, the horizon empty but for the distant wrecks of abandoned and burned-out oil rigs, the white blades of ageing wind farms dancing like synchronized swimmers in the cold air, the island further still.

Cooper was not alone.

The sand on the beach was coarse, littered with vast strings of seaweed weeping like fingers from the dark sea. A crab moved along rocks out on the bank. If she went close to it, it might disappear beneath the surface. No one might ever see it again. A small group of gulls crowded together on the sea-wall, leaping into the air and diving, not progressing much beyond.

There was a stiff cold breeze. The sea swelled and retreated, the tides moving in and out.

'How many?' Cooper asked. It was 7.15 a.m. She wore her green coat, a larger, thicker one she'd bought for these colder days. She had a splitting headache, a reusable cup of coffee in her left hand.

'A dog walker found the first one,' the inspector said.

No one ever seemed to call him 'Harry'. Cooper had tried for a little while, and he hadn't seemed to like it.

'The inspector' it was.

His black trouser legs were flecked with sand. Cooper wore her boots.

Salt drifted into their throats.

'It was around an hour or two ago. Dog had a collar on, one of those glow-in-the-dark ones. Ran right up to it, green halo all spinning. It must have looked strange.'

'The dog or the walker?'

'What?' He looked at her.

'What looked strange?'

He did not answer. He just shook his head and kept walking. Eventually, he said, 'Two.' There were two that they knew of.

They continued their walk along the shore. She could not see any bodies, not yet.

'They smell,' he told her. 'It wasn't like I thought they'd smell.'

They had been in the water for weeks, moving back and forth with the tides, their bulk and their legs splayed out as if they were flying. Their skin had been pecked by fish beneath the waves, by birds once they had made their journey back to their home shore.

'There,' he said.

She squatted down on her ankles next to one of them, a vast curve of hooves with no head or tail. Just flesh, bloated, decomposing, pale, bitten, mutilated in a frenzy, the skin separating in places from the body like a piece of clothing that did not fit. The other body had not been cut beyond its lack of skull and tail, its fleshy long neck extending to nothing.

Later that day, out in the large animal shed in which she had once dissected sixteen heads, Cooper would confirm it.

These two strange bodies, these blood-drawn leviathans from beneath the waves, were two of the animals whose heads had once been buried on Well Farm. Three more bodies emerged in the days to come. No others ever did.

You can do anything if you decide something isn't human.

They floated forever in the dark waters, their flesh becoming food.

The food becoming life.

The life becoming death.

Hours passed and a van drove onto the beach. They loaded up the bodies.

A man stared, a few hundred yards away.

Legs eleven, the bingo cried.

'He's stable, now.'

'What?' Cooper turned. 'Who?'

'Alec – he's been up for hours. Seems to be doing better.' The inspector hesitated. 'You want to go talk to him, don't you?'

She watched as the van pulled away. She didn't say anything.

'They questioned him this morning,' he said. 'Asking all kinds of questions about his bins. About how he treated his boy.' He turned to her. 'If you have any kind of sway . . .' He sighed. 'I don't know . . .'

Still, she said nothing.

'He'll be grieving, soon. We all know it.' The inspector scratched his arm. 'And you know as well as I do . . . he had nothing to do with this. Nothing to do with any of this.' There was a faint grimace upon his face. 'That's what you're focusing on, isn't it? That's why you've been round his home. That's why . . .' He began, and then stopped, seemingly thinking better of it.

'Did you ever meet Simon, Harry?'

The inspector seemed surprised at the question. 'A few times.' He paused. 'Did you?'

Cooper shook her head. 'I didn't know Alec for very long.'

The sun continued to rise over the bay.

'Neither did I,' the inspector said, turning to the sea.

৩৫

The water, vast and grey, had long since lost its magic. Cooper and her sister used to compete to be the first one to see the sea from their car. They would swim out to rocks, they would find every pool and every cave they could. Her little sister had done these things for Cooper, to be like Cooper, to be liked by her. And the big sister would pretend to herself that she'd only realized these things growing up, but that wasn't true, was it? People liked to be admired, to be copied. Even children aren't so innocent of wanting stuff like that. Everyone tried to lose themselves in greater things.

After vet school, whenever Cooper came to the seaside some of the old nostalgia would hit, like re-watching an ancient film, but you'd remind yourself who you'd been when you'd liked it, and you'd move on.

She didn't like being in the water. That was all.

She didn't remember when she'd last been on holiday.

'Please be kind to him,' the inspector said, 'when you see him. He's not himself.'

'Who is he, then?'

They parted ways without saying goodbye.

Search parties for the missing eighteen-year-old Simon Nichols have been called off on their fourteenth night.

The boy, son of local police officer Detective Sergeant Alec Nichols, was first reported absent after his father's car crash in what has become known as the 'Sixteen Horses' incident.

'Although this phase of the investigation has ended, we are pursuing multiple active leads,' Inspector Harry Morgan told assembled press.

'We appeal to anyone who may have information about Simon's whereabouts to please—'

CHAPTER FIFTY-TWO

Alec watched the television coverage. He watched all the clips he could find from the weeks past. Videos from news reports, the horrors of Ilmarsh, of quarantine authorities, of roadblocks and face masks. He saw the boats going out to sea.

The air in his hospital room didn't feel like air at all. He kept watching.

At the press conference, journalists had asked about the rapidity of the victims' decline, the unusual progression of symptoms. They asked if this was some new form of the infection – if people were in danger.

Mentions of his son had faded through the terror, through the times.

The doctors had told Alec that he'd woken multiple times over the past weeks. Each time they'd attempted to explain his situation, each time he had forgotten once more.

He sat up in his bed, out of the quarantine ward now for days. The other four beds were empty beneath the beeping, unnatural light. He was still feeble from weeks in this place, from the sickness that had ravaged his body, the barely faded bruising of the crash. Alec did not walk much, not yet, insisting only on going to the toilet by himself. They'd helped him with his steps.

They had given him a laptop on a tray. At the time it had not felt unusual.

꿈

'When we tried to find friends we could chase up with . . . we found something sad, you understand. Your son didn't appear to have any, did he? At least not that we could find. Popular, but no one actually close to him.'

The detectives had sat around Alec's bed. It was their third attempt to talk to him, apparently. Even moving his lips felt like an effort.

'Your son wouldn't have had any reason to run away, would he?'

'What?' Alec had tried rising in his bed, but—

'We found glass mirror fragments in your back garden bin. We—'

'What has that got to do with anything?'

They'd stared at him. 'How did the mirror break?'

'Who gives a shit about a fucking mirror? Who—'

'We found blood on the mirror. Why did we find it?'

Alec's nostrils had flared, his breathing harder. He'd tried to control his words. He tried to— 'Who is in charge of the investigation?' he'd asked.

'You'll have to be more specific.'

'Who is looking for my son?'

꿈

Alec found the answer, soon. No one was looking for him; not successfully, anyway.

A quarantine of two weeks had provided no answers. No trail from the car.

No body.

When he eventually managed to get a photo of the crash, he saw Simon's airbag had inflated. He read the report: based on where the stag had been found, he'd lost control after hitting the animal, exacerbated by a growing delirium from his infection. It had been a perfect storm.

Though a small trace was found, there was not enough blood in the car to suggest that Simon had suffered any fatal lacerations in the crash itself.

There had been no trail into the woods, though it was possible the boy had wandered there.

The only other way out would have been the road itself, just a few dozen yards behind them.

There was not enough time for a boy on foot – an injured boy at that – to clear the long road to town before the police had tracked Alec's car. Someone would have seen him.

Why wouldn't he have remained and searched for his father? It did not make sense that he would leave.

※

So what, then?

Before emergency services had arrived, someone must have picked Simon up.

That was all Alec could see. All Alec could think about.

He wondered why no one else seemed to join him in believing this, in *knowing* this.

He found no reference to abduction in any report, in any document, in any news clip, at least none that was available to him.

CHAPTER FIFTY-THREE

It occurred to Alec that these people, they thought he might be lying about his son's presence in the car. That the disappearing boy might never have been there at all.

He wanted to see a friend.

He wanted to see George. He didn't know why he wasn't on the case.

He didn't know why they were doing this, why they thought so little of him without knowing him.

He'd only ever tried to do good.

Day Twenty-Six

CHAPTER FIFTY-FOUR

Outside the train station, dark and dismal and thin, a vast blank billboard had been filled with a message for those who had been caught outside the quarantine and roadblock: WELCOME HOME.

The expected homecoming never occurred.

Instead, after a small initial influx of disaster tourists unable to keep their distance, residents had begun to leave. Restaurants open for decades began to close. Old people in care homes were left there, unvisited.

※

Louise Elton was eventually traced to her son-in-law's home on the Isle of Man over a hundred miles away; she claimed she had not known of her husband's activities, that he had hidden his paedophilic inclinations that had led to their blackmail threat. Cooper had got hold of the interview transcripts, had read them in between waiting for updates from Ada.

'Please . . . just leave us *alone*,' the stable owner had pleaded.

Her purported innocence was a load of shit, of course, but Louise had a good solicitor, and she was right: there was no hard evidence of any further involvement, at least not that would necessitate her immediate return.

Ilmarsh's few remaining officers had the task of talking to each and every child who had attended the riding school throughout the past few years. No images of any of them were found on Charles Elton's hard drive; all of the files appeared to be downloads from other users.

There was not, and never would be, any evidence that he'd molested anyone himself.

ॐ

Cooper ended up speaking to a small group aged between fifteen and eighteen with the attending officers. It had been difficult to get their permission, her limited professional currency almost spent.

She asked them about two people, showed them photographs of these people, told them stories.

Simon?

The teenagers had seen him at school. He was well liked, charismatic, but none of them had grown particularly close to the boy.

Rebecca?

Most didn't know the name. One of them recognized her photo, though. A boy named Peter. She'd been in his class at school. Hadn't seen her for a long time, but for a single meeting.

'She came to a lesson at the stables – months back.' The student hesitated. 'Why?'

Rebecca had been happy, the student said. She'd said she'd come again, but never did.

Rebecca had never ridden before, beyond a carriage-ride at the beach.

CHAPTER FIFTY-FIVE

Seagulls perched on top of paint-flaked facades and black iron lamp-posts. Neon logos screamed ST GEORGE'S CHARCOAL GRILL, TROPICAL CAFE, CAESAR'S PALACE. Empty amusement arcades blared *waka waka waka* chiptune music and flashing lights.

There were no other trailers, no caravans left along the seafront.

No strangers in unpeopled Ilmarsh.

It was all left for Michael, now.

The sky was grey. Waves lapped against the shore.

Cooper walked up to his door and knocked upon it.

৪৩

'You're not with the police?' the carriage driver asked. They sat on the sea-wall nearby, watching the ebb and flow.

'I'm a contractor,' she said. 'I work for myself.'

'So you're a private detective, then?'

She hesitated, then nodded. 'I suppose so. For now, at least.'

'I always wanted to be a detective,' Michael said. 'When I was young, at least. My dad claimed he was one, back before I was born, but I don't know . . .'

He took a packet of cigarettes and held it out towards Cooper. She shook her head after a moment and he put them back in his pocket.

'You can still have one,' she said. 'I'm not going to—'

'You've given up. It wouldn't be fair.'

Neither of them said anything for a little while. Seagulls landed on the sand nearby, watching them.

'Show me this photo, then.'

Cooper reached into her coat pocket and retrieved it.

He nodded at Rebecca's image. He hadn't known her by name. 'Took a ride for her birthday, ages back. Came again a couple of times. Said the first one was a present.'

'Her birthday was in September, so—'

'No, no. This was a year ago. Nothing that recent.'

Another boat moved in the distance. All the fishing vessels had gone now.

'Did you talk about much?' she asked. 'I know it was a long time ago, but anything you can remember . . .'

'Why are you asking me this? Who is this girl?'

Cooper scratched the back of her head.

'Was she involved in what happened? Did she do this?'

'She's been in hospital for almost a month,' Cooper said. 'Only recovering just now.'

'She was infected?'

Cooper nodded.

He looked away, and down at the photo again.

'She was happy, happier than most,' he said. 'And I liked that. She wanted to stroke Annie, seemed to have a real thing for the whole experience, even had someone filming it. She—'

'Who?'

'What do you mean?'

'Who was filming it?'

He paused, looking down at the photo and up again. 'A man, I suppose.'

Cooper got her phone out and found a picture of Albert Cole. 'Him?'

Michael shook his head.

After a moment, she found a photo of Alec and showed it to him.

Again, a head shake.

'He was in his mid-twenties, I think.'

An image of Simon produced a similar shake of the head, but Michael stiffened. 'The missing boy?'

Cooper nodded.

'I would have said something if I'd seen him.'

'How far away was the man standing? Where?'

'Near the old cinema.' Michael handed Rebecca's photo back to her. 'Just the first ride. I asked the girl why he didn't join in, but she didn't . . .'

'Didn't what?'

'I don't know.' He looked tired. 'She might have said he was afraid of them.'

'Might have?'

'Like I said, I don't know. It was a year ago . . . and honestly, I'm not sure I'd know his face to look at.'

He took his cigarettes out again and this time he lit one, shuffling a small distance away from her.

'Did that man . . . did he do this?'

Cooper did not know.

'Did he hurt those animals?'

She nodded.

They talked and they talked, the cold day getting colder.

৩৩

'I was thinking of leaving, you know.' He turned back to the water, smoke rising into the guilty air. 'Everyone's been leaving my entire life, and I never thought – I never thought I'd want to.'

He dropped ash down onto the sand.

'This town . . . it was always waiting for someone like this.' His voice was thinner, now, and he coughed.

'Someone like what?'

'No one wants to continue,' he said, no longer listening. 'No one's going to live here, not in ten years, not in five. I wouldn't be surprised if this . . . if this was all of us. Most of us. Hurting each other. Hurting ourselves.'

There was a long silence.

Queen Bee. Under the tree.

The sound of bingo made him laugh, though Cooper did not smile, did not understand.

'We'll disappear. The process . . . the human process . . . it will be over, one day, and we'll disappear. It will be as if we'd never been here. We'll be like we were before we were born. And it will be over.'

After a few moments, he got up and went inside his caravan.

Cooper remained on the sea-wall, looking out.

After a few minutes he came out again, his clothes changed, and left down the shore towards the pub. There was no goodbye here, either.

And her phone buzzed once more.

A message from the hospital, wondering why she hadn't come.

Wondering if she wanted to rearrange for the next day.

Yes, she said, and sent it. **Early afternoon.**

She went back to her hotel room.

CHAPTER FIFTY-SIX

Frank sat in the vet office alone, Halloween decorations taken down, sitting in a box on the far table. Dirty mugs sat around the sink. *Crazy for Ewe*, drawn in ink on the side of a blank cup.

The police had torn the business apart. Drugs had been confiscated, pending an investigation of Kate's illegally sourced ketamine, the wires stolen from their shed, sedatives used without oversight or control.

He left and locked the door.

Their customers fled to the next town over. The only work left was emergencies, and even then, numbers had declined.

People he'd known his whole life avoided him in the street.

This had been his father's business.

He went out to the river.

ॐ

The director of the vet practice tried to find beauty in the world.

He watched the birds. He loved this spot, had come here when he was young. There were white swans back then, but he had not seen any here for a while. Just ducks.

Everyone and everything that had come to this place, a part of them remained in the water, in the soil. Evidence of life. Whispers of knowledge. Collections of voices, caught at the edge of all meaning, like a machine of people, like history in a jar.

He imagined them all as they must have been.

Warriors step off boats on the beach more than a thousand years ago, their faces full of salt and spray.

The king's men ride to pillage monasteries, to eradicate European influence, to ensure all loyalty to the crown.

Planes drop bombs for a distant state.

The River Sedge starts eighty miles to the west of Ilmarsh, it runs through the town, and it ends far to the south, spilling out to a different bay despite its proximity to the sea itself. From the hills it flows in three directions, but only one runs to its mouth.

The River Sedge runs through everything.

The Norse called it Garsecg, spear-man. The river itself was shaped like a trident, twin spokes trickling from the hills and going nowhere while the central stream carried on.

The Tudors called it Sedg or Sedge or Sege. They were not particular.

The Luftwaffe, they called it nothing.

The vet sat for a while longer, wondering if what he had thought was worth thinking. He did not know what to do with his thoughts, sometimes. His face grew red with embarrassment.

He threaded along the trail. Light shimmered from a break in the clouds, dancing on a small group of shivering branches.

He thought of phoning her, of going to see her.

He was a man in love.

PART THREE:
A BIRTH OF SMILES

Day Twenty-Seven

CHAPTER FIFTY-SEVEN

When Alec dreamt, he dreamt of his boy linking paper clips across their lounge, his wife making spaghetti in the dark.

He dreamt of arguments and fights, of disappointments. He dreamt of picking his son up from his maternal grandmother's. The first Christmas alone. He'd been lonely. They both had. Out here in the country, you really needed a car. When Simon was old enough, Alec had bought him lessons for Christmas, and the boy never passed, of course he hadn't, he hadn't applied himself, had never taken it seriously, perhaps *because* it had been a gift, because it had been from *him*. Alec would say he loved him. One day, the boy who'd played with paper clips stopped saying it back.

Alec dreamt of these things. He dreamt of wanting him to go. When he woke up, Cooper was there.

ॐ

They said nothing, not at first. Alec stared at her – her red, sleep-deprived eyes, her hand and the cup within. She put it down on the table.

'They let you bring coffee?' Alec croaked, his throat dry.

'It's not coffee.' Her voice was soft.

'Can I have some?'

The air was slightly cold and artificial, pumped by hidden engines.

'No,' she said. 'It's mine.'

'Oh.'

He thought back to walking through those fields, to leaping over the ditch and splattering his legs.

He thought of driving along a road at night.

'No one's visited me,' he said. 'Just . . . just people asking questions.' He hesitated. 'Anyone visit you?'

'Doctors.' She didn't say much more.

'Doctors aren't visitors.'

'I'm a doctor. I'm visiting you.' She paused. 'I didn't get sick. They checked me out, but . . .'

'That's good,' he said, trying to sit up. 'That's lucky.'

She said nothing.

He smiled, briefly, and then he remembered. He remembered he had not smiled in weeks. 'I didn't—' Alec's vision blurred as he shook his head, not quite sure what he wanted to say. 'I don't—'

She paused, her expression softening.

She got up with a sudden movement and poured some of the mug's contents into an empty glass by his bedside. It was red. 'Have this.'

Alec nodded and drank, the motion hurting his arm. He'd thought, briefly, that it might be alcohol, the way Cooper was guarding it.

But it was just some kind of fruit cordial. That was all. It was strange. It reminded him of being a child again.

He didn't know why he expected much else. It was a hospital. She wouldn't be drinking. She wouldn't be allowed to bring spirits in here.

Yet he'd hoped, all the same. He needed something.

He did not feel like himself.

'What happened to us?' he asked. 'What—'

She showed him the letter.

You—

You could have saved him.

CHAPTER FIFTY-EIGHT

She watched him as he read.

These things I did I did and no one knew until I let them. I have held the dancing plague. I blossom, now.

His face was tired more than anything. His eyes drooped, barely recovered from their bruising. His cheek now bore a fresh scar. His hair had only just started to become more than a buzz cut. There was so little of the man she'd so briefly known. She'd made more of him from three weeks of reading than three days of partnership. She had mythologized him, just like she always did.

Here he was.

He didn't cry.

He didn't even shake, not much.

He just held the letter loosely, like he couldn't remember how to read.

After what felt like an age, he began to speak, his head turning slowly, the paper still held in his hands.

'They think Simon's dead, don't they?'

Cooper said nothing.

'They think the person who wrote this letter took him.'

There was laughter in the hallway. The silhouettes of nurses moved past the translucent glass. There was no indication they had seen or heard any of their conversation. They were just happy.

'Why are you still in town?' he asked.

A light was blinking, now, across the chamber.

'There's something else,' Cooper said, and Alec opened his eyes again, not realizing he'd closed them, not realizing he'd almost dozed off. But there would be no true sleep there, not now. It had taken a car crash and anthrax to cure him of his long insomnia, and she – she'd brought it back. 'This number.'

She passed him another piece of paper.

He took it, sitting up fully this time before looking down.

'Whose number is this?' She hesitated. 'Why was this in your handwriting?'

'Because I wrote it,' he said, his voice gaining some of its old strength. 'You found this in my home.'

She nodded.

'I asked you a question, Cooper. Why are you still here? You were supposed to – you were going to be here for four days. You—'

'Tired of me?' She tried to smile, and he surprised himself by smiling too. He liked the way she smiled. He liked her.

He didn't say anything back, and her smile faded.

'Your son phoned that number,' she said. 'And the person with that number phoned him.'

'When?'

'Over the last year. Hundreds of calls.'

He noticed it then, in Cooper's face.

It wasn't just sympathy. Wasn't just pity.

It was curiosity.

She wanted to see how he responded. Releasing information every so often . . . seeing how he coped . . . seeing what he gave away.

'Are you telling me everything?' he asked, and after a moment she nodded, but it was there, wasn't it?

A delay.

A flicker of an eye.

'The phone number – I got it from the farmer and his daughter. I brought it back the night we found the horses. I didn't – I didn't have time to follow up, it didn't seem like a priority. I tried a couple of times, but—'

'Who did the number belong to, Alec?'

'It was the mother's number. Grace Cole.'

'You did nothing wrong.'
She sat, shivering.
'You did nothing wrong, OK?'
She did not look.
'This is the beginning, not the end.'
A hand touched her face, touched her tears.
'It's not over. It's—'
'I love you,' she said.
'I love you.'

Day Twenty-Eight

CHAPTER FIFTY-NINE

(Woman, 36)
He pulled Rebecca out of school a few days after his wife left him. We tried fining him for the absence, but he had her registered as home-schooled and that was that. There was nothing I could really do, I suppose. Nothing that anyone could have done. It was a shame.

(Man, 49)
Most companies around here, they run on account, usually – farm supplies, vets, shearers – you don't always have to pay immediately, everyone understands how things can be. But I don't know a single business around here who'd let him buy on credit. Fool me thrice, shame on both of us. That was all it was.

(Woman, 35)
Portugal or somewhere. I think Grace is happier now. It's hard to know. It must be nice. She posts these lovely photos.

No one had seen Grace Cole for over a year. Phone calls to her number had all reached a full voicemail box, the line most likely disconnected. Attempts to communicate with her on dormant social network accounts also failed.

All that Cooper could find of the woman were the memories of others, recorded in phone-ins and reports about the whole family in those early days of the quarantine. These accounts focused more on the farmer than on his prodigal wife.

It was plain to many, the poison of marriage.

꿈

(Man, 28)
I don't want to talk about this. He's dead. People are dead. This is—

(Woman, 35)
Was it him? People are saying it was.

(Man, 49)
I know he sold a lot of his flock out there a while back. There'd be way too many animals to a field, just way too many – not sheared, too, June and full fleeced – not enough water, not by a long shot. He was struggling, I think, when Grace went.

(Man, 23)
Is his girl OK? There's not been any news.

(Woman, 41)
I don't gossip.

꿈

Local officers interviewed Grace's old employers from those few brief jobs and extra shifts she'd taken since the farm had begun to fail. A launderette out near the Wooden Bridge. One of the arcades on a day shift. They'd let Cooper come with them, thankful for the new spirit of shared information.

It was difficult finding anyone to talk to at the arcade, the halls dim and dark, but a manager had finally emerged and answered their questions.

'We have a lot of staff turnover,' he said. 'Hard to keep track.'

No one seemed to know the woman.

Like Simon, like the farmers, like Alec . . .

They had been apart.

They had been alone.

(Woman, 53)

No question it was that farmer. No one knows who he is. He's been here, what, seventeen years? Eighteen? And no one knows him. No one can say what he did before any of this, why he even came out here. His wife leaves him. He hurts his daughter – God knows what he did to her, what he planted in those fields . . . And then he goes and kills himself, just walks out of hospital like that? I know what sickness is. It's guilt. I know guilt. It's guilt.

(Man, 28)

A lot of people are making assumptions.

(Woman, 53)

I heard Albert hit her, the police got called out . . . took a few hours, of course. The wife denied everything. The daughter, she kept her mouth shut. It's just a tragedy.

(Man, 49)

I hope the girl is OK. I don't know about her dad, that's not for me to say, but . . . I hope she gets through this. We all do.

(Man, 32)

Men like him . . . personalities like Albert's . . . they're what grow, what always grow, in places like this. A certain kind of person, alone with their thoughts. Something ends up giving. Something sort of . . . fake, happens, for you to keep going. And everyone around you knows it, they know something's wrong, even if they can't name it.

(Woman, 35)

You can't rescue yourself.

ॐ

The daughter had woken, just a few days before.

When asked by the doctors about her mother, Rebecca had just repeated what she'd already told them: she'd left a year ago.

Did you ever see her with a boy?

They showed her a few photos of Simon Nichols.

And Rebecca just stared at them, and told them no, she'd never seen her mother with a boy, with anyone.

Grace Cole did not go out much, not in the end.

She wasn't well before the end.

Her medicine had been – it had been making Grace unwell. She hadn't been herself.

Rebecca had looked down at the photographs again before they'd left.

'Who is he?'

He's lost, they told her.

They told her to get well soon.

ॐ

(Woman, 36)
She'd tell me about them, those final months before she left school.
She wasn't always so distant with everyone. All the teachers, all
of us loved her.

She'd play games on her computer all the time. Tried to do her
class project on one of them. Worlds where you didn't watch a
story, but you made your own decisions.

I think the escape appealed to her. I think that's what it was
. . . well, probably what all stories are. They're escapes into the
lives of others. That doesn't have to be a bad thing. We'd die if
we couldn't escape.

That girl had dreams. And maybe . . . I don't know if she kept
playing, but maybe it wasn't enough any more.

Maybe whatever was happening to her, maybe she couldn't
escape it. Maybe no story was enough. You consume media where
there are heroes . . . where beautiful people win the day and, you
know, do the things beautiful people do . . . You start viewing life
like stories. More than a year of that, alone, her mother gone,
that awful man her only friend . . . What if it stops working?

What if the things keeping you alive, what if you're numbed to
them? What if they break? Who's going to save you then?

Her dad tried to kill us.

He brought his filth and his lies to this community.

And now he's dead, isn't he? Now he's dead, and we're not.

And I'm happy with that.

I'm happy.

ॐ

All throughout this day and the days that followed, Alec kept
messaging Cooper. He kept asking if he could help. He kept giving

her suggestions – kept telling her the best way to do things. Kept asking her to come round and see him. To let him help. To talk to the doctors, to tell them he was needed, to tell them—

To tell them what?

Cooper stopped answering, after a few times.

He could barely walk.

And this . . . all of this . . .

Who knew what his release might precipitate?

The fingerprints . . . the letter . . . the son . . .

The dancing plague went on.

Day Thirty

CHAPTER SIXTY

Alec remained up late one night, thinking it all through.

Though his bones ached still.

He thought of the circles.

He thought of the heads.

The crates.

What lay within.

W A T C H.

The number.

§⊚

Why had his son been speaking to this stranger?

What had he got himself involved in?

Why hadn't Alec known?

These questions had swarmed around the pity of half a dozen faces, their sad gestures, their awkward smiles.

Cooper herself had barely asked, which had felt worse, somehow.

He had offered to help.

He had done everything he could.

And they'd kept him here, hadn't they?

He closed his eyes in the dark.

His son was out there.

His son was out there, and he—

ॐ

It kept going around his mind.

The piece of paper on the table.

The night of the break-in at his home. The muddy footprints on the stairs.

The farmer, walking through the fields.

You won't fall, he'd said. *Not afraid of a little dirt, are you, Sergeant Nichols?*

And the man was dead, now, wasn't he? Collapsed in the fields they'd walked in so long ago, no blackmail initiated since, no further development in the case after the two suicides.

No trail, nothing that anyone would tell him but that which they'd had to: the number of a woman.

In her photo, in her profiles online, Grace Cole had red hair. Standing on a beach with her back to the camera, a classic tourist shot.

Other officers had messaged her again and again, trying to phone, trying to force her social networks to give them information about her account access.

He'd thought about what Cooper had said, so long ago.

That this – all this – wasn't about the animals.

It was about the moment of discovery.

Of witnessing the pain in the face of the owner.

You could have saved him.

The smile is yours.

It was about him, Alec knew, somehow, some way.

This is what Cooper wasn't saying, after all – this is what no one was saying.

Why else would they ask him the things they had asked?

Why else would they look at him the way they'd looked?

There was more than just the phone number: there was something else that linked Alec to these strange events; not enough to condemn him completely, but enough.

He sat in the dark and took his phone.

He logged into his profile and removed all of his friends, setting the account to private.

He went to Grace's profile and added her as a friend.

If a game was being played, he'd play.

He'd do what he could, until he could do nothing else.

CHAPTER SIXTY-ONE

[00:18] *Grace*: Hi.

[00:18] *Grace*: I got your message.

[00:21] *Grace*: Do we know each other?

[00:21] *Alec*: No.

[00:21] *Alec*: I don't think we do.

Finally, a hit.

CHAPTER SIXTY-TWO

[00:32] *Grace*: How do I know you're a real policeman?

[00:32] *Alec*: I'll ring from a registered number.

[00:33] *Grace*: Is it normal to contact someone this way?

[00:33] *Alec*: Not usually, no.

[00:33] *Grace*: Unless you're friends, I guess.

[00:34] *Alec*: We tried your phone number but it wouldn't work. I understand you're no longer in the UK.
[00:37] *Alec*: Are you still there?

Day Thirty-One

CHAPTER SIXTY-THREE

[07:12] *Grace*: You don't have many photos.

[07:20] *Alec*: What do you mean?

[07:21] *Grace*: On your profile.
[07:21] *Grace*: Did you look at my photos?

[07:41] *Alec*: No.

[07:50] *Grace*: Some good ones.

[07:52] *Alec*: Why did you leave Ilmarsh?

[07:58] *Grace*: Didn't my husband talk to you?

[07:58] *Alec*: He did.

[07:59] *Grace*: Where are you now?

[08:00] *Alec*: In my bed.
[08:00] *Alec*: Where are you?

[08:01] *Grace*: Sitting near the beach.

[08:02] *Alec*: Why can't people reach you on your phone number?

[08:02] *Alec*: If you give me a new number, I can ring.

[08:03] *Grace*: They wouldn't want to speak to me.

[08:03] *Grace*: I'm not that interesting.

[08:04] *Grace*: What really happened there?

[08:08] *Grace*: What did Albert do?

CHAPTER SIXTY-FOUR

In the early hours of the morning, the house at Well Farm burned.

The fire was not seen until 4 a.m. By the time the fire brigade arrived, it was too late to save the structure.

That the empty house had followed the culling of the flock – it seemed natural, somehow. The end of the Coles' story, written in flame.

Alec read about it on his phone. The local town group had noted the event.

Cooper did not tell him.

The inspector did not tell him.

No one did.

So he phoned a cab and left the ward without informing anyone in turn.

He'd been doing better, much better.

He was better.

He knew he was.

He knew.

Just a few months ago, Alec had seen a documentary. Most days, Simon had usually just gone straight up to his room once he returned from school, but this time, the boy had sat and actually watched this film with his father. It had surprised Alec. It had expanded his idea of his son, this thing he'd made, that *was* him, half of him at least. All that would be left of him when he was gone. All that was left of parts of Alec that had already faded. He could see it as the boy grew up, ghost echoes of a way he'd seen himself smile in photos, sounds he'd heard his voice make in old recordings.

So they'd watched this documentary together.

They'd sat there as the dark images on the screen passed by, as slow lines were read out by the croaking voiceover. The film was about plans to bury nuclear waste so that future cultures would understand not to approach. The plans involved building vast spikes in a maze to warn interlopers of the material within, planting signals of danger throughout time. In the centre there would be these words:

This place is a message, and part of a system of messages. Pay attention to it. Sending this message was important to us.

We considered ourselves to be a powerful culture.

This place is not a place of honour. No highly esteemed deed is commemorated here. Nothing valued is here.

What is here was dangerous and repulsive to us.

The danger is still present, in your time, as it was in ours.

'This message is a warning about danger,' he murmured, watching the snow coat the ruined structures.

The long level fields were white, too. Bleak, flat, barely textured.

The driver stopped the car and opened the gate, jumping back in. Alec had promised to give him fifty extra pounds for this. The police would stop them soon, he knew, but no one had been at the barrier.

They drove the same way the horses had most likely come.

They saw the vans parked in the distance, the cars, Cooper's own.

Alec got out, his legs still weak, and she turned.

❧

Markers stood against the white snow, crimson spears shot into the ground to delineate the points of burial, almost a mirror to the spurs of the sheep-pyre opposite, though here they were thin, spread out, elegant, almost metallic in their red. They had been harder to see from the road.

Alec thought back to the moment he had first caught sight of the glassy eyes, the coiled tails of these creatures.

Have you ever seen anything like this? he'd asked the farmer. *It's—*

Grotesque.

Beautiful.

No. Have you?

That's murder, the farmer had continued, his voice soft. *Just look at them. Look.*

Alec walked through the void. Smoke rose from one farm over.

Cooper would explain it all to him later.

The firemen had not been able to save the home.

At dawn, before they left, one of them had wanted to see the place where sixteen horses had been buried.

One of them had wanted to see the place of death.

He'd come here, right up to the red spears.

And he'd seen it.

Alec didn't know this. He didn't know anyone had seen anything. He just saw a stolen investigation.

He just walked on towards the horror, glad to be out at last.

Glad to be breathing fresh air, glad to be using his limbs.

Glad to see the looks on all their faces, the disgust, the horror that he'd deigned to return to his old life without permission.

He would be who he'd been again.

He would help.

He would mean something.

There had been something in the grass and snow, near the base of the metal. Something red.

Cooper had knelt down and parted it, taking forceps from her coat.

She'd found a human nail.

⟡

Alec approached, Cooper already saying something to him, but he couldn't understand, he couldn't hear her, he couldn't hear anyone.

Blackened, weeks old, its rot had been slowed by the cold.

Upon the closest spear, a finger had been placed. A hole incised in its centre, just before the bend. Enough to prevent it falling.

It hung, human flesh. It had been amputated with a knife, sawing through bone.

There was nothing else. No letter. No note. No photo.

Just this.

The final bloom.

DNA testing would confirm that both the finger and the fallen nail belonged to Simon Nichols.

Twenty Years Ago

CHAPTER SIXTY-FIVE

London

How do you know if you love someone?

It is 16 June.

An off-duty police officer meets his future wife.

He stands at the edge of the South Bank with his jacket over his arm, his feet squeezed tight by his new trainers. At long last, the sweat on the back of his neck is beginning to fade. He stares out at London.

The low sun ripples its light through the thin trees of the riverbank, mingling with the breeze. People huddle on green and patchy grass by the sides of buildings. They clink glasses. They hold wrinkled hands and hot dogs on benches that bear the names of memorialized and anonymous dead. These benches are curved to stop the homeless sleeping. The Thames spits itself out into the distant sea.

In ten minutes, he will walk along and say, 'Angela?' to a woman whose name is something else.

She will apologize for not being Angela. 'Met online?' she will ask, and the police officer will nod, sheepishly. She will wish him luck. She will go for a coffee with a friend.

He will remain in the area for an hour, alone, wishing he had put on sunblock.

By the time he will finally think of leaving, the woman mistaken for Angela will walk past him once more, and – surprised at his persistence – will ask if he is OK.

He will lie and say that he is.

She will ask his name. 'Alec,' he will say.

'Elizabeth,' she will answer in turn.

They will have their first date two weeks later.

In three months, he will ask her this question.

How do you know if you love someone?

They will move in together, shortly after. They will start a life.

It is 4 November.

Alec meets Elizabeth's parents for the first time. She cooks spaghetti sauce with bacon lardons. Within two years, she will become pescatarian. Within five, she will become vegan. Within eight, she will have given it all up again, living life in a cloud.

The parents come to their flat, a small place in Tottenham Hale. Throughout the meal, Elizabeth repeatedly stresses how sorry she is that the place is so messy. It is, as far as Alec can tell, immaculate. He was the one who cleaned it. She does not chastise him about it, then or after.

Before he goes home, Elizabeth's father will remark that Alec is 'better than the last one'. He will do this when he thinks neither his daughter nor Alec can hear. He will talk about their age difference – she is twenty-five, Alec is twenty. He will resist his wife's protestations that the man seems nice. He will say they don't have to pretend this is permanent. Their daughter's new boyfriend doesn't even have a degree. How much does the man even earn? He knows his—

Elizabeth will walk into the hall.

They will all pretend nothing had happened.

The past infects them.

And that night, as they lie in bed together, Alec will talk about his own parents for the first time.

He will talk about the scars on his back, and how he got them.

He will do all this to try and make Elizabeth feel better.

ॐ

It is 8 June. It is almost their anniversary.

He looks on her phone while she showers.

He unlocks it with her PIN. He has seen her enter it a dozen times.

She had been a mystery to him, lately.

He finds a message. She had sent it to her ex.

It is a photo of her, almost naked.

He puts the phone back down.

When she is out of the shower and in her pyjamas, they watch television. She goes to make herself a drink. 'You want one?'

When she is in the middle of pouring it, he appears in the kitchen doorway, and tells her he thinks she has a problem with alcohol.

She is surprised.

He tells her that he'd like her to pour the drink down the sink.

She tells him to fuck off.

As she passes him, he grabs the drink from her, spilling some over the glass's edge, and throws it in the sink, shards flying across the metal.

He never mentions having seen the message or the photo, not then, not ever. The ashes of his own faithfulness give him a strange and secret comfort. He had been better than her.

She never confesses.

He never finds anything like it again.

ॐ

It is 5 January.

Elizabeth asks Alec what he thinks of having children.

When they'd pass babies in prams, or little children being lifted up by their parents, swung along in smiles, he'd smile too, sometimes.

At Christmas, when a boy had pointed at Alec's reindeer jumper – at the giant cotton red nose stuck to its surface – Alec told Elizabeth about it, all those hours later.

She asks again now, sitting at night in their lounge.

'We could call her Angela, if she's a girl.'

He smiles at this, but his smile is hollow.

He talks about the world. About everything happening. How could they bring a kid into this?

She talks about all the things their child might do. That who knows? They might help fix the planet. They might be denying a prodigy, or a prime minister, or a scientist discovering a cure for cancer. They might set the world on fire, creating unimaginable art, great works of which others could not even conceive. They might—

He wonders, aloud, if they'd be good parents.

She is silent.

He realizes he has hurt her. He does not know what to say.

He says he will sleep on it.

It is 6 January.

After she leaves for work, Alec finds a pregnancy test in the bathroom bin, partially hidden. It is positive.

He has the day off. He creates an online dating profile. He has never done anything like this before, not during their relationship. He talks to women and men throughout the early afternoon. Three hours before Elizabeth gets home, he deletes the profile.

He wonders what friend he can talk to. He wonders who he has.

He thinks of phoning his own mother. He does not. They have not spoken for months. They will not speak again. She will die of a heart attack four years later. She will never meet her grand-child.

It is evening.

He tells Elizabeth that he has been thinking.

About what he said the night before.

Of course she'd be a good mum, he says. He didn't mean to ever say she wouldn't be.

He—

'You'll be a great dad,' she says, quietly, nervous, trying to smile. 'If you want to be.'

He tells her he doesn't know.

It is 9 October.

A blade pierces a mother.

A boy is torn from her womb.

Minutes later, a nurse passes him to his father.

He holds his baby's hand.

Day Thirty-One

CHAPTER SIXTY-SIX

Partially rotten, heaving with bacteria, found impaled on one of the red spears marking the burial site of the sixteen horses, DNA testing confirmed the flesh to be Simon's own.

His ring finger from his left hand, it had likely been fractured before the point of its severing, possibly infected, too. It had been taken with a heavy cutting tool, perhaps an axe, in a single fast motion a number of weeks before.

The soft tissue had started falling away.

Days after the car crash, the boy had been alive.

Alec would ask to see the finger, back at the station before nightfall.

He asked to hold his only son.

They told him, again and again, that he could not.

That maybe he needed to take some time.

That he'd been through a lot.

Go home, they told him, again and again.

The mess with the hospital – the discharge – that could all be sorted out.

He needed to get better for his son, they told him.

But Alec – Alec had no idea what that meant, now.

No idea at all.

A patrol car, driven by a man Alec had never met, brought him to his house.

The neighbours had Christmas lights up all around.

He went inside the cold, empty building and took his phone out.

He read the messages of the morning, sent and received within the cab on the way to Well Farm, now held within his shaking hands.

ॐ

[09:18] *Grace*: Do you miss your son?

[09:32] *Alec*: How do you know I have a son?

[09:41] *Grace*: We're friends.

[09:42] *Alec*: You're friends with my son?
[09:51] *Alec*: Grace?

[09:53] *Grace*: Lol no. WE'RE friends. I can see your contacts.
[09:54] *Grace*: Are you going to keep me on here?

[10:01] *Alec*: I don't miss him. He lives with me.

[10:02] *Grace*: Message me whenever you want.
[10:02] *Grace*: I'm by myself a lot.
[10:04] *Grace*: What's it like there, anyway?
[10:14] *Grace*: Raining probably.

[10:16] *Alec*: It snowed.
[10:16] *Alec*: But the sun is slowing.
[10:17] *Alec*: Sorry, meant shining, autocorrect.

[10:19] *Grace*: Take a photo.

There was a knock on his front door. The bell hadn't been fixed, not for a while.

Alec realized, then, that he'd been crying. He didn't know for how long he'd been doing it.

Alec wiped his cheeks and got up.

It was snowing, still.

The snow would be gone by midnight. It never lasted.

He pulled the door open.

It was her.

It was Cooper.

CHAPTER SIXTY-SEVEN

'What are you doing here?'

She hesitated, looking past him into the house beyond. There was a smell of meat, like pasta and Bolognese, though she would not find any evidence of cooking while she was there.

He hadn't switched any lights on, even though night had now fallen.

'I was – I was worried about you. I wanted to see how you were doing.'

He stared at her. He seemed shorter, somehow, standing in that doorway. When they'd met, he'd been tall and stocky. He'd seemed strong, handsome even, his jaw full of stubble and his restless eyes full of questions.

Those first days, he'd soon shown her part of who he was: he'd shown her nervousness, anxiety, a concern over his position, a wish to do right. All these weeks later, the end of the year soon to be upon them, he displayed none of that – all the good and all the bad gone, as if it had never been.

He was just empty now.

He turned and walked back into his home, leaving the door wide open.

Cooper followed, clicking on the light.

She removed her coat, holding it over her arm. She unwound her grey scarf, long and wide. 'Shoes on or off?'

Alec didn't answer. He'd disappeared into the kitchen.

A kettle boiled, somewhere beyond.

She took her shoes off and lingered by the sofa, not quite sure whether to sit or stand, follow or wait.

She waited, standing.

Eventually, she heard a croak. 'Tea?'

'Coffee,' she said. 'I can make it, if you—'

'No milk, no sugar?'

'Black is fine.'

Time passed.

He brought the coffees through one at a time, his own with milk and two sugars.

She looked around.

'You've got a, er . . .' She frowned, smiling just a little, trying to make herself comfortable, not knowing what to say. *A lovely home.* She'd been here a dozen times without Alec's permission and still she had no idea how to describe it. 'I don't know how people compliment houses. Sorry.'

'It's OK.'

They fell silent, drinking their hot drinks. Outside, snowfall started to pick up in the night, more and more falling through the air, drifting in vast plump flakes.

'You all . . .' he said, staring at his cup. 'You let my son die.'

He shook his head.

She said nothing for a moment, her face frozen, her eyes wide.

The snow continued to fall, accumulating on the grass, on the windowsill outside. Colours flashed on and off in the dark, Christmas tree lights in the garden opposite.

'I've been doing everything I can, I—'

'Then it wasn't enough.'

The family photograph appeared to have been moved from its original place in the kitchen. It now sat on the mantelpiece.

Alec had a thick beard in that photo, not just the stubble he had now.

Simon had been a little boy.

His wife beside them both, her arm around her husband, his arm around her in turn. Both of them smiling.

'Everything you've done . . .' Alec said. 'It wasn't enough.'

Cooper put her cup down.

'Why did you make me coffee, if you feel that way?'

'It's . . .' He scratched his eye. 'It's what I do.'

'What you do? I don't understand.'

'When people come round . . .' His hand was shaking, the cup spilling liquid splashes on his trousers, on the fabric. He didn't seem to notice. Suddenly, his expression changed. 'Please—' he pleaded.

'Alec?' She got up.

'Please – let me help,' he whispered, the cup falling from his hand. 'Please—'

CHAPTER SIXTY-EIGHT

Cooper was going to go to sleep on the sofa, then she'd head back in the morning. She refused to leave Alec alone in this state.

'We can talk about the case,' she'd told him, not intending to talk about it at all.

He took the other sofa, the stairs still too much for him.

'I used to have trouble sleeping,' he said.

He almost smiled, but the moment faded quickly.

She left and went to find him a blanket. She passed a shadow on the wall, where once a mirror had been broken.

She went up stairs once muddied by a stranger.

When she came back, he was changing into a T-shirt from the wash-basket. His back was covered in old scars, too old to have been caused by the crash, by any of this.

'You don't have to stay,' he said. 'I'll be – I'll be OK.'

She sat on her own sofa, still dressed.

He sat on his own.

'I asked you once – I asked you the worst thing you'd ever done,' he said.

'You did.'

He lay down to sleep. He didn't say anything more, not until they'd been there for a while.

She lay down, too.

He looked so small, so feeble.

'I do need your help,' Cooper said, quiet, watching how Alec's eyes couldn't keep still, even as he looked at nothing. 'Of course I need your help. Of course I'll involve you, you just . . . you just needed to get better. And now . . . and now you're better, aren't you?' He turned away as she spoke, and her voice grew gentler. 'We'll find him – we'll find who did this, we'll find your boy . . . everything's going to be OK.'

He did not answer this, did not turn back to her.

She went to switch off the lamp on the small table nearby.

Time passed before he spoke again.

'It was what I did to her . . .' he said, barely more than a murmur. 'Elizabeth . . .'

No other words came, not really. At one point, she thought she heard him saying something about Christmas, but there was only silence after that, and she decided she might have dreamt it.

The night passed.

In the morning, Alec asked questions about the island. About anthrax. About the crumbling buildings, the fires that had raged there, the pit, and the father who had done all those terrible things. He asked, not once acknowledging he'd lied to her about his prior knowledge, not once apologising. And Cooper let him ramble. He needed connections, he needed hope. He looked into other outbreaks, about how the government had tested weapons against sheep on distant shores, and how they had failed to clean up the work of all their bombs. What if this too had been a test? What if it wasn't just incompetence and neglect? What if they were being lied to?

He'd ask these things, in the days to come. He'd wonder about these other fathers who had died in their farms, whose children had lived on forever changed.

For now, sitting at his dining table over breakfast, he just asked about the first.

'Did it happen to him, too?'

Cooper didn't understand. 'Did what—'

'I mean . . . what if he was targeted, too? What if whoever's doing this to me did it to him and his family?'

'There's no evidence anyone else was involved. No one has even—'

'His daughter survived,' Alec went on. 'We should go and speak to her.'

'She can't speak.'

'Can't, or won't?' Alec finished his coffee and shook his head. 'It's a lead, isn't it? Maybe her parents knew Grace . . . maybe they met her, or, I don't know . . .'

She hesitated. She tried to show him pity. 'We'll look at it . . . it's worth thinking about. And just . . . don't worry, OK? We've got plenty to look at. You'll get sick of being in the car with me, by the time this is over.'

He smiled weakly. He went to put his coat on.

'We'll find him,' Cooper said, and Alec nodded.

In the car, he kept talking about it, kept repeating himself.

Some force in the world had taken notice of him, had ruined his family like it had ruined so many others. It was not his fault.

None of this was his fault. Everyone would see.

Cooper said nothing for a while, as she turned down the drive.

'I don't think you're viewing it all the right—'

'The right what?' Alec scowled.

'What happened on the island . . . what that man did to his own children, to his wife . . . I know you think you're like him, but you're not.' Cooper paused, trying to find the right words. 'He destroyed everything. We know he did it, we know he meant to do it. We know he's dead. There's no culprit there, nothing to uncover, at least not that I can see. If you're looking for something to blame . . . it's just his mind. It's just what happens to people, I don't—'

'What happens to people?'

'Whatever changes us,' Cooper said.

'Evil, you mean.'

'Call it what you want.'

There were things people owed to each other.

The days passed, and she tried to help him.

She tried to help a man who had never helped himself.

CHAPTER SIXTY-NINE

Alec was not officially reinstated, nor was he reimbursed for his time beyond sick pay; all he did from then on he did as a private individual, even with the inspector's reluctant blessing. No one seemed to have the heart to stop him any more. The department itself was continuing its dissolution; after their temporary re-inforcements had left, after the dead, there were now only four officers on duty for the entire forgotten coast.

Harry told Alec, before he left the station that first day, that George's widow was asking to see him, if he was up to it.

※

As for things with Cooper, they had changed for the better. Though there were still things she hid from Alec, though she was still evasive about her employers, she took him with her on her rides. The role reversal was strange. He was jealous, he supposed, and he'd never wanted to be jealous. He'd never thought of himself that way. He wanted to be someone who did a good job, that was all.

Her main focus appeared to be a camcorder, now, and so it was his, too.

'One of the horse owners saw Rebecca Cole being filmed on a horse-carriage ride.'

'Which owner?' Alec had taken a sip of his water.

'Michael Stafford. The coach—'

'I know who he is. You don't have to explain everything.'

Alec had then asked Cooper if she'd been aware of his record. Of the man's former crimes.

She'd not said much to that. Her look told Alec that she didn't much care, either way.

He didn't mind. He was just glad to be out of those hospital halls, that artificial light, that strange beeping.

No one understood, but the work helped him.

It had always helped him, with everything. He'd try to keep going, not think of anything he'd done or would do.

He'd just think of the mystery. Of all the people who must be out there, waiting to be caught. He imagined rituals, robes. He imagined a network of adversaries, blackmailed or otherwise, an evil pressganged from all this history, all this soil and flesh. He imagined it, witnessing nothing with his own eyes.

Ilmarsh gave Alec this nothing. Its seas were empty, its streets deserted. So many had left since the quarantine, even if there were no official figures to mark it – the homes were just abandoned. A slow exodus had become a calm before a storm. It had become a rapture.

Who could tell them if they'd seen Grace, if they'd seen a camera man, if they'd seen anything at all?

There were so few left – even some of the horse owners had fled, terrified of potential retribution.

One night they'd gone to see a former councillor, a would-be member of parliament that George had interviewed before his death.

※

Posters stood behind glass. Many of them showed a bright-eyed woman with dyed, dirty-blonde hair, a red jacket and a wooden sign in her hand, the kind you'd find in a front garden announcing a house sale. They showed the woman shaking hands, standing next to government ministers, slogans from her failed election, her last campaign. JO MARSH. JOANNE MARSH. MARSH. Whatever testing demanded. Headlines on papers. Flyers. Promises to remain.

The former politician lived at the end of the cul-de-sac, a long road in the woods leading only to her home and the trees beyond. To take the horses, a van had needed to drive around the building itself and back the same way.

෯

They had gone to ask the politician about the camera man, if she'd seen anyone strange those past months, if she recognized their photographs of Grace.

There had been wine bottles on the counters, old unwashed glasses on the table.

'I didn't see anything, I didn't hear anything. It's not my *fault*—'

These things people said. They spoke to her for a while. They exhausted one of their final leads. They said goodbye.

Alec sent another message to Grace, out in the night near the car.

He made sure Cooper did not see. They drove home without speaking. She dropped him off, and words kept spilling round his head, as he walked up his drive, to a door he'd once found open, to stairs he'd once found muddied, to a place that had once been a refuge.

Whatever changes us.

He closed the door. He drank his own wine in his own kitchen until he couldn't feel a thing. He went to sleep.

CHAPTER SEVENTY

The police wanted to conduct a search of his house.

Frank walked the pier.

The blackened wooden boards ran one hundred feet out into the sea, the legs of the pier still holding up, even after all this time. Even after fire, even after abandonment. There was a sign telling people not to go out here, there were alleged plans to demolish or redevelop the site, but nothing had happened for a decade, now. So children still went out, sometimes. So Frank went.

The pier had ended with Frank's childhood, somehow. He hadn't even been in Ilmarsh when the fire had blazed. His mum had sent him to live with relatives for a while, passed around from home to home. When he'd come back, sometimes he'd sit in the vet practice, waiting for his parents to be done. They'd both worked as vets. It was hard to meet people outside the profession. His parents had not been married. She had been the head nurse at the practice. His father's wife had worked elsewhere. Everyone knew. Kenneth and Jennifer. He had been well liked. The nurse had been feared, frequently jealous of others who had joined the practice, the young in particular. It was the way of his industry, of all such industries.

All they had left him – their only boy who had survived birth – all that was gone, now.

Frank had put his vet practice up for sale. Perhaps a corporate would come in and rescue them. Perhaps no one would. He'd changed the name before he'd done so, hoping against hope that the bad press might be harder to find.

All these people they'd let down.

He'd come out here a few times with Kate in her early days, seeing how quiet she was, seeing how little she'd integrated with the others – others who had never come back to work, others who had betrayed him, when only the dead had remained loyal.

They'd come out here and they'd bought chips by the sea.

Day Thirty-Five

CHAPTER SEVENTY-ONE

Rebecca watched television, mostly, during her time in the hospital. She'd wanted her phone, but no one could find it and – unused to making demands of adults – she had not asked again. Who would she have messaged, anyway?

Who was left?

Investigators had come and gone. At first they'd asked about her father, who was dead, which was strange and which she tried not to think about. She knew she'd have weeks, months, years enough to remember him, whether she wanted to or not. They said awful things about him, implied them, anyway, and while she had not liked her father, he had loved her.

He had protected her. Had kept her safe against a world that might have taken her away.

And she had taken that time – that last gift – and what had she done with it?

She knew her dad hadn't understood the games she'd played. Why she'd spend all her time in other worlds than this one.

She didn't do it for fun.

Pretending, it was all she'd had.

She'd found the horses at 5 a.m. not because she woke that early, but because she rarely went to sleep before six. She'd been awake when the phone call had come, telling her to go outside.

When the voice of the man who had once filmed her on her

birthday, who had walked with her in woods and distant places, came back at last.

ॐ

The voice was sorry for all the messages.

Everything they had done would be for nothing, if she didn't come outside.

So Rebecca had gone.

She hadn't known how to argue.

She'd taken the dog with her that night, not for a walk.

She'd taken it because she'd been afraid.

She'd gone out towards the eyes in the earth.

She'd gone out, and she knew it, now, all these weeks later – the doctors telling her about the new life that awaited her in the morning, about the foster parents, about a place at school once more – she knew, now, deep in her bones.

Her father had found it in himself to love her, this past year.

And she'd killed him, hadn't she?

All of these people . . .

It was all her fault.

Day Thirty-Nine

CHAPTER SEVENTY-TWO

Rebecca followed the rest of the road, having been dropped off by her foster father and mother. She insisted on walking the rest of the way, even if she still felt weak – how else would she get better? Grey and potted, warped with every heatwave and every round of frost, the road snaked past abandoned factories, un-inhabited and unused for at least fifty years. To the edge of the woodland, green like Christmas trees, like ponds.

After weeks of illness, a year after her father had begun to home-educate her, Rebecca was going back to school. They'd thought it might be good for her, take her mind off things: she'd only known these foster people for a few days but already they'd created a rota for her, had pulled strings to get her three days at school before it closed for Christmas.

Once she'd dreamt of having a different family.

These people were pleasant but quiet, absorbed mostly by their end-of-year accounts, and Rebecca quickly felt – even in the span of a few days – like one more column in a spreadsheet. They hadn't noticed how she'd—

She—

She walked on.

The trees were separated from the school's own fields by a chain-link fence along their far edge. In places the roots had pushed the land up, had made the metal warp and flex towards the sky. In other places children had used to climb over the fence or force their way through holes, out to play in the trees, to smoke, to go far away. There were rumours people had sex in those woods.

Along the playground edge there were other trees, deciduous, leafless oaks that crested the whole boundary. They rustled in the low wind. There was no one else in sight. She'd got there early.

It was the first time she'd been to this place in over a year. She didn't even know if she'd do her GCSEs or not. They hadn't said anything either way.

How did you find the horses? Why were you out so early?
Why did you touch one?
Did you see or hear something strange?
Do you know why someone would want to do this?

A crow screamed from the chain-link.

She walked into the playground. There were grids for cars, but cars were never allowed to park here, not normally, but for parent evenings. Sometimes car boot sales, too, every other weekend in the summer. Townspeople and parents would sell old DVDs and board games and other flotsam from their homes. Her mother and father had once sold their things here, back when they'd still thought they could tame Well Farm, that they could let go and clear space.

She went inside, the doors unlocked, the long metal bars cold to her touch. The hallways already had their lights on, sterile fluorescence reflecting on the cheap shiny floors. Images splayed themselves across the white walls. There were old headmasters, all men. Photos of football teams, of rugby. Some posters by the Year 9s. A few old trophies in a cabinet. The hatch for reception was closed. It all felt smaller than she'd remembered it. It all felt minuscule, shrunken in the wash.

She went to the girls' bathroom, passing row after row of orange lockers. She shut the door and approached the mirrors.

She looked at her face, lit up by the light. There were no windows. Her face was caught in a mix of shadow and freckle. She'd put her hair up in a ponytail before she'd left. It was how she'd always worn it at school before. It was ridiculous but she wondered if things were different, a year later, if this was somehow wrong.

She played with her ponytail, trying to look right. She pulled it round so it tangled over her shoulder.

It looked like a tail. Like the twist of a snake.

She pulled the band off, letting it all hang loose. She brushed it behind her ears. She went into a stall, shut the door, and sat with her new phone in her hands. She sent messages until people could be heard in the corridor.

She opened the door and went to class.

CHAPTER SEVENTY-THREE

Rebecca was early to school, in the classroom without permission.

She removed a print-out of a poem from her backpack. She took her red water bottle out and put it on the table in front of her. The whole place smelt of pencil sharpening. She had been told to make notes on this piece. They had emailed it to her. She did not know if other people would have gone through this poem already, or if she was being keen. So she read it and made her notes. They were going to do one prepared poem and one unseen piece.

No one had really remained in touch with her after she had begun home-schooling. They said they would, but they didn't. She had a few friends on the internet that she did not really care about. The few friends she did care about fell silent after initial bursts of enthusiasm about meeting up and doing stuff together. Her father had refused to drive her into town, most times she asked.

Other people began to enter the room. A few faces she recognized, a few names. Falling out of touch with people was worse than never knowing them.

To have drifted apart was a limbo, a shadow of the thing you once had been to another, and what they had once been to you. You couldn't sit next to a ghost.

So Rebecca ended up sitting alone in that classroom, even as dozens arrived and spread across the seats. Even as some looked at her, even as they smiled and whispered, even as the final few were forced to come close, clearly not wanting to. She sat alone, not knowing a thing but the words on the page in front of her.

They talked about the prepared poem for eight minutes. 'Porphyria's Lover'. A piece by Robert Browning about two lovers who held each other, who wanted the moment to last forever, so the man took the other's hair and strangled her with it.

They talked about the life of the writer. The ways it could be interpreted. That the speaker of the poem was most likely mad, and with such madness, whether he could truly have loved the woman he was holding, or if it was possession he sought through her murder.

In the year since she had left school, Rebecca had not read any poems that were not in her game. She had not been asked to.

They had twenty minutes to write some additional answers in their workbooks, and then the unseen poem came up on the interactive whiteboard in front of the class.

'Stopping by woods on a snowy evening'.

They were going to go along as before and read a line each.

The work began with the poet standing before a forest, before trees owned by a local man. The poet thought it was unlikely he would be spotted here, since the land's owner lived in town, away from this property, from this lonely road. The poet knew he should not be seen watching the man's trees, his possessions. The night was almost silent. The snow rested among the trees, settling on each branch, each root, each hidden creature.

The next line was about a horse.

Or, more specifically, how the poet's horse probably found it strange to stop like this so far from any human habitation, near a lake, on this coldest, blackest night. Except it wasn't the horse that thought it strange – it was the poet, expressing his ideas through the imagination of an animal. Animals didn't think things were strange. Animals didn't think at all.

But something was wrong, wasn't it? Something was wrong with the person speaking.

It wasn't Robert Frost who spoke, at least not now. He had lived
and died long ago, leaving this creation, words on a page that couldn't
speak. All these voices, they existed only in the reader's mind.

It was *them*. Rebecca, her teacher, this whole class . . . they
were much like the horse itself: imagined proxies for an abandoned
thought, dancing in a mirror in a mirror in a mirror. The old
words skipped through time. When they read aloud, they were
puppets of the dead.

She imagined the man's hands in her skull, moving her neck,
opening her jaw.

From across the class, a girl turned briefly, looking right at her.
The expression on her face was different from all the others.

Rebecca picked up her water bottle and drank.

Then the horse asked if something had gone wrong. There
was no answer but its own asking, and the soft fall of snow in
the breeze.

Her father had slapped her across the face, a month before he
had died.

They focused a lot on Frost's final lines.

> *The woods are lovely, dark and deep,*
> *But I have promises to keep,*
> *And miles to go before I sleep,*
> *And miles to go before I sleep.*

'What is this poem about?' the teacher asked.

No one answered.

'What do you think it is about?'

No one answered.

The teacher, frustrated, began to talk through the poem. She
told them that on the surface, it seems like it is about a man and
his animal, going through the dark, maybe a little lonely, eager
to get home.

She asked people how it made them feel.

'Sad for him,' a boy said. His voice made Rebecca go cold. It had changed, these past months.

'Why do you feel sad for him, Peter?'

'It's – it's like you said. He seems lonely. His horse seems kind of, I don't know, it seems worried about him.'

Something about Peter made Rebecca want to run, to cry.

'Why would his horse seem worried about him?' the teacher asked.

'He's thinking of going into the woods,' said her former friend. 'It's dark and cold.'

'The darkest night of the year,' the teacher said. 'What could happen to him?'

No one answered.

'What's the worst that could happen to him?'

'He could die,' another boy finally said, across the room.

'Yes.' The teacher nodded. 'He could die. So what do you think this poem is about?'

No one answered.

The teacher looked around the room.

'If he knows he could die, if his horse is concerned about him – or if he is acting *as if* his horse is that concerned, if his mindset is that distorted that he can apply compassion to other, non-human creatures, but not towards himself, then what could be going on here? What is he thinking about?'

Rebecca stared at the screen. Her eyes were dry for staring, pinned in place, unable to move.

She thought about her carriage ride, long ago along the shore.

She thought about birthdays.

The camcorder, watching her from the street.

She thought of all that had been done to her, all she had done in turn, and all that remained.

'Suicide,' she said. 'The poem is about suicide.'

CHAPTER SEVENTY-FOUR

[08.51] *Alec*: What else did your husband believe?

[08:52] *Grace*: That I'm a bad person.
[08:52] *Grace*: An unfit mother.
[08:53] *Grace*: Probably that the world is flat.
[08:54] *Grace*: I don't know.

[08:55] *Alec*: Is that why you left?

[09:03] *Grace*: Did I leave because the world is flat?

[09:04] *Alec*: Because of what he felt about you.
[09:05] *Alec*: You left your daughter. You left your whole life.
[09:05] *Alec*: Why did you do it?

[09:06] *Grace*: What would you have done?

[09:07] *Alec*: I would have tried to do what was right.

[09:07] *Grace*: And what's right?
[09:07] *Grace*: How do you know what's right?

CHAPTER SEVENTY-FIVE

Once, nine hotels had been located around Ilmarsh.

Five had been repurposed for council housing and temporary accommodation over the last few decades, while two, beyond the point of repair and economic benefit, had been left untouched for the homeless and the lost.

The company responsible for the conversion of the unused hotels was part-owned, following the severance of the majority of its foreign contracts, by the government itself. The shares were to be sold off soon at a likely loss and would be bought up by the friends of those politicians who had made the decision to sell.

The buildings in this distant town leaked humanity. People left every day, not wanting to live here any more. So other distant cities sent people they did not want, by train and by coach. It sent them to the emptiness, to the towers.

Beds and tables were crammed into spaces far too small. The walls between rooms had been altered to form inner doors. The people who came here had arrived from across the country, from other countries, too. They were told to be excited. They were going to see the sea.

Vulnerable people were told housing would be given to them not where they lived, not where they knew people or loved people, but here, and only here. They would come, these strangers, and find themselves giddy, sometimes, happy at the whimsy of the buildings, at the small shops packed full of candy and inflatables and sand shovels no one ever really bought from muttering old men who never really said anything. It was as if the government had sent them on a form of holiday.

Few of these temporary residents could ever afford to leave that cold sea and its side. There were no jobs, though to qualify for their benefits, they completed the work of the council. They helped pave. They helped dredge. They cleaned the streets of moss and syringes and sand and blood for less than minimum wage. Sometimes they drowned. There was something in Ilmarsh that grew into agony. Old couples lived out the dream of their lonely retirement in surprising, awful silence, barely able to heat their homes.

There was a sign outside.

THE WHITE ROOMS.

Cooper and Alec stepped up to its doorway, its old name visible only by the torn lettering, the shadows those words had left behind in the paint.

CHAPTER SEVENTY-SIX

Rebecca's foster parents had agreed to let them speak with her if they could wait to let her settle into her new life a bit.

'Just give her a few days.'

ॐ

Now they went inside the tower to find a lobby full of cracked tiles, a checkerboard pattern of black and white. There were awful rolled-up red curtains behind what had once been a front desk, and which now stored only boxes of God knew what.

'Which room?' Alec asked.

'I don't know.'

'It's on your phone.' Alec craned his neck around as she spoke, sniffing the air.

'It's on your phone, too,' Cooper said. 'Check your own phone.'

He grimaced and got his mobile phone out. It always annoyed her when people did things like this. When they wanted the time from you, forced you to act, when there would be just as little effort to find it themselves.

'Third floor, number thirty-nine,' he said.

They went over to the elevator. There were no signs warning it was out of order, but they hesitated.

'What do you think?' Cooper asked.

'The stairs would be safer.'

'Are you sure?'

Alec nodded.

If they used the elevator, they could be stuck for hours, or worse.

'It's only three floors,' Alec said.

Only three floors.

Cooper kept pace, ready to help him if he stumbled.

He had to pause halfway through the second flight. 'It's OK,' he said, seemingly as much to himself as to her.

They went up through the dust, the spray-paint on the walls, black bags of rubbish lying openly outside doors.

On the third floor, they came to number thirty-nine, and knocked.

CHAPTER SEVENTY-SEVEN

When Simon was ten, he'd found his mother throwing up in the sink. She'd been so careful about what she ate. She had grown thinner and thinner, until one day she had left him and his father for a couple of weeks.

Alec knew these things not because Elizabeth had told him, but because his wife had left behind diaries after her death.

When his wife came back to the house after her few weeks away, there were no pills or diets. She began to cook more again. She took up meat, though when Simon asked about it she'd go quiet, she'd seem guilty, on-and-off as she had been, and Alec would change the subject.

Alec kept saying how proud he was of his wife.

He'd sit there, making comments about the women on television in turn. He'd talk sometimes about their bodies. He did what anyone did.

She'd been worried, sometimes, that Simon didn't eat enough. That he was too thin, that he'd leave food on his plate, that he'd refuse cake on birthdays and drink only water. She managed to wean him from some of this behaviour throughout his teens, and in trying to help him be better, she helped herself. The impulse never entirely left him, though, however big and strong he grew, and it haunted his mother, to know she might have sparked it in him. That something he had seen might have damaged him. You didn't know – you just didn't know—

Years later, Alec had read Elizabeth's diaries. All of them had just been lying about for anyone to see, all of them now packed in the many boxes of her things reclaimed from her mother, who had no right to any of it – they were Alec's, after all. They'd never got divorced. They belonged to him; they were the last things Simon would ever have of his mother. They were part of how he would remember her. Of how he might remember his father in turn.

Alec had read these books, and then he had burned them.

CHAPTER SEVENTY-EIGHT

Four wooden crates lay far along the shore, hidden in a clearing in the trees.

None of them moved any more. Within, animals began to rot. Flies flew nearby in strange arcs.

Rain had begun to seep into the sides.

Along the shore, a house began to shiver.

It shuddered with each wave, its pink pastel shifting, its beams groaning.

The walls fell.

They fell, even though no one was there to hear it.

They fell, crushing a human corpse within, cracking its bones and flesh.

All these things went into the sea.

An empty crate blew against a tree trunk, skipping around in the wind as if it were playing.

The water grew closer and closer.

The rain went on.

CHAPTER SEVENTY-NINE

Rebecca looked so different from the girl Alec had met at the farm all those weeks ago – scrawny, emaciated, she'd had a horrified look in her eyes – she'd told Alec all she had seen, how she had found the heads, what she had been doing out so early. She hadn't been able to sleep. She'd taken her dog for a walk, an animal who was missing, now, who had fled in the confusion of the days that had followed.

Her eyes had been the first to see.

In the White Rooms, she stared at Alec once more. She now wore a school uniform, a white blouse and a blue tie, her cheeks red and her eyes hollow.

There came muffled noises from the floor above. A woman shouting for her keys, hushing a crying baby.

'Hello, Rebecca,' Alec said, not knowing what else to say.

Rebecca looked at him, and then Cooper. She was anxious all the while, holding on to the doorway as if it was the only thing keeping her up straight.

They made their introductions.

They walked through. Rebecca brought them plastic cups of water.

Her foster mother sat at her laptop in the corner. She had headphones on. They invited her to sit with them, but she shook her head. It wasn't her business, she insisted.

The walls were thin. The yellow thatch wallpaper was flaking in the corner of the lounge, children's toys everywhere on the cheap lino floor. Alec stepped on one of them by mistake on his way in. He swore under his breath, then apologized to the foster mother, then realized she was so engrossed in her spreadsheets that he might as well leave it. They all sat down around the clear-glass coffee table, a remote control, a stack of magazines. It reminded him of a waiting room.

They asked their questions. Rebecca promised to answer what she could.

ॐ

She confirmed that she'd had a riding lesson. 'Just one. Months ago. My dad – he doesn't . . .'

She hesitated.

'It's a shame you stopped,' Cooper said. 'The other kids spoke highly of you. Said you were really good at it.'

Rebecca blushed. 'I don't think I was.'

'It was your first lesson, though, wasn't it?' Cooper asked. 'You—'

'Why didn't you tell us about it?' Alec rubbed sleep out of one of his eyes.

'What?' Rebecca turned, confused.

'You had a link with horses. You went to one of the places they were taken. Why didn't you tell us? It's OK you didn't. I just wondered why it didn't come up.'

Rebecca didn't know. They mentioned names of other kids . . . Maryam . . . Peter . . .

'It was months ago,' she said, drinking her water.

ॐ

Rebecca told them about the farm, about her mum and dad's separation. The summer before Grace had left them, Rebecca's paternal grandfather had died. That event had in turn marked a change. They'd flown out to the funeral as a family, but coming back . . . Rebecca didn't know why, but they all grew more distant. All went about their business and chores and farm work without asking the others for help, without crossing paths, without even sitting together in the evenings sometimes, if they could help it. It was gradual, this fragmentation, but inevitable once it had begun.

'I don't know if they loved each other,' Rebecca said. The more they were alone, the less they remained themselves.

One day, after they'd gone out hunting deer, her mother had walked to her office out by the side of the house.

That had been the last time either Rebecca or her father had ever seen Grace Cole.

'It took three days for us to talk about it,' Rebecca said, looking down at her drink.

'How do you know she was gone, if you weren't seeing each other much?' Alec put down his cup.

'She didn't cook. None of us . . .' Rebecca paused. 'Neither of us cooked until she left us.'

⚘

'It's strange that we were . . . that we were all in there at the same time,' the girl said.

They talked about their sickness. About the hospital. Cooper did not correct her; if it gave Rebecca some kind of closeness to believe Cooper had been sick too, then fine.

On the floor above, an argument was beginning. Low voices had become raised; words became unintelligible shouts.

'I'm sorry about your father,' Cooper said, her eyes rolling up briefly to the ceiling, more noise flooding through. She realized, immediately, that it must have looked like she was being insincere by looking up. Her cheeks flushed. She didn't know what to say.

Alec went on instead.

'Did you receive any letters at the farm, the weeks before all this? Any photographs? Anything strange, or—'

'Letters?' The girl seemed confused.

Alec took out his folder.

He showed her photocopies of the newspaper sheets.

WE KNOW.

Images of crates in the woods.

Cooper was briefly afraid he'd produce worse, but he stopped it there.

'Some of the horse owners received these,' Alec said, his voice low and gentle. 'We . . .' He hesitated.

Rebecca stared at the photos of crates.

'Does this mean anything to you?' he asked. 'Rebecca?'

'No,' she said, lifting her eyes up with a sigh. 'I don't . . .' It seemed as if a fog had been lifted. 'I don't know. I don't think so.'

There was a long pause. The shouting continued above.

'Is there something you're not telling us?' he asked. 'If there—'

'I've told you everything, I—'

'My son is missing,' Alec said. 'You must have seen the news. You must know.'

She nodded, her eyes wide, her breath sharpening just a little.

'We need to find him. We need to make sure he's OK. Whoever did this – we need to find out who they are, we need to find out why they're doing it.'

When pushed on it, Rebecca grew quieter.

'That carriage ride you took at the beach . . . who paid for it, Rebecca?' Alec asked. 'Who filmed it?'

She said nothing.

'We know it wasn't your dad. Was it a friend? A neighbour? Someone from one of your online games? We—'

'I don't know what you're talking about. No one was filming me.'

The noise intensified on the floor above.

Cooper tried not to look up, keeping her eyes on the girl and the girl alone.

'Michael – the man who rode the carriage – he said—'

'It was my dad who paid. It was a birthday present.' She blinked. 'I don't know about anything else.'

⁊☉

'Do you need any help with washing these?' Alec asked, holding up his plastic cup, realizing as he did so how ridiculous the question was. Rebecca shook her head, looking at him with an odd, sad affection. She took them to the door. They had been there an hour. They did not have much more to ask.

'Are you OK here?' Cooper asked, as she pulled on her green coat.

Rebecca nodded.

They opened the door to go. Outside, the hallway was colder now. There was no noise from other rooms. The sun had started to go down, and the halls were darker. Alec wondered what it was like at night, to wander here.

As Cooper said goodbye, Alec turned.

'One more thing,' he said. 'Your mother. Has she contacted you, recently?'

'Why?' Rebecca asked, looking at them both. She didn't say anything else.

'We've been finding it difficult to get any kind of contact information,' he lied. He put his coat on. 'Only a Facebook profile.'

'We'd like to—' Cooper began, but Rebecca cut her off.

'Don't you have her phone number?'

Alec stared at her.

'It doesn't work,' Cooper said. 'We—'

'Why do you want to get hold of her?'

Alec tried to smile. 'Wouldn't you rather live with her than in a place like this?'

Rebecca hesitated. 'I don't think she—'

'If you're able to get us in contact, a phone call or a meeting, we can—'

'A meeting?' Rebecca stared at him. 'How would you meet her?'

'Like we met, just now. If she's back in the area, we can—'

'She's in Portugal,' Rebecca said. 'She lives in Portugal.' She shifted her weight, irritated, upset.

It hung in the air. A fact. An undeniable statement of truth.

'You could live with her, still,' Alec said. 'You're her daughter. Don't you want to see her?'

Rebecca's eye twitched. 'I can't see her. She's in Portugal. I . . . I live *here*.'

'But if we can just—'

'You're talking to her anyway, aren't you?' Rebecca said. 'Why don't you ask her herself? Why don't you ask her why she doesn't come here, hm?' Rebecca's face grew slightly red, her words trailing away. 'Why don't you ask?'

'She's talked about me?'

Cooper put a hand on Alec's arm. 'Maybe that's enough for—'

'She said you wouldn't leave her alone,' Rebecca said. 'She said you were obsessed with her.'

Down the stairs, there was a noise of footsteps.

Alec breathed slightly faster, just slightly. 'What do you mean?' he asked. 'Can you show me your phone?'

Rebecca glared at him, but it was more than that. It was a mock show of anger.

She looked close to tears.

'What did she say to you?' Alec shifted slightly closer. 'What are you even saying?' His face twisted. 'This is all—'

'Thank you for your time,' Cooper said, flatly, stiffly, and took Alec's arm again, somewhere between a pat and a tug. 'We'll leave you to your evening.'

Rebecca said nothing.

Alec, halfway down the flight, looked back up, vaguely ashamed, vaguely guilty.

Rebecca was watching him.

She turned, suddenly, and shut the door.

ॐ

The lonely parted, and all around, an emptiness blossomed in the air.

I once asked a question: would you rather be careless or cruel?

But there was a secret, wasn't there? There was a choice beyond choice.

A wonderful thing was happening.

I found myself dancing, that night.

I found myself.

CHAPTER EIGHTY

They had parked up by the wreckage of the old pier.

The wooden boards ran one hundred feet out into the sea. It had not collapsed, not yet.

'I went on holiday here when I was little.' Cooper blinked. The wind turbines twisted the skyline, far away. 'Isn't that strange? I was here and didn't even know. My mum told me. Phoned me yesterday.'

'How was it?'

'The pier hadn't burned down yet. We—'

'I meant the phone call with your mum. How was it?'

'It was fine,' she said, dismissive.

He nodded, and she went on.

'We were on holiday, anyway, the last time I came here. We threw balls at coconuts, ate doughnuts, tried to avoid seagulls. It looks different now, I suppose, but I don't know how well it was doing, even then. The arcades, for instance . . . a sight like that when I was ten would have been magical. I would have loved it, I think.'

'I can't imagine you'll come back again,' Alec said, quietly. 'Not after this stay.'

She smiled, but her green eyes didn't. 'Why not? Tons of excitement for all the family.'

He looked at her, and there was a moment.

Alec's voice grew lighter. 'I never got to know anyone here. George, maybe – maybe he was a friend, I don't know. Harry, a bit, but never as well. And then there's . . . there's you.'

Still, she said nothing.

'I saw you, the night before you came to Well Farm. In the pub. I was thinking of speaking to you, but . . .'

Cooper stared at him. 'Why were you going to speak to me?'

He looked back at the water.

Neither spoke for a little while.

'Rebecca's lying, of course,' he said, and Cooper nodded.

'What did she mean? When she said you'd talked to Grace – did you?'

There was a pause. 'I don't know what she meant. But it's interesting, isn't it? She claims she hasn't spoken to her mother for a year, then seems to know about her messages. It doesn't fit.'

'Nothing fits,' Cooper said, turning back to the sea. He almost thought she was annoyed at him for a moment. 'Everyone who could help us is dead or lying or gone. This case, it—'

'Sun's going down.'

She scowled. 'And I don't like how much you interrupt me.'

'You're just tired, that's all. I'm really not interrupting you.'

She scratched her neck.

'Go back to your hotel,' he said. 'I'll hang around a bit, go to the shops before they shut.'

'How will you get back? What are you—'

'Need to get Christmas presents,' he said. 'For when Si's home.'

She said nothing.

'For you too.' He winked. Later he would cringe when he was alone, wondering why he'd winked. She just smiled at him though, strangely, differently.

They said goodbye.

CHAPTER EIGHTY-ONE

Something in Alec preferred the cold to the heat – the way it felt in his lungs, the way it brushed his face – and with the sun, both things were bearable, in perfect balance. The breeze had started to slow.

In the usual teeming square, only three stalls were set up. Seagulls looked for food and found little. Soon they would starve, and many would fly away forever.

All your old favourites. ICE CREAM, TEN FLAVOURS.

PAPA TEA.

SHOE & KEY REPAIR. WHILE YOU WAIT.

AMERICAN CHIP SALON.

All were closed. It did not even cross Alec's mind that some of them might be closed indefinitely.

The military surplus stall was still there. The angry man that had run it was no longer angry. He smiled as if it was Christmas morning itself.

The streets were mixed with slush and grit in case of ice. It was hard to tell the two things apart.

An empty motor scooter stood, abandoned, by the only open coffee van.

Alec went on to the Local. Maybe he'd find something there.

Inside, only one checkout was open. A stranger cried near the frozen food. Alec did not know whether to say anything, whether to do anything.

'*Chcę iść do domu*,' she whispered to her phone. '*Proszę . . .*'

Alec found a chocolate bear in the sweet section, a tiny Christmas bell around its golden wrapping. This would make a start. He bought a bottle of whisky too, a good one. Cooper had bad taste. They could drink it together.

He went to the checkout, and paid, and left.

§

The trees stood against the clear blue sky all around.

Alec looked ahead, thinking of Cooper, reassessing her, wondering what his son might think of her in turn when they met. Wondering if they'd get along.

Wondering if, after all this, she might somehow stay here.

She made him smile.

Seagulls perched on top of paint-flaked facades and black iron lamp-posts. Neon logos screamed. Empty amusement arcades blared. It was all for no one, no one at all.

§

Cooper went out for a run before the day ended, pulling on her purple university hoodie, the big white letters of the Royal Veterinary College on the front below a crest. Animals danced around a picture of a crown.

The air was cold and dry.

She headed back along the seafront, past empty sands, beneath a crimson moon. The tides moved, back and forth, back and forth.

She passed through the park. The trees were lovely that belated autumn day. The leaves had fallen like fire, rapidly, in the false starts and strange beginnings of new winter. They lay in heaps upon the path and beside it. She passed a couple of dog walkers, but no one else. Small greetings in the new dark, even as the sun shone above the dense overgrowth. People said hello, but only their dogs meant it.

She was already sweating through her green top, despite the crisp chill air. Her purple hoodie hid it all. Thank God for the RVC. She'd been happy enough in her time there. Most of her friends had been American, on the international programme, and had gone back home now. Something about the other British people put her off. Her grades had been middling; she had been involved in far too many extracurriculars at first, too many societies and clubs, her skill in practical application, not theory. It was perhaps strange she'd ended up in the line of work she had, but then she'd always thrived in the unexpected. You find yourself disappointing people enough, you find new people.

So she ran, her dark hair tied back in a ponytail, her grey trainers sinking into the soft mud of the track.

She felt joy in stretching her legs, in seeing these things, to be out here alone at last, away from all their failures, to be out here in this beautiful air.

Somewhere in the trees she heard the cry of a crow.

She kept running.

Everything around her spiralled into a great silence, the sea shifting, the noise of the waves and the arcade echoing away into empty buildings, into empty streets.

Ilmarsh died, as it died every day.

She kept running.

༅

When she came back to her hotel room, a package was waiting for her outside the door, an envelope with no name upon it.

She went down to reception, but she couldn't find the manager.

She went back upstairs and picked it up. She went inside her room.

The curtains were drawn wide as the red sun set. Fresh towels and a bar of soap lay upon the neatly folded bedsheets.

She went to the desk and felt around the envelope. There was a small object inside, a few inches wide, rectangular.

She opened the envelope, knowing she should wait.

But she had to know.

She had to.

She opened it, and found a small, black, old-fashioned camcorder videotape.

'I think I'd die if anything happened to you.'
'Why?'
'I don't have anyone else.'
. . .
'What?'
'What am I supposed to say to a thing like that?'
'Nothing. I just . . .'
'Come here.'
'OK.'

'I'm older than you.'
'I know.'
'Rebecca, I—'
'I won't tell anyone.'
'You don't know anyone.'
'Exactly. So it will be easy.'

'Who did this to you?'

CHAPTER EIGHTY-TWO

Years past

A camcorder begins filming.

The town is in spring, at first. Petals fall from trees around a flaking pavilion in the park.

There are occasional gaps of static, of blue light in the flow.

There are happier moments recorded around town, glimpses of strangers, some homeless women in sleeping bags on the beach, playing cards and laughing, telling jokes. The camera records them from nearby each time. No one speaks to the camera, or seems to know they're being filmed.

Night comes.

It is not clear where the camera films now. Not at first. It is so dark.

Wind braces against the microphone.

There is a stone building, rising from the ground. There are fields, far away and all around, trees in the distance.

It is Well Farm.

All around, reeds shake and shiver.

Voices talk about the sickness of the world.

They talk about a need to do something, anything.

They talk about an island.

They talk about being watched.

Bonfire Night

It is night. The filming goes on, all those months later. The colours of the hotels become visible in streaks as the occasional firework thunders in the sky. When they were converted into residential blocks, each building was given the corporate branding of a thin cladded facade on one edge, a great vertical of colour to rejuvenate the homes, to give a new lease of life to the town by the sea.

The camera moves around, showing how they curve, how they loom around the field in their midst. It almost looks as if it is flying off the ground at one point, but it is just being held out of a window.

Something moves in the field below.

It is larger than any person.

It is frightened.

December

The last shots are of Alec and Cooper, sometimes together, sometimes apart.

The torsos are washed up upon the sands.

A dog in the woods, wooden crates all around.

The beach in the evening. Alec and Cooper sit side by side from far away, their backs to the film, talking about something the filmmaker would never hear, never know.

There is one final scene.

It is indoors. It is dark. The only light is thin, seeping from the fairy lights of the promenade, from the reflections of the arcades, the seams around the curtain edges.

Cooper leans forward towards the screen, her lips parting, her eyes wide and dry.

In the film, there is a woman, dreaming in a bed, turning beneath the duvet covers.

The lens watches her.

It watches Cooper's sleeping face in the dark, captured by that camera, witnessed from the corner of her hotel room some anonymous night, just a few feet from her body.

I had been with her and she hadn't known.

Day Forty

CHAPTER EIGHTY-THREE

The tape finished.

They sat in Alec's home. It was a little after dawn.

She hadn't been able to sleep in her own place.

'We can't stay here.'

Shadows moved as light danced along the trees outside.

'I can't stay in that hotel. You can't stay in that house, you – we're – we're what this person wants. We're what he's watching, now.'

There was a birth of smiles, once, in a town by the sea.

'It came through . . . I got permission, just like you wanted. It's been arranged.'

'What's been arranged?' Alec stared at her.

'An interview. A meeting . . .'

There was anger in me once.

I have held the dancing plague.

'I feel like I'm – I feel like I'm losing my—'

PART FOUR:
SIXTEEN HORSES

CHAPTER EIGHTY-FOUR

On the final day of school, Rebecca walked towards her locker. She had waited in the bathroom at the end of the day, had sat in a cubicle until the sound of movement and clanging had ceased. She had just been on her phone.

She went to her locker. It was so new she hadn't even got a padlock for it yet. The whole place looked duller than it had in her memories. Her mind had made the drab beige something bright and terrible. She only had her books with her, nothing expensive.

She looked down the corridor. A teacher left his room and headed towards reception. A cleaner had started mopping the waiting area.

Rebecca opened her locker and white powder tumbled out, entering her lungs, filling her eyes.

CHAPTER EIGHTY-FIVE

Alec and Cooper were halfway there, now.

The girl from the island – the girl whose father had destroyed her entire family, who had poisoned them, who had set their homes and farm alight – the girl who had not spoken in all this time . . . Alec thought was his one last hope to find an answer to these strange events.

Cooper didn't know. But he was right, in a sense. They were running out of options. And however unlikely it was that a child might hold their solution, at least they would be out of Ilmarsh. At least they would be far away from whoever hunted them.

This girl waited for them, far away.

'At least you have a reason, now.'

'For what?' Alec asked.

'For doing what you do.' She slowed down in the traffic. 'The day after we met, you told me you just fell into this work. That you'd lacked imagination.'

'. . . And how about you?'

'What do you mean?'

'What's your reason for all this?'

'It's my job. And . . . and I want to help you, too. We're friends.'

'Are we friends?' he asked. 'Is that what we are?'

'I . . .'

She said nothing else.

It would be night by the time they arrived, only a few hours left for visiting.

They kept going.

He looked at her, every so often.

CHAPTER EIGHTY-SIX

The first and only sign of what had happened on the island had been the choking smoke from the fires. Passing boats had reported it; others had come to investigate; soon infected, they had received swift treatment. They had only found the little girl by accident; she had been hiding in a corner of one of the collapsed barns, had coughed, violently, having held her silence each time strangers had passed by before.

She had not spoken. Not then, not after, not now.

Their family had not always been so isolated. Her great-grandfather had been a regular sight at markets in town; people remembered the jokes, the easy manner, the occasional temper of her grandfather. It was the final son who had broken with society; strangely so, considering he had left for university, then a successful career in a government lab. He'd come back one day, bringing with him his children, his pregnant wife. And as the decade had unfolded, whatever rift had separated him from this old life had faded, and it was the new life that was cast aside.

Strange materials were found in his home.

Writings about heaven and hell.

Scriptures of his own devising. Life had been sin. They'd live apart.

They'd find a new way. People didn't do things to a place. A place did things to people.

And the father, he killed them all.

Trauma never ended. It just spread its spores.

Only a girl remained.

She couldn't speak.

ॐ

Niamh was now ten years old.

The staff had asked Alec to wait outside. Men made her nervous.

'I'll be OK,' Cooper had told him.

Children liked Cooper, generally speaking. She knew if her sister became a mother, her niece or nephew would think she was great; of course they would. Cooper tried to treat kids like people. She tried to pay attention to what they liked, what they didn't. She tried to be normal.

This girl, she liked drawing. There were crayons all across the table when Cooper came in.

Cooper explained who she was, why she had come here. In the middle of her story, she mentioned the word 'horse'.

So Niamh drew them. Her T-shirt was blue and was covered in images of puppets. Her hair was short and red. She—

'That's not a very good drawing,' Cooper said.

The girl looked up, eyes wide. Her shock turned to annoyance, and Cooper grinned.

'I'm sorry, that was mean. Can I try drawing one?'

The girl looked back down at her paper and kept going.

'Hold on,' Cooper said, and opened her bag. She removed her notepad and pen. 'Here we go.'

Cooper drew something that looked like a tube on cylindrical stilts, a ridiculous smiley face drawn on the end.

'How's this?'

Cooper handed her the piece of paper.

The girl looked at it. A flicker of a smile crossed her face before she saw Cooper smiling in turn, and immediately it vanished.

'Yeah, that's what your horses look like, I'm afraid,' Cooper said. 'You shouldn't draw stuff from imagination. You should draw stuff you can see. You'll learn more that way. Like . . .' She put her thermos on the table. 'This. Draw this.'

The girl and the woman both drew the thermos.

'Now you see how the light catches against it, the shadow? You can fill that in. It makes it more lifelike, it gives it depth.'

They both began to fill theirs in.

'I used to draw all the time,' she said.

They finished.

The girl's was better. She looked up at Cooper for approval.

'This is better than our horses. We're definitely getting better.'

৪ᦦ

Alec chased up the visitor records while they spoke.

There had been no family, no distant relations that had come to claim Niamh. Social workers had visited her; court-appointed staff and other authorities immediately after the original incident and the aftermath.

No one else.

He searched through the database for other names.

COLE.

Nothing.

ELTON.

Nothing.

NICHOLS.

Fifteen times throughout the last twenty years, he'd come to this place, apparently. Not for this girl. For patients with names he did not recognize.

'Nichols, Alec.'

He did not remember coming here.

He did not understand why his name was in this system, who he was supposed to have visited.

He asked a clerk.

'I didn't visit,' he said. 'I've never been here before, I don't—'

They couldn't help him.

How could they help him?

It was just what the computer said. Records had been transferred to a new system from across the region's services. They—

'This isn't just this institution, then?'

It wasn't.

He let them leave.

He looked at each name, wondering why he could not remember them. He must have visited them for cases he'd been working on, back in his old district.

Had they meant so little to him?

Or had something happened to his mind, too?

How many things in a life really stayed with you? How many days did you really live enough to remember them?

Alec came back to the observation room. Cooper was still drawing with the girl. It had been forty minutes, now.

There were horses across the desk. Pictures of her thermos. Now pictures of each other.

Still they did not talk of anything.

What was she doing?

They didn't have time for this.

'Can I go in there?' Alec asked.

The social worker told him it would not be a good idea. These things took time. 'Your partner's doing well.'

He waited for twenty minutes in a hard chair, watching through the one-way glass.

⚯

He'd forgotten his own laptop. He took out Cooper's.

She'd let him use it briefly in the car, surprised that it didn't make him motion-sick. So he used her password now.

He got it out, logged into his email, his notes.

He'd listed all the meanings he could find, just days ago.

Sixteen:

A unit of measurement. A square number, four times four. The base hexadecimal of all computing. The number of pawns on a chess board – for that matter, the precise number of pieces you start with in any game, elegant, mirrored.

The tarot card for the Tower.

Destruction. Revelation. Higher learning. Change.

The age of consent.

The number of completion.

Divisible by one, two, four, eight, and itself.

The number of waking hours in a day.

The date of the Boston Tea Party, the first Academy Awards, Marie Antoinette's marriage, the day of her death, the number of her husband, XVI.

The atomic number for sulphur.

The age of Rebecca.

It meant everything and nothing.

He had images contained in the document. Photos of the heads. Of wooden crates amidst the trees. The Tower card, showing a collapse, two people throwing themselves from a building.

A finger. A nail.

For the horses themselves, there were other combinations:

Riding. Rescue. Racing. Work. Pet.

War. Pulling the chariot of the sun. Glue.

Hunting. Meat. Power. Friend.

Horse burial as a ritual could be found in a variety of cultures, symbols of Odin, of fertility, of wealth, of death.

In Shandong province, six hundred horses were discovered in a pit, centuries past their deaths.

In the Trojan war, a wooden gift had been given at a gate.

There had been a plague. The Greek forces had been lost at sea, sick, dying without hope of reclaiming lost Helen.

A deer, sacred to Artemis, had been slain.

The plague of the place was of their own making, a reward for all they were and all they had been. It drew attention to their crimes, serving justice, restorative and punitive.

To end it, the Greek forces had to provide a sacrifice of equal value to the dead deer.

The Greek king had to slit the throat of his daughter Iphigenia.

The war would end, years later, with men hiding within a horse.

The king would go back home, victorious.

He would kiss his wife and walk on purple sheets.

He would look on all he had done, and smile, victorious.

He would never wake.

The wife would kill him in his sleep.

ॐ

Before Alec shut down the laptop, he went into Cooper's own email using the same password. He wasn't surprised when it worked.

He read all of the private correspondence he had time for.

He saw emails from her sister.

He saw emails arguing Alec's innocence, reporting on the contents of his home. He saw emails requesting that he be allowed to re-join the investigation, attempts to argue against what someone called Ada Solarin thought to be Alec's 'instability', his negligence, his incompetence.

He saw emails about bird necks.

He saw emails about his own fingerprints, found on plastic.

An obsession with a mirror.

He got up and put the laptop away in Cooper's bag.

He went through to the hallway and opened the door.

⳹⳨

'Alec?'

He walked past Cooper and pulled one of the chairs from the opposite wall, placing it across from Niamh. The girl flinched at the noise of its metal legs dropping down onto the floor. She avoided eye contact with the both of them. Her drawing slowed and shifted.

'Alec, we're—'

He ignored Cooper. 'Hey, Niamh. I'm a policeman. My name is Detective Sergeant Alec Nichols.'

The girl blinked as she drew.

'We're here to ask you a few questions about your family.'

'This isn't—' Cooper turned, forehead creased. 'Do you want to talk about this outside?'

'No, no. In here is fine.' He kept his eyes on the girl. 'You see, Niamh, something happened to me, too. I got sick. Just like you got sick, just like your dad, your brother, just like everyone. We've all been through the same thing.'

Still, she did not look up. She kept drawing, faster now.

'This isn't appropriate,' Cooper said. 'There's no sign she even knows anything about this.' Still he did not move. 'This – this isn't fair, come on, Alec, we're—'

'You can leave if you want,' he said, still not looking at her. She did, after a pause.

It was just him and the girl, then.

'And I survived, just like you did,' he said. 'I survived, but someone's still missing. My son. My boy. He's the same age your brother would have been, if he'd lived. And I – I need to know where he is. I need to know who's doing this.'

She said nothing.

'Did someone – did someone visit you all, before what happened? Did any of your animals get hurt, any letters in the post, any photos?'

There was noise in the hall.

'Was anyone in your home who shouldn't have been there?' he asked.

Still she drew.

He reached across the table, hesitating before he did it.

He snatched the crayon from the little girl's hand.

There was no resistance.

No response.

Her empty hand just hung loose in the air.

ॐ

'Why was your house set on fire?'

The door opened. Two care assistants walked in with Cooper, followed by the director.

'Mr Nichols, you can't be in—'

'Detective Sergeant Nichols,' Alec said.

'I have to ask you to leave.'

He looked up at them. Cooper stood behind the others. He'd never seen her so angry. Had they watched him? Had they been out there?

'Niamh, I—'

He turned. She had her crayons again.

She drew a wooden house.

She drew another, and another.

They took him from the room. He stared at her, as the security guards' fingers gripped his arms. He tried to count the houses.

She stopped at five.

୫୭

There was no answer for his own crime, not here.

Not that he would find. Not that he would know, that he *could* know.

The Hail Mary, she was just a ghost.

She was just a little girl, lost in a life of burning men.

CHAPTER EIGHTY-SEVEN

Rebecca walked far from the pier. Her blue-white trainers pattered past the arcades and their screaming noise, a few children inside just watching her, not playing games, just watching: younger, angry eyes. She'd been to the arcade a few times with her boyfriend. They'd played light-gun games, mainly, sticking coins in machines with silly names and pointing her red and black rifle at the faces of velociraptors and zombies. She'd keep looking at him all the while, keep smiling, and he wouldn't turn to her at all, he'd be so fixated on his task. They'd put as many coins in as they could. Rebecca had barely been able to afford it, but they'd done it anyway. It had made him happy, even if it hadn't been her kind of game. He'd let them both buy hamburgers as a treat. She hadn't wanted to – they were so full of fat – but he had told her to eat her burger, so she had eaten it.

Months after her last birthday, they'd lain in the fields of the farm, far from the house, far from her father, from strangers.

He'd asked her what she'd wanted, and she'd not known.

She'd just talked about that carriage ride along the beach.

She'd talked about happiness, about what it might mean.

Months later, now, Rebecca sat on the sea-wall and knocked the heels of her trainers back and forth against it.

She had told no one about the powder.

Her locker would be opened a day later and the authorities

would be called. They would analyse it, and find it was just flour, put there by cruel students playing a careless prank. Rebecca did not know this as she walked.

Rebecca took out her phone and sent some messages. She had no friends left, not now. Maybe she'd never had them.

Maybe all this time, all this absence in her life, had just been a dream.

꙱

She did not know what she had breathed. She did not know if it was happening again, she did not know who hated her.

She got up and went into town. She had brought a coat, a backpack full of her things. She went into the market.

There, a few people in mobility scooters had crowded near the chip van. Most of the stalls were shutting up for the day. A stern-looking man stood near a rug upon which military memorabilia was laid. Old, impotent guns. Medals. Clothing.

'Is any of that real?' Rebecca asked.

'Huh?' The stern man looked up. His face was mottled by acne scars and sixty years of too much sun, but his voice was surprisingly croaky. He did not sound as stern as he looked. 'What?'

Rebecca kept walking. She did not answer him, heard him muttering behind her. She went to a pub where once a policeman and his friend had sat, where once that man had wondered if anyone liked him. She knew none of this, but she sat in the same booth. It took on meaning, this place. It woke up. She opened an app on her phone and ordered a drink from the bar. Vodka and Coke.

It came, half to her surprise. The barman hesitated.

'My mum's just in the bathroom,' Rebecca said.

He nodded and went back to the bar. Rebecca drank it, and hated it, and was surprised by how easy it had been, not the ordering, but the lying. She just said it and he believed her. She ordered dinner: chips, a burger, everything.

She ate it all and left, a man at the bar winking at her as she got up.

She left, wondering if the man would follow her.

CHAPTER EIGHTY-EIGHT

Each day, another person left.

Within three years, the train station itself would be gone. The rails themselves would be torn up for scrap.

The vet surgery was never sold. The people there, they found jobs in other practices. Their customers – few as they were, the population dwindling by the day – travelled to adjacent towns to get help.

Frank thought of all the things he had done for them. All the things he had done to them. Standing in fields, telling men their livelihoods were going to be destroyed. Telling them of infection, of Foot and Mouth, of fire and captive bolts. Telling them what had to be done.

His girlfriend hadn't wanted to speak to him any more. He should never have dated someone younger. He'd been flattered at the interest. He'd lost himself.

Everyone had been on edge for so long. Everyone was afraid.

'I'll talk to you soon,' she'd said, but she hadn't meant it.

People thought he was arrogant, he knew, they thought he was rude, but if you didn't pretend to be confident – if you didn't make yourself into what the world wanted of you – what kind of man were you?

He'd gone round to the American diner late at night to surprise her, one last attempt to win the woman's heart, but using his key in the pitch black had upset her, had frightened her, and the true end had come.

༄

He passed the alleys of a thousand years, the narrow streets, the land forever remembering what it was, what it might be again. The pattern had been there always, for those who looked, for the worst of us.

He passed the carriage driver, leaning against a caravan, his face shaved, his eyes clear. The man nodded at him, and the look made Frank feel sad, though he did not know why.

The vet went to his car, a few of his possessions in the back.

The police had come again, this time with sniffer dogs. They kept thinking he had drugs, wouldn't leave him alone about it.

Everyone knew where they came from. Everyone knew but didn't say. He wondered how much they'd paid the inspector. He wondered if this was it, if he was to take on all the sins of these arcades and empty streets. If he'd be blamed for things he had not done.

It was the problem at the heart of his profession. How to save the animal from the owner.

He remained still for a while sitting at his wheel, staring at the curve of houses opposite. He couldn't see anything through the windows of the houses, not from this far away. The lights were low inside.

He'd gone to the market that morning. He'd sat amidst the scooters, he'd listened to the cries of the seagulls, he'd seen faces he'd not seen for decades.

An old woman had spoken to him, turning her head, twisting her body in a sharp, dramatic motion.

'Something is happening.'

CHAPTER EIGHTY-NINE

Rebecca kept thinking, as the sky grew dark, her legs and feet tired, the hours moving past, about her father and how they had found him, after his death.

He had not had his shoes, apparently.

He'd taken them off; they were lying in the reeds nearby. They'd thought briefly that someone might have taken them from him – Rebecca had asked this, certainly – but no fingerprints, no other evidence was found. Why he had taken his shoes off, then, became the question in her mind.

She walked through alleyways her father would have killed her for walking down, dark, untended. It was night, now.

From one street she heard noises, a cry.

She kept walking.

She came across a car and a mass of people. From what little she could tell, a man had stumbled out into the road and a car had not expected him.

'Daft fucking sod,' a voice had said.

The voice, the man's friend, would tell the ambulance what a character the dead man had been, how he would always do things like that. Others in the road took photos of the man as he bled in the rain. The car and its driver had fled. Rebecca's hair was getting wet. She walked away.

Nothing in her life was what it could have been. This struck her, as she thought of her father's shoes, lying there without feet.

Brown leaves scuttled along the pavement.

There was blue light, decorations glinting overhead. Redness coiled around puddles, around building-sides, like pale fire.

Her last memory of the sky that night would be starless, empty, black, for her and her alone. In school as a little girl, she'd always drawn the night as dark blue, not black, and had told her teacher he was wrong for thinking it was so. It was light blue in the morning, dark blue at night. That was how existence should be. That was how cause and effect should operate.

There was still a Rebecca who thought there might be more, after we were all gone, after we'd killed the world. But what if what God had made was not enough? What if her grandfather had been wrong about everything? Her father had thought so. Her father, who stood so tall in her memory, even next to him. Her father, who was mad, yes, who was strange, yes, who had ruined all that was good for him, who had suffered evil, had allowed evil. Her father, who she missed. Her father, who had helped save her from what she had done.

What if we had done too much?

The names we took, the things we called ourselves, the ways we lived our lives, they made the world bearable, didn't they? It was easier to be a process than a person.

She thought again about what it meant to be good. Surely if you were good, it would be easy to be good. It would be easy to stay that way, to do those things. You would not have to make yourself anew, and damn the old, damn all that you were. You would not have to die.

She passed a bar, and there were men laughing outside, a stag party of some kind. Some of them wore ape masks as they toasted their friend, pints of beer in hand.

She lingered, watching them, and one of the men seemed to spot her. He kept looking at her.

He came over, eventually, and asked if she liked the masks.

She said they were weird.

'Why aren't you wearing one?' the man said, his voice strange through the plastic. He went back to the table and took one for her.

'Leave her alone,' one of the men said, watching their friend.

'What? She wants a mask.'

'She's like twelve.'

'She's not twelve.'

The other man shrugged.

She left.

She continued down another side street, the sounds of her birthplace like numbness. She was seized by the impulse to laugh, but nothing came out. She walked right out into the road and wondered, briefly, if this might be the moment her body would shatter, that she would be gone before anyone could know about her mother, about the things Grace Cole had done, before anyone could know what she had said before she'd gone, before anyone knew what Rebecca was, really, her heart laid bare.

People kept their selves with them, they never lost what was good about them, but there was more than that, wasn't there? There was more you could show yourself than what was right.

No cars came. The road was empty, and Rebecca had found herself already on the other side.

She kept walking, all those hours.

She kept walking and passed through the wreck of her old home.

She passed the red spears in the earth.

WARFARIN TABLET(S) 10 MG.
ONE TO BE TAKEN DAILY.
TAKE AT THE SAME TIME.
SWALLOW WITH WATER.

CHAPTER NINETY

The roads were slick with water on the way back, red and white reflections rippling in puddles by the kerb, the signs of the city at night, its shops and chains and crowds and Christmas lights mingling into a blur past the rapid movement of the windscreen wipers, the pooling mass of acid rain ebbing down each window-side. The satnav took them through it all – all Cooper had left behind, all Alec had abandoned forever. No one knew anyone in the city, wasn't that what people said? But Alec had known no one in his small town, far away.

He drove on. He'd wanted to drive, had pushed for it on the way back. There was more stopping and starting than he'd thought there might be.

Cooper didn't say much. She just looked out of the window to their left.

They reached the open road. One straight line, breaking out into the flat plains, and then Ilmarsh. They were going to book a couple of rooms in a bed and breakfast on the outskirts of town. Neither felt safe sleeping in Ilmarsh itself.

He turned his head to her. Her lips were curled. She stared at nothing.

'You all right?' he asked.

'. . . Yeah.'

He did not like her when she was like this.

There was not much out here. Office parks, occasionally, close enough to the city to commute. A mile out, they passed a partially constructed power plant, its three towers sitting dormant after its funding deal had been blocked by the government. Foreign interference was now feared.

He wondered what went on in those halls. If anyone still guarded the building, if it would be dismantled for parts, if they were just waiting for the baton to be passed again, for power to be needed, for the atom to be split at long last.

'Sorry about back there,' he said, his mouth dry. 'Sometimes you just, you know—'

She shook her head, gently, still not looking at him, still saying nothing. The motion interrupted.

'What?'

She was silent.

'What was that?'

'What was what?'

'You shook your head.'

'OK,' she said.

They kept on. He felt hot in the car, but he couldn't turn down the fans or it'd mist up.

'You were going absolutely nowhere,' he said. 'All you were doing was drawing. You barely asked a single question about the case, and—'

'The girl hasn't spoken to *anyone*, maybe ever. We were told men made her nervous. What did you think was going to happen, Alec?'

'I get that. I get it. I do. But we only *had* a few hours. You aren't a therapist. You were wasting time.'

She didn't answer. She was just leaning back, now. She moved away slightly as he shifted the gear stick.

'There's no need to be emotional,' he said. 'You're sulking because I had to take over. That's all this is.'

'Fuck you.' Cooper's face twisted. '"Emotional",' she scoffed, rolling her eyes. Still she did not look at him.

He turned.

He kept his own eyes on the road from then on. His stomach in knots, his legs, his ankles, his feet aching with the dull pressure, he tried to concentrate on everything that was outside himself, and nothing that was within.

They drove past hamlets full of Christmas lights, trees displayed in the windows of cosy homes. Was there a connection between the place 'hamlet' and the play *Hamlet*? Between small groups of houses and princes avenging their fathers by killing their uncles? He didn't know. English was a strange language. 'Pepper', for example, referred to vegetables, seasoning, the action of scattering, chillies, and far more – all unrelated, all disparate. He thought about Christmas.

He had not got Simon much, yet. He was last-minute, every year.

He wondered if Simon had got *him* anything, before his disappearance.

Maybe he was like his father. Maybe he had left it late, also.

He gripped the wheel tighter. The rain fell lighter and lighter.

He ticked the wipers onto a lower setting and switched on the radio. Cooper used to fight over it, those early days, used to debate what station, what songs to listen to. Alec liked the news, talk shows, that kind of thing. They helped quiet his thoughts.

She did not touch it now.

An unseen voice talked about the ethics of artificial meat.

'Look, I'm . . .' he began, and hesitated.

Twenty seconds passed.

'What? You're what?' she asked.

'Nothing.'

'You're not yourself,' she said.

How would she know?

How would anyone know?

The radio show went on and on. The host asked if a guest would ever consider eating a steak if it was grown in a lab, if no animal really suffered.

The guest told him that steak was still very complex and hard to get right. A hamburger would be easier to grow. It—

Cooper leant forward and changed the radio station, clicking it a few times past Christmas songs until she just switched it off. They drove in silence after that.

The world thinned as they approached the outskirts of Ilmarsh.

୫୭

Only one room waited for them at the bed and breakfast – two beds, at least, but still, not what they'd booked.

There was no other option, though, unless one of them wanted to sleep in a room without any bed at all.

'We're doing renovations,' said the woman at the desk.

They took the key and went upstairs.

CHAPTER NINETY-ONE

She didn't face him. She didn't sit up. She just lay on her bed, still wearing the clothes of the day. She stared at the ceiling and began to talk.

'What happened today . . . it can't happen again.'

He did not answer. She did not know if he was still awake.

'You're careless, sometimes, Alec.'

Thin light came through the blind slats, the street lamps still on outside. The place smelt like all such places: musty, mildewed. If other people were staying there, they'd barely heard them.

Cooper turned from him and shut her eyes.

৪৩

At some point in the night, she woke. She had no idea if it had been two minutes or two hours.

Alec was talking, now. She didn't know if he'd said much else.

'—rather be careless than cruel.'

She turned her head.

'My dad used to say that, when I was younger.' He was staring up at the ceiling. He didn't look over at her. 'Meaning to do good, he thought it was more important than . . . well . . . he wasn't clear on what. Just that meaning, it was better than . . . than not meaning.'

His voice was hollow, worn, gentle.

'The car you scratched . . . did you mean to do good?'

Cooper rubbed her eyes. 'What?'

'I asked you the worst thing you'd ever done. You told me it was—'

'Scratching the car,' she said. 'Alec, it . . . it wasn't that. But I'd just met you. And asking a question like that, it—'

'You've been asking the same question all these days. Ever since the hospital, you've been wondering about me. I know you have.'

There was laughter, somewhere, distant through the walls.

'Mine was Elizabeth. What I did to her.'

Photographs, hung around bodies.

Patches of skin, displayed on a board.

Cooper watched Alec, just like she had watched all these things. She had pulled them apart, every life a mystery. She had tried to help the dead.

'She hid the diagnosis from me at first. A year to live,' Alec said, quietly. 'Cancer.'

Still, she said nothing.

'She took three years to die. So I . . . I left her, one year into the three. I left Simon, too.'

He told her.

He told her about how hard it had been.

ॐ

He told this woman the same things he'd told himself a thousand times before.

He—

'Men whose wives get cancer, apparently it's . . . it's common for us to leave them.' He took a deep breath.

Still, Cooper said nothing.

'My whole life, these things I did, that I do . . . they're just things other people do, aren't they? If I'd died, what would have been lost?'

He blinked. His eye twitched uncontrollably. A nerve trapped.

'I've always been alone. What did I want?'

He closed his eyes.

'You asked me why I did it, why I'd chosen this life. I didn't lack imagination. It wasn't . . . it wasn't that.'

A door opened somewhere outside.

'Why did you do it, then?' she asked.

And what was her voice?

What was it but more coldness, more curiosity?

What was he to her? What was he to anyone?

He—

Cooper listened to her friend.

He turned over towards the window. She didn't know what to say.

She didn't know what to do that would make him better.

She just listened.

She kept closing her eyes, she—

'—wanted to feel powerful, I—'

I wanted to feel like I was good.

CHAPTER NINETY-TWO

He thought of the letters on the crates.

He thought of Grace's face, her photos.

He thought of Cooper.

He thought of the eyes in the earth.

He got up half an hour later and took Cooper's laptop with him through to the hallway outside. She did not stir.

A renovated room without a bed lay opposite; he needed space if he was going to be able to think about this, to think about *all* of this.

A solution lay ahead. He knew it did, he just had to work hard. That's what he'd been told. That's what everyone had been told.

Work hard. A good life would be yours.

Maybe this – maybe this would make him better.

Maybe this would heal them all.

He poured himself a glass of water from the tap. He thought about messaging someone. It didn't even have to be Grace. It could be anyone. He wanted to talk to everyone. He felt light-headed and so he drank more, shaking his head. The quicker he was back to work full-time, he knew, the better. He went to the desk of his new room. It smelt of paint, even though the walls were dry.

He opened the chat with Grace.

He scrolled up.

[10:04] *Grace*: What's it like there, anyway?
[10:14] *Grace*: Raining probably.

[10:16] *Alec*: It snowed.
[10:16] *Alec*: But the sun is slowing.
[10:17] *Alec*: Sorry, meant shining, autocorrect.

[10:19] *Grace*: Take a photo.

He thought of Cooper, how they had met.

I was the one who found the horses, Alec had said. *Well, after Mr Cole and his daughter, of course.*

Cooper had then snapped the bird's neck.

He thought of the animals, his lungs weak, his chest sore.

He thought of his life here.

He selected a picture of the crates, of W A T C H, of the rotting animals in the dark wood, and sent it to Grace Cole using his phone, now charging from the socket next to him.

There was a draught, somewhere.

A window was open.

He looked down at the laptop. He was still logged in on his social media and email from earlier in the day; he needed to be more careful.

He went to the tabs.

He went to close them.

And then he saw it.

CHAPTER NINETY-THREE

He had a friend request.

CHARLES ELTON.

Another. KATE BABBIT. Another. Another. Names he recognized, names he didn't.

Some of them had been dead for weeks.

He accepted all the faces of the lost.

A message came through from Grace, thirty-four minutes later.

A location arrived on his phone. She had shared it via the app.

The map and the pin would remain active for an hour, then expire.

She was close to Well Farm. The woods, it seemed. Had she been there all this time? He did not know.

Come alone, she said.

Do you have Simon? he typed.

Ashamed, upset, he shook in his chair, wondering what to do. Telling himself he was all right.

Telling himself he could do this, that he *needed* to do this. He could not wait for the others to be ready. He could not allow them to stop him. He could not risk her running, and he *knew her*. They had never met, but he knew Grace, just as she knew him.

She was the solution to everything. Maybe the others were right.

Maybe one person had done all this, after all. Or maybe . . . maybe she, too, was their victim, whoever 'they' might be.

Yes, she typed.

She had his son. He just needed to find her. He smiled, thinly, and stood up.

He gathered his things.

He left, alone.

CHAPTER NINETY-FOUR

Alec arrived at Well Farm for the last time. The location shared on his phone was past here, or so his map said – into the woods, half an hour by foot from the stone ruin at the farm's edge. A path ran from there to a small lake.

The gate was open. He didn't know if the others had forgotten to close it when they were last out here or if someone else had driven through in the interim. He looked ahead, his car's engine still humming. He had barely driven since the crash, had been worried he might somehow have forgotten how or that the experience might panic him, but earlier that day no trauma had manifested, not like that. He paused at the edge of the land. He drove onto the soil as the van must have done that November night, its occupants ready to lay the horses to their final rest. He imagined it as the wheels of his own car turned on the scrub, designed for none of this. There were forty-three minutes remaining on the location share on his phone.

The forest became clear as he moved towards it, its blackened mass now outlined in columns of shivering bark, of needles splayed out along the heavens. He stopped the car and switched on its light.

He had a flashlight. A truncheon. Some pepper spray, cuffs, too.

A kitchen knife. If he needed it.

He checked his phone. Forty minutes left, now. He turned back to the road and saw a flash of electric red and white in the dark. The reflection of passing traffic lit up the markers of the buried heads, the red spears in the ground behind him. He grabbed his coat and opened the car door.

It was winter, now – true winter, the kind that scoured skin and dried your eyes and scraped at your bones.

It was the darkest evening of the year.

He buttoned his coat up tightly, shivering slightly already. He hoped walking would make him warmer.

Did he know Ilmarsh now, at last? These strange weeks had felt like a year in themselves. One more year and he'd meet Elizabeth's prediction, that it took four to belong in a place, in any place.

In forty, Ilmarsh would probably be underwater.

His torch flickered. He looked for some batteries in the back but he'd packed quickly. He supposed he could use the light on his phone, if it came to it.

He turned towards the treeline. He remained there for a moment, unmoving, cold in the winter breeze.

CHAPTER NINETY-FIVE

Cooper woke up, half delirious.

Alec wasn't in his bed when she looked over. The sheets seemed smooth, barely slept in.

He wasn't in the bathroom either, though she splashed her face with water while she was up.

It was then she realized his bag was gone.

Her laptop was gone, too.

She put on her shoes and muttered to herself. She left into the halls, already typing **Where the hell are you?** on her phone.

The light across the hall, the open door, and the 'under construction' sign seemed to give her a pretty good idea. She found only her laptop there.

The screen glowed blue-white in the semi-darkness.

There was no noise but her own, the night quieter than she'd ever heard it.

No one stirred in that building, nothing moved but Cooper's fingers.

She shut down the tabs Alec had opened.

She hit upon his profile, last of all.

A message window flickered in the corner with new notifications.

She read it. Saw the photo of the crate.

The location. The message.

Come alone.

CHAPTER NINETY-SIX

Torchlight caught small mounds of stones, massed in puddles. The trees, seething, anomalous, blocked any light from the moon. Alec possessed only what he could hold.

He pushed on, his socks beginning to soak through. His feet felt sore; his arches felt like they had collapsed, his calves on the verge of an everlasting cramp.

He wiped his forehead of sweat, but found none there.

He kept on, checking his phone when he could.

There was, somewhat surprisingly, phone signal out here, though it came and went, and he supposed Grace must have some too.

Alec had never been out this far.

He never went to places like this at all, not even as a child. He'd had no interest in the wild, in nature, not then, not really. Simon had gone camping and hiking, back when Elizabeth had looked like she might get better. He'd even taken his mother with him once, one brief day, one walk through the hills. These two years in Ilmarsh, Simon hadn't once wanted to go out again, he hadn't once wanted to explore. Not until he'd started to make friends.

The trees moved faster.

There were things in these woods.

Alec had passed a pebble-encrusted structure early on, surrounded and ornamented by leaves. It was only when he shone his torch above it that he saw the cracked wooden boards and realized he was looking at an old well. It had not been used for decades, aluminium soft drink cans with old depreciated branding all nestled around its base like votive offerings, enthralled in a nest of weeds.

He saw a wheelbarrow tipped on its side further along. Further still, great thick wooden poles that could almost have been trees if not for all the metal up high. They looked like loudspeakers, like air raid klaxons. Why they were here, he did not know.

Around it all, an almost invisible world proceeded. In places where the trees had grown apart, plants and flowers stood tall, some with very few branches except up the top, despite their height. Top-heavy in their arms, they shook even in the light wind. And there were bees, somehow, swimming through the night ocean. He didn't know they could live in the cold. Maybe they couldn't. Maybe they didn't know. Maybe he was wrong and they were something else, these flying creatures, but what else he could not fathom. They were fading clockwork. An anonymous droning issued louder and louder from the insects, the longer Alec remained, the more he listened.

Minutes left, now.

All this, grown around human mistakes.

All defined by absence, in the end, these structures throughout time, these stories of the things we had left behind, that we had ruined.

The feeling that someone was watching us.

He was close. There was no signal left on his phone but he had to be close.

It was us, always.

All of us, more scared of ourselves than anything.

He heard the water ripple through the trees.

He shone his light ahead at the twist of the path, the wide parting of the branches.

He hesitated, checking his phone again.

There was a single bar of reception.

If Grace was beyond, she had not moved, though he could see no light, not yet.

He gripped the knife within his coat with one hand, his light with the other.

He walked on.

He saw the lake.

CHAPTER NINETY-SEVEN

The hissing struck him first. The low drone of all the insects in the reeds. A cold that smelt of apples, somehow, somewhere. The strange dust that hit his skin. All who had ever lived here and died here touched the policeman's neck. The water haunted the stars, holding their reflection in its black enormity. Some plants and reeds crested round the edges of the lake, like the first hairs of a beard. The water, as far as the light stretched, looked like a crescent moon fallen to the world, but that wasn't right at all.

The more he looked at it, the more it seemed like a smile.

There would be so many colours, if he'd come during the day. Flies sang around the air. One drew blood, and another, though Alec did not even know or feel it. He didn't feel so cold any more. He even felt warm, even as he stood so stiff, even as his shivering came to its final end.

There were just trees and the lake, just plants, and the shell of a rusted car thirty feet to Alec's right, a torch lying on the ground nearby, pointed back in a horizontal at the treeline. It had not moved. It had not even flickered the entire time Alec had been standing there, pointing his own light.

'I'm—' he began, his voice coming out as a croak, as a quieter thing than he had meant. 'I'm here.'

No one answered.

The rusted car shell, when Alec shone his torch towards it, seemed briefly as if it were occupied.

Three figures within.

But they were just seats. The fourth was missing.

He'd heard it, just a few days ago, reading about the search for patterns, for symbolism, for numbers. He'd wanted to understand 'sixteen'.

Pareidolia.

Seeing a face in that which had no face. Hearing a message in a howl of wind.

It was so dark in that place that the edge of his vision was pure black, now.

'Is anyone here?' Alec asked, more tentatively than he'd meant to once again, but who could make him louder? Who was going to make him someone he could not be? His words carried across the dark waters, and no reply came. The wind did not blow harder from the world. The trees did not shiver or shake. Reality was indifferent to the sound of Alec Nichols's voice, his footsteps as he finally moved forward, as his light shone onwards, as every noise became like death.

He came closer and closer to the torch on the ground.

He did not know it had been just like this when the horses had been buried.

He had not seen it, would never see it.

He came closer still to the torch.

He still heard no one. He saw no one. His own light bobbled and stuttered in its focus, unable to remain steady when the hand that held it had already failed, crumpled in cold and terror.

The beam briefly caught something.

There was a camcorder on the ground.

CHAPTER NINETY-EIGHT

Tufts of cloud burned black in the night.

The world was silent as Cooper pulled up alongside Alec's abandoned car. She'd had to beg for the use of another vehicle, desperate enough to give the front desk manager a hundred pounds to borrow it, plus her passport as a safety deposit.

Insects pulsed along the reeds.

She opened the door.

The silence was more than silence. It seethed. It was manifest.

Ilmarsh watched her, its last and final emissary.

The people of this place would leave in the coming weeks, the coming years, as the tides grew higher, as the world grew warmer.

She'd wanted to help people, unable or unwilling to help herself.

She got out of the car, calling Alec's name.

She'd phoned the police already, told them where Alec was, had shared the final messages from her computer. She'd phoned her client. She'd phoned everyone.

And everyone? They'd asked her to wait.

She went into the woods, regardless.

There would be no more abductions.

No more mutilations.

The town's pain was over.

There was no one left to feel it.

It was over.

CHAPTER NINETY-NINE

Alec thought of his son, long ago, sitting in the kitchen corner, playing with paper clips, stringing them together, tying them round wooden chairs, hanging his toys and action figures from various hoops. He thought of tussling his hair. He thought of holding his wife as she cooked spaghetti, how they made fun of each other.

'You're just copying me,' she'd protested.

'*You're just copying me.*'

'I think Alec Nichols is very sorry for whatever bad thing he did.'

'*I think Alec Nichols is bla bla bla blah.*'

Simon had laughed at this. Alec had smiled too, in spite of himself.

'Hey,' he'd said, touching his wife's arm, gentler than before. She'd turned, clearly tired. 'I think Alec Nichols doesn't know how lucky he is.'

CHAPTER ONE HUNDRED

There was a small, almost imperceptible red light upon the camcorder. It had been propped up on a small pile of clothes. Beside it, something else. Alec moved round the lens, trying to stay out of its focus.

There was a small mobile phone, cheap, battered, leaning against a pair of jeans. The clothes were women's clothes.

He felt, for the last time in his life, like there was someone there.

His hands shaking, his face numb, he took his own phone out. Its battery was at seven per cent. How was it at seven per cent? He'd had it charged.

He wouldn't make it back to his car before it ran out. He stared at his contacts, at all the people he knew, at all those he liked and thought he loved.

He saw Elizabeth's number, a few places below Cooper. He'd never deleted it.

And Grace, just a few places beneath them in turn.

The mother of all this.

The number his son had phoned a hundred times, two hundred—

She—

She was out here.

She had his boy.

And Alec, as terrible, as disgusting as he knew he had been – he could be better, he knew.

Everyone could be better, and that was it, wasn't it?

You could do anything, if you pretended to heal the world. If you told yourself you had a plan. If you told yourself all that was wrong could be right.

If you had hope.

He stared, tapped her name, and waited for his phone to ring her number.

A moment later, the phone on the pile of clothes began to ring and vibrate, a stock ringtone, nothing personalized at all. Nothing like he imagined.

It rang and rang.

He turned and moved closer to the lake, trying to shine the light further across.

He thought he saw a shape, briefly, but it was just leaves.

He leant down and looked at the camcorder.

Another noise, at his right, the crunching of a twig underfoot.

'Who's there?' he asked, staggering round, his grip on his light loosening. It flickered.

A light came on in the darkness, further ahead.

His heart pounded all the faster, his sight blinded by the sudden ray. It shifted, whoever held it now moving towards Alec from within the trees.

'Grace?' he croaked, gripping his knife in his shaking hand, his own torch falling to the ground.

The light shut off.

He picked up the flashlight next to the camcorder. He shone it in the direction of the departing visitor.

Tree branches coiled back, a thin shape moving away into the darkness.

Alec called out, his 'Stop!' tearing his vocal cords, his face shivering with the cold.

He ran into the night. Somewhere along the path he would

lose his phone, fallen from his pocket as he in turn tripped over a branch. Still the shape disappeared.

'Please—'

He gripped the knife, trying to make sure he did not hurt himself.

His breathing grew faster and faster.

He began to cough as he came to the clearing, his vision blacking out.

There was something there. Something—

He moved towards it, far away.

ॐ

There was a crate. A wooden crate. He shone his light all around.

There was no one there. There was—

He felt it, its edges, its splintered sides. There was no lid on it. Nothing within. It was empty.

Breathing grew heavy behind him, in the cold night.

The smile of the forest contracted.

He turned and saw, fallen by the treeline, hunched, moaning, a pale figure in the light.

Alec approached, shaking.

He looked at the face, pupils contracting.

He saw Simon, and Simon saw him.

The father went to his boy.

'I'm so – I'm so sorry,' he choked, hugging his almost limp, shaking body. 'I'm sorry—'

Simon did not say a word. His eyes seemed lifeless, despite the flowing tears.

His face was dirty, cut.

Alec grabbed at the boy's hand. His ring finger came to a stump, bandaged round. His little finger was missing, too.

'What did they do to you?' Alec whispered.

The boy shook. The sounds he made were guttural, almost unintelligible. 'I – ah – a—'

'Where are they?'

'Here . . .' Simon croaked, his face anguished, his arms suddenly hugging at his dad all the tighter.

'We have to – to go.' Alec looked around, shining his torch into the trees. 'How many of them are there? Are they armed?'

His boy did not answer.

He turned and shook him gently. 'Si, I need you to – I need you to pull it together. I know it's hard, but we have to – we have to get you to safety, OK?'

Simon nodded, blinking, unseeing.

'How many of them are there?'

'F-f—'

'What?' Alec's head darted around.

'They're – they made me—' His son gasped as if for air. 'They made me—'

'Are they here, Simon?'

He shook his head. 'T-two are gone.'

There was anger in me once. I dreamt at times of being better. We killed to help and in helping I tasted something in me.

Kate.

Charles.

Alec nodded. He walked on, just a few steps, and realized Simon wasn't following. He turned to see the boy staggering back to his tree.

Alec grabbed the boy's good hand and began to drag him along. Still the boy wept.

'It's OK, OK?' Alec tried to calm him. He hushed him, stuttering, trying to pull him close, his son's skin cold against his own. 'It's OK.'

He did not know where to go. He did not know which way he had come, did not—

I have burned fires. I am awake and no one saw me and no one will.

'Did they say anything to you?' he asked. 'Before they left you. Did they say anything?'

'Grace, she – she—'

Simon did not finish his sentence.

They kept going through the trees. Alec grinned when he caught sight of the crunched branches, the signs of his trail.

'This way,' he said.

I have held the dancing plague. I blossom, now.

They went back to the lakeside.

The hissing struck Alec once more, mounting as they came closer. A cold that smelt of apples, somehow, somewhere. The strange dust that hit his skin. The water, the smile of the lake.

His son let go of his hand as Alec walked towards the camcorder. He needed to take it with him. This was not over, not until he found them all. But he had his son back. He had mended the fallen mirror. He had fixed it, he had fixed everything.

The dark trees seethed.

The smile is yours.

Alec turned.

Simon was not there.

He stepped towards the rusted car shell.

Something was inside.

He heard a snap of a twig behind him, low in the earth.

He twisted.

He—

You could have saved him.

CHAPTER ONE HUNDRED AND ONE

Cooper arrived at the lake.

She did not cry out any name.

She did not shine her torch blindly into the dark.

She'd switched it off, a minute before, relying only on the low light of her phone.

She watched.

She waited, the trees shaking, another light left low on the ground, a red dot before it.

No one appeared to be there.

She stepped forward, shivering as she came closer.

Near a pile of clothes, there stood a wooden crate, splinters rough around the edges, its shadow long past the light of her phone.

೫

It was like something from another reality, a made thing amongst the dying of the wildland, amongst the wreck of all those things that had come before. The rough, almost yellow wood of the crate seemed black, somehow, against this light.

It felt like it had been waiting for her, all these years.

She looked around and saw nothing else, heard nothing else.

She rang Alec's phone.

She'd sent a dozen messages, but nothing, no response, no 'seen' ticks.

And still he didn't answer.

The crate stood before Cooper, her phone's light held upon it all the while. The water of the lake still rippled gently against the banks.

Her heart tight in her chest, she hesitated.

She looked through her phone and found Grace's number.

She dialled it, as if in a dream, no longer looking, no longer seeing.

She rang the number, and something shook along the rocks, right by the water's edge.

It buzzed to life in the dark.

The lakeside sang with the ringtone, strange and beautiful.

She moved towards it.

As Cooper bent down to pick it up, she felt a sudden force hit her skull. She wanted to be sick. Blood came dripping along her hair.

She crumpled into the water.

જ્જ

Everything fades.

There are flashes.

There is a hand in the water, a shaking body.

The fire of a distant red above the rippling, the coast so far away.

Her throat would fill with water, and her body, it was so cold, it—

A man watches her from the shore.

She tries to climb up, and hands push her back down beneath the surface.

Reality falls.

She pulls her pathology knife from her pocket and digs it into the man's hand.

His other plunges into the water, his face, his hair shifting side to side. He tries to free himself.

She pulls him down further, her other hand grabbing on to his skull, her fingers crushing against his eye socket. He screams, he falls with her, into the dark.

She gasps air, briefly, before falling once more.

She has lost her weapon.

The world pulses black.

She sees the face, looking up at her from the deep.

It is full of hate, of malice, of death.

She gets to the shore.

As she pulls herself up onto the lake's bank, as she coughs, as she staggers towards the crate, towards the light, the figure follows her.

He grabs at her, lunges at her.

She turns and pushes him.

He staggers, falling, hitting his head back against the rocks.

Cooper, shivering, her fast, palsied breaths now close to a scream, comes closer.

The man is wearing Alec's clothes.

She comes closer still.

Blood is pooling, though she can barely see it in the dark. His eyes are twitching.

ॐ

He could barely move, let alone stand. She bent down at his side and sat with him. His face was blank, as if he was tired, but there was water in his eyes.

There was silence, but for croaking.

'Ph—' he coughed. 'Ph—'

୫ତ

Cooper opened the wooden crate. The lid was loose, not yet nailed down like the others so long ago.

There was silence, but for croaking.

She looked at what was inside.

She stood there for a minute, numb, and then went back to the lakeside.

'Ph—'

'Sssh,' Cooper said, propping the man against a tree. She took her torch and shone it around the head.

There was blood at the back, a fracture in the skull.

'Ph—'

She held it, gently, her fingers tracing the line of the cut.

She imagined it, plunging her thumb within.

She did not.

The body shook.

'Sssh,' she said.

When it grew still, she got up, and left Simon where he lay.

He was dead.

It took a few moments for her eyes to adjust.

The sun was starting to rise.

CHAPTER ONE HUNDRED AND TWO

Two divers had entered the lake. The clothes and camcorder had already been bagged up, and Cooper already knew what they'd find. She'd watched the tape herself.

But still. She had to see.

As the sun rose, the drone and hiss of the insects renewed itself. Birds chittered and sang. Along the edge of the lake's smile, a kaleidoscopic biomass faltered. What seemed briefly red and green and blue, what seemed teeming with health, revealed itself at last.

What is here is dangerous and repulsive to us.

The minutes passed.

From the water, they emerged with a pale, soaked figure, dark hair spilling around her shoulders, her whole body bare but for the muddy water.

They lay Rebecca Cole on the ground and covered her. She had died three hours before Cooper's arrival. Evidence of strangulation.

The second body took longer to remove.

The face was unrecognizable, but Cooper already knew, had known for hours now.

They removed the body of Grace Cole.

Dead for a year, they'd tell Cooper, soon.

She'd never gone to Portugal.

Never gone abroad, not her whole life, but for Ireland, once, on a plane.

Grace had never left her family, had never fled her daughter, her husband, her home.

Grace had never left at all.

The bodies were removed.

The wooden crate was taken, too. A body had been left within, naked, stripped of its clothes.

Hours later, others would find the head, buried in a copse seven minutes away, a single eye exposed to the light of the sun.

ॐ

The videotape had shown Cooper's room, a stranger watching her as she slept, weeks past.

It had shown the night of the horse burial, Kate's hands shifting along the soil, the filmmaker wearing protective gloves while she wore none.

The tape cut to the sea at night, further and higher along the coast than Cooper had ever been. Rebecca looked over the edge of the clifftop and turned, shaking. 'Please,' she said, weak, quiet. 'Please.'

'We killed her,' a voice came. 'We—'

'I don't want to—'

'I love you,' the young voice whispered, tender, hissing in the poor microphone of the camcorder. 'All I've done, I've done for you. You—'

The tape cuts to the girl, riding through the Eltons' stable yards.

It cuts to her, riding along in a carriage by a beach.

It cuts to her, discovering the horses at morning, shaking, crying. A phone rings, close to the camera.

It cuts to her, walking towards a lake.

It shows Alec, last of all.

ॐ

Three final shots.

In one of them, Simon is arguing with his father. His dad is asking him when he'll take a driving test again. That he needs a licence.

Simon tells him he'll book it soon. He's almost ready.

Alec asks him to do it now.

Alec gets in his way, blocks his path up the stairs.

Simon shoves him to try and get past, causing Alec to bash his elbow on the bannister rail. Alec winces, turns, and stops him, the two pushing against each other.

The boy gives way. The father slams him into the wall, his son's head hitting the mirror behind him, cracking it in turn, but not shattering it.

Simon is frozen against that glass, and Alec, stiff, steps back, releasing him.

'I'm . . .' Alec starts. 'Just . . . just book the test. Just—'

The second shot is of Alec walking past a camera by a lake.

The third is of him talking.

'They were only animals,' Alec whispers, his eyes wet.

'How will you help me?' the voice asks.

'Do you understand what you've done? You'll spend your life in prison – you can't throw it away,' Alec says. 'I won't leave you,' he says.

'You left Mum. You left me.'

There is silence.

Alec tries to smile, and he does not know why. He still carries a blade within his right hand, limp, forgotten.

'The others did this to you. They made you do it,' he says.

The voice makes a noise, as though it is trying to speak, but has no idea what to say.

Alec shushes it.

The son walks into the camera shot.

He hugs his father, crying, convulsing. The father hugs him all the tighter.

'It's OK,' he says.

It's OK.

Simon holds his father, gently takes the knife from his father's hand, and cuts his throat.

EPILOGUE

As I passed by the old infirmary,
I saw my sweetheart there,
All stretched out on a table,
So pale, so cold, so fair.

Let her go, let her go, God bless her,
Wherever she may be.
There'll never be another like her.
There'll never be another for me.

Sixteen coal-black horses,
All hitched to a rubber-tyred hack,
Carried seven girls to the graveyard,
And only six of them are coming back.

'Those Gambler's Blues'
(Songwriter unknown)

1.

'Why are we here?' her therapist asked.

There was no clock in the small, fluorescent-lit white room.

Cooper had forgotten to bring her watch that day. She didn't know why, and wondered, if she told the therapist, whether the woman might then ascribe some meaning to it. Some twist of fate, on today of all days. She felt naked without it, kept looking down for the time, for an end.

She kept gripping at her wrist.

The hum of the air conditioner continued as the therapist wrote in her notebook.

Cooper drank some water from her bottle. 'We pieced it together, from the tape. We found notes in the boy's bag. He'd left the Grace account unlocked. He—'

'The son was Grace?'

Cooper did not move her head. 'Yes. Rebecca, before him. She . . .'

The sun kept on shining outside.

Cooper had been back for almost a year now.

જ

One night a few weeks ago, Cooper had gone online and pretended to be someone else. She had found a photo of a stranger and had talked to other strangers in turn. Had shared fictional stories of abuse and trauma she'd never experienced.

She had not talked to many people after that. She had not answered her sister's calls. She had not been on the internet since.

2.

The therapist watched Cooper talk, watched her eyes flicker, occasionally darting towards the ceiling lights.

'Can we – I'm sorry . . .' Her patient hesitated. 'I—'

'What?' She waited, and Cooper said nothing, just looked down at her own lap. 'It's OK . . . What do you want?'

'It feels brighter in here. Can we—'

The therapist rose from her seat and turned the dial on the light switch. It was darker now, but for slivers of red sun through the window.

'Is that better, Cooper?'

She did not nod, did not say yes or no.

'You were telling me about the children.'

'Simon wasn't a child,' Cooper spat. 'We all acted like we were looking for a boy, but he was *eighteen*. A man.'

Outside, cars moved along the street. People went about their days, did their shopping, headed back from work.

She scratched at her arm.

'He thought he loved her. She thought she loved him. And – and that was the start of it, wasn't it? The start of everything.'

There were stories we told ourselves, more than we told other people.

Rebecca had, with Simon's encouragement, started giving her mother more and more of her medication. Warfarin, typically used to help manage blood-clotting disorders in humans, could also be used to murder rats. Administered gradually – in addition to the normal amount prescribed by the doctor – they had tried to rescue Rebecca from her life of humiliation and pain. They tried to make Grace sick and weak enough to leave her girl alone.

Cooper turned away from the window's light. Her voice was flat as she told their story, at least at first.

'Alec wasn't a careful man. So he didn't think other people cared either. He'd bring his work home and leave it on the table, on his desk, in his room. He thought – he thought his son didn't read any of it, didn't notice *any* of it, didn't take an interest in who he was, laid out in plain sight. So when Alec took home evidence of what had happened on the island . . . the fire . . . the poisonings . . . photographs . . . reports . . . it's how Simon learnt of it all. It was how hate became more than hate.'

She dug her nails into the skin of her arm.

'From the messages we found on the phone by the lake, it . . . it made Simon feel special to know the things he knew. The kids, the—' She paused. 'They felt important, knowing about the infection. Knowing what people could do.'

She rolled her sleeves down, playing with the fabric.

'One day Grace died. No physical trauma was found on the body, beyond its deterioration in the lake. Whether it was a function of the gradual dose, whether it was something the kids meant to do, I don't know. The thinking is, her husband pulled his daughter out of school to cover it up. Albert Cole didn't seem to have known about any boyfriend. He might even have thought what happened to his wife had been an accident. They hid the body, and life went on.'

Her eyes were empty, red as she spoke. Her arms bore scratch marks, from today and other days. Cooper held her breath as she talked about hurtful things, things she had been told not to think about, things she had tried to move on from, things that just kept coming back and back. Sympathy passed like a fever, and when she tried to aim it at herself, when she tried to show compassion for her own regrets – her failure to get to the woods fast enough, what she'd had to do to that boy – all forgetting ended in the memory of the wooden crate, of the head in the soil, of the hole in the skull.

The gut lived on after death. The microbiome bloomed and bloomed. But what had lived by that lake . . . what had germinated in the broken families of sinking Ilmarsh . . . Being there had changed her. And now Cooper was broken too.

Sitting in this room, talking about the case of the sixteen horses, Cooper's words were so specific, so chosen, that the therapist couldn't help but wonder if she'd rehearsed them before, to herself, to others. She said things like 'the thinking is', or used the pronoun 'we', the more their sessions went on.

Her breathing did not get better. It continued on and on. She kept drowning.

'How did it make you feel, to find his body?' the therapist asked.

'I'm talking about Grace,' Cooper said.

'I know you are. I—'

'Rebecca took control of Grace's account,' Cooper went on. 'She pretended her mother had left the country. Maybe she was dealing with her grief and guilt in the process, I don't know; the chat logs suggested it was more than just a decoy. She developed entire friendships with people, posing as the woman who'd brought her into the world, who'd tortured her in turn.'

'Cooper?' The therapist stared at her. 'I asked you a question. How did it make you—'

꽁

Cooper held her breath again as she went on. How did it make her feel? She felt interrupted as she tried to explain. She felt like a husk.

'They broke up, eventually. They couldn't stay happy. Rebecca returned to her old life a while later. She had a horse-riding lesson; she saw old friends; she even considered a return to school. She was trying to change, she—'

'Why aren't you answering my questions?'

'I'm trying to . . .'

'Try to focus on how you're feeling,' the therapist said, not unkindly. 'How you're holding yourself. You hold your breath when you tell these stories . . . your feet curl around each other. You know what it reminds me of?'

'What?'

'The way you described the dogs in the crates. The way you said *they* looked, the way *they* must have felt in their last hours.'

Cooper said nothing.

'I think you're more emotionally invested than you let on, and it's OK, Cooper. It's OK to care, to show people you care. This is a safe place.'

Cooper's face grew more and more stern as she sat there. Anger and sorrow swarmed within her, but it was more than that.

She ignored the therapist, when she next spoke.

'Simon discovered something in himself. He'd helped kill for Rebecca, and now he was all alone, profoundly alone. All he had was a man he hated. A man who had – as far as he was concerned – killed his mother. A man who slept less and less. A man who took all the early morning cases. These two . . . they were Simon's targets, no matter who else would die, no matter who else might get hurt. It was his father, and his love. He came up with a solution to a problem.'

'What problem?'

'The problem of other people.'

The therapist wrote in her book.

The red sun began to fall.

Cooper picked up her water bottle. She looked at it a while.

'He stole Grace's account. He stole all that girl had left of her own mum. All he did, he did for those people who had left him all alone. For those people he had loved.'

They reached the end of their time. The therapist did not say anything. She looked concerned, but it was the end. They would never see each other again.

'There were sixteen horses,' Cooper went on, her voice distant. 'One for each year of Rebecca's life. Circles . . . like candles on a cake.'

3.

The sun was red over London.

'Are you happy, Cooper?'

She shook her head.

'Were you happy *before* the horses? Before Alec?'

There was a longer pause, and she shook her head again.

'In our first session, you told me you helped people. That what you did prevented evil, that you rescued animals, that you were proud of your life.'

'I was. I am.'

Cooper looked away.

'What would your inner self say about you, if she talked to me right now? How would she tell me you treated her? What would she say about your relationship, your life?'

'Don't be sad?' Cooper shrugged.

'What would she say, Cooper?'

'She'd . . .'

&☙

She'd say I'm killing her.

4.

Her journey home took an hour and a half, some of it on the Underground, the rest by bus. Much of it involved standing, jostling, trying to make sure she could board each vehicle, and that others could get off. She had to bash a man to the side to let a young mother off. He had his headphones on, wasn't turning, wasn't listening, was just blocking the door, even as it was about to close. He didn't even turn around, didn't confront her. Just lazily moved aside.

The bus was easier. It emptied as it drew closer to her stop. The area was beautiful, red-brick, moss on long walls. The streets were full of cafes, of music in places. The summer went on and on.

She drank a bottle of wine at home, all by herself. She had her favourite ready-meal, oven-baked meatballs. She even boiled some broccoli. She chopped each stalk in half, boiled it for four minutes, drained, salt and peppered with a dash of lemon. It was, she knew, good for her.

She finished the bottle and watched some television.

She got ready to sleep. Her flat was small, unshared, fashionable, a studio space with unpainted walls and, once upon a time, multicoloured fairy lights above the fireplace. She hadn't switched them on since she'd come back, not once. She wondered if she might take them down, but she didn't do that, either.

She brushed her teeth, put on her pyjamas.

She switched on her sleep music and turned from side to side as the minutes passed.

5.

Cooper woke up. It was early light and she was splayed across the sheets uncomfortably, the duvet half on the floor. Her pyjamas were twisted round. Her neck and shoulders were hurting.

Her phone was ringing.

She pulled herself up, wiping sleep from her eyes. She blinked and reached for her phone in the semi-darkness, almost knocking over her glass of water as she did so.

'Ye—' She cleared her throat. 'Yes?'

There was another assignment for her at last. They put her through to the officer in question.

She thought of all the therapist had said to her.

What was the worst thing they had ever done?

Alec had told her about his wife, his boy.

She thought then about her own answer.

She'd keyed someone's car. She'd seen the owner kick his dog, and so she keyed his car. She'd been thirteen.

The only problem was, it wasn't his car. She'd got it wrong.

She would smile whenever she thought of it. It was silly, but she would smile at who she'd been, who she still was.

For a brief moment, she wondered if she should put the phone down. If she should end the call, and go to her mother's like she'd planned.

She should go.

She hadn't seen her family for months.

All of this – everything she had done, everything that had happened to her in that strange place – she'd told them none of it.

She'd told no one but that woman.

She should have a sign by the door, she knew. Like the one in the hotel.

NO BEING AFRAID.

NO HATE.

NO ALEC.

NO HORSES.

NONE OF IT.

She could write these things. She had a permanent marker, somewhere, but sticky tape, that'd be a problem. She—

The voice on the other end of the phone asked if she was there.

Cooper?

Cooper?

She had killed someone.

She had killed a boy. Not a man. A boy.

༄

When she thought of Alec, when she tried to remember, she thought of the crescent smile of the lake. How he'd stood there in that dim video, how he'd walked towards the water, towards Rebecca, towards his son.

Cooper would go back there one day, before her own end. Her hair would be dark grey. A dog would walk at her side. She'd return to where she'd first taken a life. She'd walk the empty town, walk the abandoned streets one final time.

She'd go back.

She'd stand by that lake. Thinking of all the things she did not know. Wondering if anyone else had been there that night. Dead fears and old doubts would never stop blooming. She would carry them with her, and they would infect her, again and again, until she could not sleep at night, until all she could see were figures in the dark, haunting her dreams.

She'd imagine Alec by her side, asking another stupid question, interrupting another idea, smiling at her with his silly smile. She'd imagine others all around, the ghosts of a hundred cases wondering why she was still here, and they were not.

This was the life that waited for her if she said yes. If she did not go home. If she did not tell herself she could be happy, that she could be more than a function, that she could still change.

She didn't want to be afraid.

People lived on, they passed themselves on, the good and the bad.

Alec – all that he was, all that he had become – lived in her mind.

He had thought he had loved her, she knew.

And he had thought he had loved his son, too.

What was the secret of life, the answer to the question of happiness?

It was simple, Cooper knew. It was a trick.

It was never having to ask the question at all.

She held the phone to her ear and spoke.

ACKNOWLEDGEMENTS

Thank you to my friends G. C. Baccaris, Jose Borromeo, Sarah Longthorne, Anna Wharton, Patrick Weekes, Valerie Price, Gary Kings, and my classmates at UEA for your invaluable feedback and suggestions. Thank you to Claire McGowan, Doug Johnstone, and TLC for your insightful comments on early draft material. Thank you to Dr Harriet Brooks Brownlie for your incredibly useful and in-depth guidance on veterinary pathology, and also Graham Bartlett for your expert fact-checking of the book's police procedural elements. Thank you to Giles Foden – your early support of the novel, and suggestion that it be called *Sixteen Horses*, shaped its future course.

Thank you to my agent Sam Copeland. My life changed when I sent through a (coincidentally) 16,000-word sample to your inbox; without your feedback and guidance over the last two years, I might have joined the horses and lost my head. Thank you also to Peter Straus, Stephen Edwards, Sam Coates, Tristan Kendrick, Katharina Volckmer, Natasia Patel, Honor Spreckley, Madeleine Dunnigan, my adaptation agent Michelle Kroes, Arian Akbar, and everyone else at RCW and CAA for all you have done for *Sixteen Horses*.

Thank you to my editor Maria Rejt for your incisive, thoughtful and caring edits – for helping to create not only a better book, but a better writer as well. I would also like to thank the rest of my UK editorial team – Josie Humber, Sarah Arratoon, Rosie Wilson, Alice Gray, Samantha Fletcher, Claire Gatzen, James Annal – and my US editorial team, including my editor Zachary Wagman, former editor Noah Eaker, Lauren Bittrich, Maxine Charles, Katherine Turro, Lisa Davis, Jonathan Bush, Marlena Bittner, Samantha Zukergood, James Sinclair and Jason Reigal, for all your hard work in getting *Sixteen Horses* into readers' hands.

Thank you to my parents, Tricia and Glenn, and my sister, Amy, for your endless support for my writing and for making me who I am (even if that means sending you five billion drafts of various stories since the age of eight!). Writing a novel can be an exhilarating, exciting, rewarding process, but it can also be a lonely one. You never failed to let me know what you enjoyed about my work, and your constant belief in my writing was instrumental in getting to the finish line. Other family members – Deirdre, Hilda, Ben, James – were really helpful in reading and giving feedback on the novel's later drafts. I would also like to thank my niece Izzy, who was born on the same day agents got back to me about *Sixteen Horses*. I hope you enjoy reading this when you are capable of reading!

Finally I'd like to thank Dr Charlotte Mahood, veterinary surgeon, real-life Cooper, for all your animal advice, emotional support, writing feedback, patience and love throughout the development of this novel. When we met in 2012, I wasn't a professional writer, you weren't a vet, I couldn't click my fingers and you couldn't whistle. While you're still working on the last one, achieving three out of four dreams isn't bad at all, and we have our whole lives to figure out the rest.

Readers – the book you have just read couldn't exist without all the people in these acknowledgements. If you enjoyed the book and ever meet them, please direct your praise in their direction.